THE CURSE OF THE WHITECHAPEL ORPHAN

ANNIE SHIELDS

PROLOGUE

Whitechapel, London
1888

Footsteps echoed off the damp cobblestones, the lone figure hurrying through the tangle of narrow alleys, slicing through the dense, swirling fog that rolled off the inky black waters of the silent river.

The stench of decay mixed with the acrid chimney smoke of ten thousand fires, though there was no heat in the belly of the city. Up ahead, the mouth of the alley glowed eerily, the illusion of safety to be found in the pools of the gaslights.

She erupted onto the narrow street, her dark cloak streaming behind her, then plunged into the next alley, determined in her mission. Heart pounding, eyes wide in the dark, she leapt over the detritus that littered the floor. The scuttling of rats running to escape her was accompanied only by the murmurs of the destitute who lurked in the shadows.

They were the discarded. They were the forgotten.

Ragged forms with hollowed-out faces, spectres of humanity hardened by a city that ignored them, driven mad by hunger. They didn't matter to her. They sank further into the recesses of the broken walls, watching as she rushed by.

She darted through the silent thoroughfares, past the dormant shops and the rickety houses that huddled with their neighbours, either for warmth or for balance. Windows blocked by boards. Their doors served as flimsy shields against the dangers just beyond the gaslights. Onward she hurried through the suffocating darkness, winding her way through the maze of streets.

She paused at the road, her breath smoking into the night air as a solitary late-night hansom cab clattered by, careening like a fleeting phantom in the night; a shower of sparks flew from the hooves of the dark beasts, each one snuffed out by the biting chill of the night air.

She danced over the stones, melding with the shadows once more.

Not much further now.

Angry bellows and coarse laughter erupted somewhere in the distance, drifting on the sinuous air scented by the putridity of the Thames. Gin palaces and taverns were swollen with the dregs of society, peddling their trades to unsavoury patrons who stumbled out into the night. Drunkards who remained unaware of the dangers that watched them.

That followed them.

Biding their time with predatory patience.

Everyone in the city had heard the stories. Had seen the gruesome, blood-soaked images splashed across the broadsheets; the tempestuous headlines screaming about the dangers that lurked down the alleyways of the Whitechapel district.

She didn't care.

This was London.

Only the righteous believed that the sanctuary of a bolted door would keep them safe from the prowling dangers that roamed this city.

She knew the dangers.

She'd seen them for herself.

She wondered if the faceless predator happened upon her this foggy night; if he was confronted by the wild madness that she held inside, clutching it to her chest like a precious gift, would he run away from her instead?

For tonight, there would be murder on the streets of London.

PART I

The name of Doyle, the seer did tell
Wealth plenty, but the death toll knell
For every man, a Doyle holds dear,
Will meet his doom before they're wed a year.
The Doyle line, no sons shall be born.
Only one daughter, her life forlorn.
She walks alone, to wither and fade,
An heiress of solitude, living in perpetual shade.
Blessed by beauty and gold in lieu
Of love's eternal kiss, the Doyle's curse holds true.

CHAPTER 1

Whitechapel,
London

1877

"Mama, please!" Kezzie Doyle hefted the crude wooden crate up onto the teak counter, the blue glass bottles inside it clinking together with her effort.

The box was stamped by the manufacturing company in Bath. They made all the bottles from her mother's shop, each one etched with a curlicue letter 'D' like a fancy royal crest. "These bottles have travelled further than I ever have!" Kezzie added with another shove of the box.

Ada Doyle paused as the glass shook and the long look that she levelled at her only daughter shimmered with her impatience. "Kezurah, you are pushing your luck today, young lady."

Kezzie heeded the warning tone but wasn't yet ready to capitulate. She decided to change tack. "Mama, haven't you raised me in amongst these herbs and salves? Haven't you taught me everything you learned from Granny, and from her mother before that?"

Ada's vivid blue eyes glinted with amusement as she tilted her head at her child. "I have."

If anything, her mother's amusement only annoyed Kezzie more. "You've said it yourself; the Doyle's have been healers in this district for generations. It's in my blood. I've watched and learned and listened. I stood beside you when you treated the sick in the back room!"

"I know this, Kezzie."

"Then why won't you allow me to make the deliveries?" Kezzie demanded, just about refraining from stamping her foot in frustration. "I'm ready. Please, Ma, let me go."

For a moment, Ada Doyle considered her carefully. A little light of excitement flared in Kezzie. But her mother's weary sigh extinguished any hope.

"We've been over this, Kezzie. Many times. When you're older, you can go. But for now, you are to stay here and study."

"But–"

"Kezzie," Her mother's tone brooked no arguments. "Enough. For pity's sake, leave it. Blending salves and tinctures under supervision is nothing compared to tending to the sick out there by yourself. It's dangerous, Kezzie. Now," Ada softened her voice. "Go back to your studies. Trust me, the time will come when you'll have plenty of opportunities to prove your worth. Not just as a Doyle, but as a healer in your own right."

Hot tears of frustration filled Kezzie's eyes, though she refused to shed them. She hated the invisible chains her mother insisted on.

Kezzie understood that the streets of Whitechapel were no place for the naive or the faint of heart, but she had seen the skinny street children out there alone. They survived every day. She was older than them. She'd also seen the horrors that city life could bring about. She'd helped her mother treat many of them in the tiny back room of the apothecary, hidden behind the heavy red curtain in the far wall. She looked at Rose, her mother's constant companion and oldest friend, seated next to the roaring fire in the corner. Rose had been a part of Kezzie's life for as long as she had drawn breath.

She had red hair that had now faded to a white colour and brown eyes that could convey a message with just a look. Rose called herself an honorary aunt to all the Doyle girls.

Though Rose's mouth flattened in compassion, she didn't offer any support.

Reluctantly, she collected the medical textbook from the table and slowly walked up the stairs that led up to the Doyle's living quarters above the shop.

The ticking of the clock filled the silent shop.

Beyond the muntin window, the thick London fog churned along the narrow, cobblestone passage.

Ada sighed heavily and shook her head, giving herself a moment to remember what task she'd been doing. Her movements were jerky with irritation as she began tidying unnecessarily. "She drives me to distraction."

Rose's chuckle was light. She pressed to her feet, refilling her cup with a fragrant herbal tea. Grateful for the heat of the liquid on this damp day, she wrapped her fingers around the cup as she peeked through the window. Figures moved through the haze beyond the glass, floating past as if in a different dimension.

"She's a Doyle through and through," Rose murmured as she approached the counter.

Ada looked up sharply. "What do you mean by that?"

Rose gave her friend a mild look. "Just that she's brilliant and bright. And that you can't protect her forever."

Ada's hand stilled over her workbook. Sadness shimmered around her brilliant blue eyes. A small acknowledgement that as skilled as she might be, she couldn't stop the hands of time.

Rose leaned in. "She's too clever for her own good, Ada. She'll work it out for herself, sooner or later."

"I know," Ada whispered, almost inaudibly. "But not yet. Please, let me keep her safe for a little while longer."

"How old were you when you found out?"

"Younger than she is now."

Rose shrugged as if Ada had proved her point. "You've done your best. To keep her caged isn't fair on her. She's not a child—"

"She's twelve!"

"Almost thirteen," Rose retorted. "My mother said that it wouldn't do me any good to hold onto things too tightly. That I should let them go. If they come back, then they were always mine," she finished sagely.

Ada paused, her hands stilling on a stack of dried herbs as her brows crunched together. "Are you forgetting how long I've known you, Rose Donovan? Your mother died when you were four. She said no such thing to you."

Rose's mouth twitched and then she pinched the bridge of her nose, eyes squeezed tight shut. "It must be all these funny smells in this ruddy shop. They're affecting my memory."

Ada couldn't stop her laughter, shaking her head in exasperation.

~

Kezzie heard their muted laughter through the polished wooden floor.

Her books sat where she'd left them, abandoned. She'd have to read them, of course. Just not yet. Temper mixed with bitter disappointment, and her thoughts wouldn't settle enough for her to take in what she was reading. Besides, her mother would check on her learning by asking questions later. It was almost as though Ada Doyle had a book where her mind was, and she could summon up that information at the drop of a hat.

Kezzie wasn't quite that quick, but she vowed that she would be.

The room had a chill to it. Kezzie ought to light the fire, but obstinate stubbornness drove her to stand at the window. Dark furniture filled the space; a table, several chairs, a desk, and a long sofa next to the hearth. All still the same furniture that her ancestors had sat on and used.

Far below her, a hand cart rattled along the stones, the image distorted through the small squares of glass. A man pulled it along, a small boy walking alongside, his hand keeping whatever it was they were carrying in place. Kezzie sighed, her breath blooming against the cool surface.

She knew that she was lucky. She had eyes in her head. People walked past their apothecary shop every day who clearly didn't have anything at all. The Doyle's weren't wealthy by any stretch of the imagination, though Kezzie knew that she had more than most in Whitechapel.

Her mother's apothecary shop stood as a testament to her great-grandfather's foresight and investment. His good business sense had not only bequeathed them a legacy of healing but also premises that had become a secure financial foothold for his wife after he succumbed to a premature death. Her great-grandmother had passed down the healing knowledge through the years, daughter to daughter. Kezzie knew that one day the shop would be hers, and that it was her duty to continue helping and healing in this city.

"Why keep me tucked away with books when there's real suffering just streets away?"

Only silence answered her.

She didn't know why her mother insisted on keeping her locked in this house. Kezzie had been standing next to her mother as she'd worked in this shop since she could walk. She knew that blackthorn treated stomach aches and fevers. For burns, you could use St. John's wort or calendula. Dandelion root for constipation. Wounds had to be cleaned with witch hazel and honey healed the skin better than anything else.

One day, just like it had come to her mother and her mother before that, Doyle's Apothecary would be hers. She loved that there was a legacy to pass on to each generation. But one day, Kezzie was determined to make her mark on this world.

And no one would be there to stop her.

CHAPTER 2

It was Kezzie's grandfather who had the idea of placing a brass bell over the door of the apothecary shop. He had seen it in one of the dressmakers in Mayfair and had ordered one to be fitted that same day.

It meant that, on days like today, when there was a continuous stream of visitors in and out, the doorbell rang constantly.

Doyle's Apothecary was a popular destination, hidden down the backstreets of Whitechapel, away from the busier main streets. A gem of a place that had built a reputation for dispensing concoctions that could cure a wide range of ailments. The customers here didn't care that the law prohibited sales of some of the items.

This tradition dated back to her great-grandfather who was proud to have trained in pharmacology and druggist healing. Of course, being a man, he was allowed to help and serve the community. His wife, and all her daughters ever since, had had to continue their healing and apothecary work in secret. Kezzie knew that her mother relied on their solid reputation so that they weren't reported to the authorities.

To the untrained eye, the shop interior looked like

organised chaos. Each wall was lined with shelves, each shelf laden with glass bottles and jars in a kaleidoscope of colours. Bunches of dried herbs, their leaves faded to a brown and curling at the edges, hung from the ceiling.

Scents of lavender and chamomile mingled with the sharp tang of eucalyptus and woody scents of bark.

To Kezzie, it was a comforting aroma. There were the same remedies that her ancestors had blended. A Doyle had stood in this shop for over a hundred years. These herbs were the smell of home and belonging.

Ada and Rose stood side by side behind the huge teak counter, its wood darkened by time and bearing the marks of countless transactions across the Doyle generations.

Behind the counter was the apothecary cabinet and several deep drawers filled with the tools of the trade. Scales for weighing out doses, brass spoons for measuring, and a collection of cork stoppers that fitted precisely into the tops of the etched glass bottles that were the Doyles' trademark.

Fat, stout bottles of scented oils ran along the back counter, sitting next to several different-sized pestles and mortars for grinding herbs into fine powders.

Ada diagnosed what ailed her customers. She measured out the products, sometimes needing to make up bespoke blends. Rose's job was to entertain them as she wrote down each sale in the ledger. She also took payment for the remedies and elixirs that afflicted the Londoners.

It was Kezzie's job to fill the standard prescriptions, scooping powders and measuring liquids with practised ease. She scaled the wooden ladder so that she could reach the higher shelves and delved into the narrow drawers of the apothecary cabinet, all done under the watchful direction of her mother. She loved days like today, loading up the baskets and predicting the diagnoses and prescriptions that her mother prescribed for those who were sick.

A potion for tuberculosis.

A bottle of favoured perfume.

An herbal tea blend.

A tincture for the red heat of fever.

A balm for the deep ache of rheumatism.

Even during the lulls, there was work to do. Ada made a note of the medicines needed by the poorer community members. These requests often came in note form. Sometimes, in person, late at night, when everyone else was in bed. It was common knowledge amongst those living in Whitechapel that Ada Doyle would help those in need, often for free. These items were left at the end of the counter, waiting until trade quietened down enough for Ada to go out and deliver them.

Thanks to the support of today's shop patrons, her mother could continue her work, tending to the sick and venturing into parts of the city where doctors feared to tread.

One customer, Mrs Partridge, held her fractious child to her hip. The child's cheeks were flushed red. Kezzie passed the small bottle of elderflower tonic to her mother, who handed it to the customer.

"Take one teaspoon every four hours, Mrs Partridge," she said. "Use a cold compress to bring down the fever. Make sure she has something to drink but don't feed her."

"No food?"

Ada nodded. "Feed a cold, starve a fever. That's what my mother always said."

"Very well," Mrs Partridge said as she set out her coin purse, awkwardly juggling the child and bottle.

"Here," Kezzie reached across the counter, pressing into tiptoes to reach the purse. "I can help you."

"Thank you," Mrs Partridge smiled. "Goodness me, you are the absolute image of your mother. Do all the Doyle women have those striking eyes?"

Kezzie's smile faded slightly when she saw that her mother wasn't as pleased by the observation.

She brushed a hand over the top of Kezzie's blonde hair. "We do, Mrs Partridge. Although not everybody is as complimentary about our eyes as you are."

Before Mrs Partridge could reply, the shop door burst inwards, a gust of damp cold air surging inside as a young man staggered in, dragging another behind him.

"Ada! Please! Please help him!"

Kezzie recognised Tim Tibbs straightaway.

As the other customers simply stared at the curious scene unfolding before them, Ada calmly stepped around the counter and assessed the situation. She ducked down for a closer look at the bloodied face. "Who's that you've got there?"

"It's Frank Armstrong. His head..." Tim lurched further into the shop, his companion leaving a trail of blood in his wake.

"Bring him into the back room, Tim," Ada commanded. "Rose, please finish up here and then lock the door. I'll need your help," she added as Tim hauled the young man through the middle of the shop. "Kezzie, fetch my sewing kit and be quick about it." Ada pushed the heavy velvet curtain aside so that Tim could pull his companion through.

The back room was small and utilitarian. A narrow yet sturdy bed was set in the centre of the room. Ada quickly lit the gas lamps. Kezzie hurried in behind the bedraggled group, leaving Rose to jostle the remaining customers out of the shop.

"What happened?" Ada shook out a worn linen sheet and then helped Tim lift Frank onto it.

"We're working down the distillery. Frankie was loading the barrels onto a wagon. A blasted strap broke, and the whole thing collapsed on him," Tim growled, swiping a lock of dark hair from his face and smearing blood on himself in the process. "He was crushed under the lot! I can't take him to the surgeon–"

"It's fine," Ada's hands were a blur, taking out scissors, and shaking rags loose out of a drawer as he spoke. She handed Kezzie a dark brown bottle of carbolic acid. "Press on that big wound on his head," Ada instructed her. "Frank? Can you hear me? This is going to burn like blazes. Are you ready?"

Kezzie did as her mother had shown her, her heart racing as she soaked the cloth. No sooner had the cloth touched his skin before Frank roared in pain, a string of profanities let loose as his hand shot out the source, sending Kezzie flying backwards.

Ada's concerned shout was lost in the pained bellows, but it was Rose who helped Kezzie back onto her feet.

"Are you alright?"

Kezzie ignored the searing pain in her hands, balling her fists instead as she nodded to her mother. She bent for the cloth, though Rose took it from her.

The older woman took determined steps towards a writhing Frank, cloth aloft, "Let's see if you knock me on my arse, ya silly beggar," she muttered.

Ada turned her attention back to Frank. Her mouth was a thin line as she checked his injuries, her hands moving deftly to clean the head wound.

"Will he live? He has two nippers at home…" Tim said as Frank's head lolled.

"Head wounds bleed a lot and often look worse than they are," Ada replied. "I think he has broken his wrist though."

Frank moaned deeply as if to confirm her words. Ada gave him laudanum for the pain. The grumbles abated and Kezzie felt the tension leave the room. She ducked out through the curtain, leaving her mother and Rose to their work.

She knew that some of the work her mother was doing was strictly reserved for physicians and that Ada would get into a lot of trouble if caught. She kept glancing at the door as she nervously washed the trickles of blood from the floor. Once done, she rearranged the bottles and jars behind the counter, sweeping the flecks of powder and spillages away.

The muted clatter of carriages passing along the main street and the echoing footsteps, as people hurried past the bay window, did little to ease her anxiety. So much so, that she jolted when Rose finally emerged from the back room, the cloth she was drying her hands on carrying the stains of Frank's blood.

"How is he?" Kezzie asked, almost afraid of the answer. It was dangerous enough for her mother to be doing the work that she did, but how would they cope with a man dying on their premises?

"He'll live," Rose murmured, tugging the curtain shut behind her. "Ada still has some work to do and he's going to have a nasty headache in the morning. How is your hand?"

Kezzie showed the scrape she'd sustained from landing on the flagstone floor. "I'll live."

Rose chuckled at the joke.

She stepped behind the counter, brushing a gentle hand over Kezzie's hair, letting her hand rest reassuringly on the girl's narrow shoulder. "You did well in there. You'll make a fine healer one day."

Kezzie smiled at the praise as relief flooded her. "I didn't do anything. Maybe next time, I'll learn to duck though."

"You did well," Rose repeated pointedly. "You remained calm and did as you were asked without question. That takes a level head, Kezzie. I'm sure Ada will say the same when she is finished putting that boy back together."

"Thank you."

The sharp rap on the door drew their attention.

"I'd better unlock the door," Rose waved at the

customer who tried the door, then meaningfully peered through the glass partition at them both. "We'll have a mutiny on our hands, otherwise."

She unlocked the door to welcome the customer with a hearty hello that sounded false even to Kezzie. "Hello, Mrs Maitland! Come on in!"

"I tried earlier. Is everything okay, Rose?"

"Sorry about that. Are you here for your usual?"

Mrs Maitland frowned at the subject change, but Kezzie's guileless smile didn't reveal anything more to the nosey customer. "Yes, please."

Rose directed the woman towards the range of perfumes displayed along the far wall then joined Kezzie behind the counter.

"Should I make a start on supper?" Kezzie indicated the basket filled with remedies sitting on the end of the counter. Mama still has to make her deliveries."

Rose glanced back towards the curtain, her mouth twisting from one side to the other with indecision. A flicker of resolve crossed her features.

She snatched up the piece of paper with the addresses on it and held it towards Kezzie. "You must make the deliveries today."

Her mouth popped open when Rose pressed the paper into her hand. "Me?"

Rose fiddled with the bottles in the basket, checking the corks by pressing them into place. "Did you not pitch a tantrum just the other day about being allowed to make the deliveries?"

Heart racing, Kezzie could only nod.

"Your mother can't step away from what she's doing. I don't want her making deliveries in the dark. She'll say it's fine, but it isn't right for a woman to be out alone on the streets at night unless she's a… a… Never mind," Rose spared her a look. "I'd just prefer it when she's making deliveries during the day. You claim to be able to do this task. You begged your mother for the opportunity," Rose tucked a muslin square over the tops of the remedies. "Now's your chance."

Kezzie hesitated.

Her mother had made her views on the subject perfectly clear. To go now would be to directly disobey her. Trepidation turned her blood thunderous in her ears.

The deliveries were written down in geographical order. She recognised the street names, the names of the people.

With a surge of determination, she said, "I'll do it."

A slow smile spread on Rose's face. "That's my girl. No payments. Read the labels to whoever answers the door. Get them to repeat it twice, so you know they've understood. Got that?"

Kezzie slid her arms into her woollen coat and fastened the toggles, which took longer than usual because her hands were shaking. This was her chance to prove to her mother that she was ready for more, she reminded herself, nodding along as Rose gave out the instructions in staccato time.

"Got it."

Rose handed her the basket. "It's heavy."

With a deep breath, Kezzie looped her arm through, bracing herself against the additional weight as Rose settled it into place.

Nervously excited, Kezzie nodded. *This was her chance.*

She brandished the list of addresses and gave Rose a reassuring smile. "Thank you, Rose. I won't let you down."

"Hurry now," Rose urged as she opened the door and scooted Kezzie out onto the foggy streets of Whitechapel.

CHAPTER 3

It was easy to tell when you were heading away from Whitechapel and towards Mile End. For starters, the throngs of people began to thin out a little. The people in Mile End were more stooped, as if the weight of the cards that fate had dealt them pulled them down closer to the grimy, cobbled streets.

Whenever Kezzie and Ada ventured beyond the shop, they travelled by coach. Life looked very different to Kezzie down at this level.

There were none of the fine, elegant shops that you found south of the river along this part of town. Instead, ironmongers and makers of oilskins fought for pavement space, all squashed in next to alms houses and a builder's merchant.

The grey afternoon air hung heavily with a drizzle. City smoke slithered along the damp cobbled streets, coiling around her ankles. She wound her way along the labyrinth of lanes and alleys, her burgundy coat doing little to stave off the dampness of the day. She tried to look as though she belonged, although her heart was in her mouth. She remembered the route she'd taken before, nevertheless, it felt very different without the protection of her mother's skirts.

Any courage that Kezzie presented to her mother within the safe walls of the apothecary shop had quickly dwindled, leaving behind a hollow ball of anxiety that gnawed at her belly. Several times, she had to switch arms, the weight of the basket making her arm ache. Each time she stopped, she became aware of the scrawny children pausing in their activities to stare at her with wide, curious eyes.

With her white-blonde hair, pretty blue dress, and fine woollen coat, she knew she must stick out like a sore thumb among their filthy rags. Each child had thin legs and bare feet, the same colour as the streets.

The deeper she walked into Mile End, the worse the stench became—an unpleasant mix of decay, the world down here blackened by soot and despair.

She turned the corner, pausing to check the crumpled piece of paper that she gripped like a lifeline in her hand.

Bone Lane.

The road ahead stretched out like a dark tunnel; any light diminished by the way the buildings leaned in on each other as if squaring off in a fight.

Carefully, Kezzie picked her way along the muddy track, stepping over broken bricks and piles of decaying, rotting waste, counting doors as she went.

She stopped in front of the door that was askew in its frame, not quite meeting the corners as it should.

Several filthy rags had been used to plug the broken window to her right. She knocked on the rickety door, the rattling sound sending a series of barks rolling along the street. A mangy mutt trotted over to her as she waited, its matted fur barely covering the ribs poking through its coat. It sniffed at her boots before losing interest in her and moving on down the street.

Kezzie was relieved when the door creaked open. Rather than an adult, though, it was a girl not much older than herself who answered. Her face was thin, her eyes large in her lean face, her lank, black hair tangling around her features. She looked at Kezzie with a mixture of suspicion and curiosity.

"Who are you?" the girl said.

"I'm Kezzie Doyle," she replied.

The girl blinked, eyes moving from basket to Kezzie. "What do you want?"

"My mother has sent me to bring some medicine for you." Kezzie held up the basket, trying to sound much more confident than she felt.

"Hester! Shut that ruddy door!" A voice bellowed from somewhere behind the girl. "It's cold enough in here as it is."

Kezzie flinched. The young girl stared. Under the quizzical look, Kezzie offered her a reassuring smile.

Hester hesitated a moment more before she pushed the door wider, allowing Kezzie to step inside. "It's my mother. She's through here."

The room was cramped and dim. Kezzie peered into the gloom, carefully inching her way forward. Gradually, her eyes adjusted to the darkness, revealing just how confined the room really was. She couldn't help but compare it to her own warm, comfortable bedroom. A thin straw mattress covered part of the floor in the corner, a pile of blankets at its centre. On it, sat a young girl with her knees drawn up to her chest eyeballing Kezzie just as her older sister had. Two rickety chairs flanked the bed.

The bare wooden floor was littered with scraps of fabric and bits of card. There were what looked like half-made tiny boxes spread around the room. Faded wallpaper peeled from the walls and the window let in more draught than light.

She could just about make out the shadowy forms of more children huddled together in the other corner; their eyes wide with suspicion as they stared at her. She tried not to stare back at them. Kezzie's breath formed little clouds in the stifling, mildew air.

A tiny black cast-iron stove was tucked into a recess in the wall, its belly unlit. In the low light that filtered through the grimy window, Kezzie followed Hester. She hadn't ventured much further inside when the sound of a woman's hacking cough echoed off the walls.

Kezzie knew a consumption cough when she heard one, wincing at the wretched sound, her heart sinking by what she knew of the pervasive disease.

No cure.

"Ma," Hester announced in the doorway of the next room. "It's the Doyle girl. She's here with the medicine to make you feel better."

Steeling herself, Kezzie pasted on a smile. Hester gave her a brief nod, stepping aside to allow Kezzie better access to the frail-looking woman leaning against the damp bedroom wall.

Bloodshot eyes narrowed as she took in Kezzie's form. "You're not Ada."

"I'm her daughter, Kezzie."

The woman shook her head vehemently. "Why has she sent you? I need to see Ada. She's the one that helps me."

Kezzie tried not to take offence at the tone. She realised her mother had tried to warn her, to prepare her for the hardships she was about to face, but seeing it was so much harder than it looked. She set the basket down on the floor, confident now because she knew which medicine the woman needed. "I can help you, too."

"No!" The woman shook her head. "I don't know you."

"I'm a Doyle," Kezzie leaned in and fluttered her lashes in her direction. "See? My mother and I have the same blue eyes. I promise you that Mother has taught me well. What's your name?"

"Hazel," the woman rasped, squinting through the gloom at her. Kezzie let her look into her eyes, remembering what Mrs Partridge had remarked on earlier. There was no denying that she was Ada Doyle's daughter.

When Hazel seemed to accept her, Kezzie lifted two

bottles out of the basket. She held up the first one. "This one is to help soothe the cough," she said. "You need to use a spoon and take two doses four times a day. It doesn't taste very nice, but it will take away the tickle that's troubling you." She remembered what Rose had made her promise to do. "Can you please repeat that back to me?"

The woman obliged; her words cut off by a fit of coughing. Kezzie handed her the grubby rag she was trying to reach and used it to wipe at her mouth. "I don't pay Ada."

"I know," Kezzie replied. "Mother's work is very important to her – to all of us, really. I wasn't expecting any payment. Now, this one is a salve. You can melt it in some hot water, and the steam will help ease your throat, or you can rub it on your chest. Try not to get it in your eyes because it will sting."

"We got no fire," Hester muttered from somewhere behind her. "We got no way of heating any water."

Kezzie peered back at the young girl. She thought about the roaring fires that filled her home, and the spikes of guilt pained her. "The best and quickest way to clear a tight chest is through inhalation and steam," Kezzie smiled and reached into her pocket, pulling out a couple of copper coins. She held them out. "I don't have much but this ought to buy a couple of pieces of coal at least," she said.

The woman exchanged a look with her daughter, her lips twisting into a wry smile. "It's not very often we see kindness in these parts, Miss Kezzie."

"It's the only way for the medicine to work properly and the fastest way for you to get better," nodded Kezzie, aware that there was no cure for consumption, especially not in conditions like this.

People needed rest and fresh air, neither of which could be found in this dark and dingy room. All she could do was make Hazel as comfortable as possible and help to keep her alive a little longer. Her eyes drifted beyond the doorway, to the children who sat huddled together in the other room. She made a mental note to bring a couple of pieces of bread for them next time.

The woman's hard, red eyes softened a little as her daughter accepted the coins from Kezzie. "Bless your heart, girl. The bairns haven't eaten for a couple of days."

Her heart stuttered as she wondered how they hadn't perished in this cold, damp room already.

No food, no fire.

It made her heart ache.

No wonder Ada felt compelled to do this kind of work.

"Here, let me show you how to do this."

Kezzie instructed the girl on how to apply the salve and administer the tincture to her mother. As she did so, a sense of purpose began to solidify. Despite the overwhelming despair and darkness of the harsh reality of living in such conditions, Kezzie hoped that this small gesture would make a difference to this family. She now understood the importance of their work and why her mother gave up a portion of her business to support these people, and she grasped the true impact of her family's legacy.

Kezzie left the dismal room to a chorus of thanks echoing behind her. They followed her back out into the cold streets.

She made three more deliveries that afternoon. Each place was as sad and haunting as the first one. But she reminded herself that this was what she wanted to do.

This was what she had been born to do.

A mission to fulfil, a legacy to uphold.

And though she felt incredibly sad for the desperate people she met; her heart felt a little lighter as she made her way back towards the apothecary shop.

She had done it.

She had proved herself worthy.

Her mind turned to the evening ahead. She wondered

if Rose and her mother had quarrelled over Rose's decision to let Kezzie go out and make the deliveries alone. Ada would be furious that she'd gone against her wishes. Kezzie reasoned that any argument from her mother would be quashed because she had successfully dispensed medicines and had completed her mission.

Dusk threaded its fingers through the air, lengthening the shadows and deepening the gloom around the city. The building conditions changed to ones in a little better repair as she walked: signs that she was getting closer to home.

A frantic energy seemed to fill the streets as people hurried by, anxious to escape the cold, damp air.

Kezzie strolled along, the empty basket swinging at her side. Cabs and carriages clattered along the streets as the thick fog from the fires and the factories tickled her throat. However, all she felt was a sense of excitement.

Surely now, Ada would let Kezzie continue to do the deliveries. Today, she'd shown her mother that she could be trusted, that there was no harm in allowing Kezzie a little bit of freedom.

She turned a corner, swallowing a scream as she collided with an unexpected figure.

The crone, her face thrown into prominence by the white puddle of pale gaslight, was twisted into a grotesque mask. She was dressed in layers of tattered rags, white hair hanging limply over bony shoulders, and a hand wrapped around a knobby wooden stick.

Startled, Kezzie stumbled back, her eyes widening in terror as she stared into the sightless milky-white orbs in the woman's face.

"I—I'm sorry," she stammered. Though before she could retreat, the woman's hand shot out to grip her shoulder, the bony grip surprisingly strong.

"Death," the woman intoned, her unseeing eyes staring piercingly into Kezzie's face with intensity. "I see it in you."

"W-what?" Kezzie instinctively tried to pull back. The grip tightened like a vice, and pain radiated out from the tight circle her fingers formed.

"I smell it on you. You bring death," she hissed. "It stalks you. Follows you."

"Let me go," Kezzie twisted in the grip. "Let me go, I say!"

"Eyes of the witch! Cursed! You're cursed, witch. Everything you touch dies. A man meets his doom whenever you're near," she yanked Kezzie closer, bloodless lips peeling back to reveal toothless gums. "It can never end. *Never!*"

Kezzie started to whimper as the crone cackled. She twisted and jerked, as the rants grew louder. Heart pounding, terror closed her throat off and a soundless scream burned there. The foggy night blurred, closing in on her, suffocating, choking her.

"Mable! Enough!" The voice cut through the tempest and a figure emerged through the mists. The tight band on her arm was released. "Honestly, Mable. Get back to the dosshouse. You can't keep scaring people like this!"

Kezzie leaned against the wall, arms wrapped around her waist and watching as the young girl turned the old crone away from her. She spoke kindly but loud enough to be heard above the ravings that continued to spew from the old woman's mouth, and she steered her along the street. She walked her over the cobbles, and down a little, standing in the pool of light once she'd set her free as though making certain she didn't come back. The old woman's cursing echoed off the walls, rags fluttering in the fog as she disappeared into the night.

"Don't mind her," the young girl called out as she made her way back to Kezzie.

Kezzie was rubbing her arm. She straightened up, her legs rubbery enough to match her jittery nerves. "Who was that?"

She waved dismissively. "That's Mad Mable. She's like

part of the furniture in these parts, though she is mad as a box of frogs. Most days she's harmless. She has a name for making wild predictions."

Kezzie's heart stalled in her chest as she recalled the venomous declarations. "She-she does?"

The girl laughed at Kezzie's horrified expression, the sound echoing in the near-empty street. "They never come true."

She looked along the black cobbles that now had a dull shine on them in the night air.

You bring death.

A shiver slithered along Kezzie's spine as she recalled the words. "I hope not."

The girl's dark eyes swept over her assessing. Her chin hitched up a little. "You're not from round here, are you?"

Kezzie frowned. "I am, too. I'm Kezzie Doyle. My mother has the apothecary shop in Whitechapel."

The girl jolted and then scrutinised her closely. "So, you are. You have the eyes."

Eyes of the witch! Cursed!

Kezzie dropped her gaze, uncomfortable with the attention, frowning as she tried to shut off the taunts that simmered in her head. "What's, um, what's your name?"

"Ethel Mooney," the girl replied.

"You're Maggie's daughter," Kezzie said.

"One of 'em," Ethel grinned.

Kezzie returned the smile. "I've seen your surname on the delivery list a few times."

"Well, there's a lot of us!"

Kezzie couldn't imagine being a part of a large family. Her father had passed not long after she'd been born. Her mother had been an only child, too. Because of the protective bonds Ada wrapped around Kezzie, she had never formed any lasting friendships with people her own age. Kezzie often watched the street urchins, seeing how they played and danced with each other, how they could find utter joy in the simplest of things with such abandon, and she felt jealous.

"Do you always do the deliveries?" Ethel asked, her gaze fixed on Kezzie's face.

A fleeting smile came and went. "Today is my first time."

"It's an important job," Ethel surmised. "Different, too. Anyway, I'd best get on. I'm meant to be out looking for my brother." She lifted a hand indicating the way she'd sent Mad Mable. "The apothecary is that way."

Kezzie wondered if she would ever get as comfortable being out in the dark as Ethel seemed to be. "Thank you."

"Watch out for Mad Mable. Remember, her tongue is sharper than her claws!" Ethel waved, skipping along the pavement.

With a steadying breath, Kezzie squared her shoulders. When she glanced back, Ethel had already vanished into the swirling fog. She hurried along the pavement, the darkness pressing in from all sides. The day's successes were lost to the scary interaction with Mable.

Her trepidation eased when she turned into East Alley and spotted the familiar radiance of the shop, glowing in the darkness like a beacon of safety for her. She knew that admitting she'd been scared by the resident madwoman would mean that Ada would lock her back up and never let her out.

No, if she was to convince her mother that she was capable and could handle the responsibility of making the deliveries, she'd have to pretend to both Ada and Rose that her day had been a screaming success.

CHAPTER 4

"You have a visitor."

She'd been so engrossed in her leather-bound tome spread out on the table before her that Kezzie hadn't heard her mother's approach, so she jolted when Ada spoke from the doorway. "Pardon?"

"There's someone here to see you," Ada announced, her tone mirroring the surprise on her face.

Kezzie frowned – she'd never had a visitor before in her life – then she realised that her mother must be referring to Rose. Relieved, she slipped down from the seat, grinding to a halt when she saw who was standing in the corridor behind her mother.

Not Rose, but Ethel, looking decidedly out of place in her filthy dress.

"W-what are you doing here?"

Ada tilted her head at her child. "This young lady claims she knows you."

Kezzie nodded quickly. "Ethel," she replied, brow furrowed. "We met when I was making the deliveries last week." She was careful to edit out the incident with Mad Mabel. "What are you doing here?"

Undeterred by the uncomfortable silence, Ethel strolled into the sitting room, eyes wide as she gazed about her with open curiosity. "I hadn't seen you about," she said, crossing to the window, angling her head to peer into the street below. "You have all your windowpanes here."

"Yes," Kezzie said, eying her mother warily.

This wariness had been prevalent since Kezzie had returned from making the deliveries and had walked straight into a terrific argument between her mother and Rose. Ada, who'd been frantic with worry, had scooped up her child and summarily thrown Rose out of the shop. Rose, furious and indignant, had slammed the door on the way out. For all of her life, Rose had been a constant.

Now, Kezzie missed the woman terribly. In the aftermath of the argument, Ada had tightened her grip on Kezzie's learning time. Which was why she was surprised that her mother had allowed Ethel into the inner sanctum of their home.

"It looks funny down below when you move your head like this," Ethel said, oblivious to the undercurrents between mother and daughter behind her.

The doorbell jingled faintly below them, a reminder that the world went on. Ada huffed, and Kezzie wondered when her mother would admit that she needed Rose, even if they were still cross with each other.

"Don't be too long, Kezzie," Ada said, sending her daughter a pointed look. "You have studies to get through. I'll be in the shop if you need me."

The door closed, leaving the two girls alone.

"She doesn't like me," Ethel moved away from the window, prowling around the room.

"Why do you say that?"

Ethel shrugged. "She didn't look happy that I was asking for you."

Compelled to protect her mother, she said, "She's very busy. My aunt Rose has... well, they've fallen out. Everything falls to my mother to do."

"What did they fall out over?"

"Me."

Ethel stopped; her dark eyes alight with mischief. "What did you do?"

She didn't want to let her know that her mother kept her under lock and key, especially when she'd pretended to Ethel the other day that she was streetwise. She wanted Ethel to like her. Pointing out how different their lives were didn't feel like that would get the job done.

"Doesn't matter."

Seemingly satisfied with the reply, Ethel wandered the room.

The sitting room was a blend of comfort and practicality. A large, faded rug covered most of the scarred, wooden floor. Bookshelves lined two of the walls, stuffed with medical texts and herbology terms, their spines cracked and faded from generations of use. The furniture was dark and well-used, strewn with ornaments and collectables. Little mementos that the Doyle women had collected over the years hung on the walls.

Ethel made her way around the room, fingers trailing along the furniture, over the faded armchairs, and the tapestries that hung on the far wall. "Do you like living amongst all of this?" she asked.

Kezzie trailed behind her. "This place—it's all I've ever known. This stuff belonged to my grandmother and my great-grandmother. It's been in our family for years. A long line of Doyle healers," she explained.

"Didn't your surname change when your grandmother got married? Or when your mother got married?" Ethel asked.

Kezzie paused, not knowing how to correctly answer, though she didn't have to. They'd reached the sturdy oak table, cluttered with papers and a dirty ink pot. Ethel's blackened fingernail traced each letter scratched into the vellum paper of the dense medical volume that Kezzie had been reading, where she'd been trying to understand the intricate details of herbal pharmacology. "Do you know what all of this says?"

"I do," Kezzie replied.

Ethel pointed to the patterns and pictures in another book. "What about this one?"

Kezzie nodded. "I've read it all. I want to be a healer, like my mother, and her mother before her. To be good at this, I need to understand it all... the herbs, plants, roots, and the trees. Rocks and metals. All of the insects and all of the minerals that go into making medicine to treat illnesses and diseases. My ancestors wrote most of these books."

Ethel's dark eyes traced her face as if trying to understand her. "I don't read. I was meant to go to school, but Pa said I needed to work. We got mouths to feed, and I learn it all from the streets, anyway."

Kezzie couldn't imagine not being able to read, the hours of enjoyment she gained from disappearing into another world. "Would you like to know how to read?"

Ethel was on the move again. She shrugged. "What would someone like me need to know how to read?"

"For work? If you were to work in a factory, or a—"

The bark of laughter cut her off. "I wouldn't get a job in a place like that. Not when my ma needs help with the little ones."

"I could teach you a few words if you like," Kezzie offered. "Might come in handy one day."

Ethel turned to stare at her. "You could do that?"

Kezzie nodded, a little fizz of excitement bubbling inside.

Ethel's eyes lit up. "I think I'd like that." Her path around the front room started up again. "It smells strange in here."

Kezzie laughed. "It always does, depending on whatever medicine has been freshly prepared. That's clove and sage you can smell."

Ethel's nose wrinkled as she sniffed the air. "Smells

better than the privy, at least. When are you making the deliveries next? I could walk with you, save you from Mad Mabel again."

Kezzie lunged for her, eying the door nervously, although she could hear the mute conversation through the floorboards. "Hush! Don't mention Mad Mabel to my mother!"

Ethel's brows climbed her head. "Alright, but why not?"

Kezzie suppressed the grotesque images that had slithered into her dreams, into her waking moments when she least expected them. Memories of Mad Mabel's ravings had upset her more than she'd let on.

"My mother... is a worrier and she's protective of me, being her only daughter. She wouldn't like to hear about how I bumped into Mable."

Mischief glinted in Ethel's quick grin, and she mimed turning a lock on her lips.

From the street outside, shouts and cries rallied up to the window, the alley filling with Ethel's name. Curiosity sparked in Ethel's eyes as she rushed to the window.

She extended a finger. "My friends are waiting."

A splinter of disappointment broke through the pleasure of having her new friend in the room as Ethel yelled back, waving. The lively voices responded, beckoning her to join in their play.

Ethel hurried to the door, her steps quick and eager. Kezzie stayed where she was, stuck in a world filled with learning and loneliness.

The young girl paused at the threshold, turning to look back at Kezzie, her face alight with an impish grin.

"You comin'?"

CHAPTER 5

Ethel was persistent.

Ada hadn't permitted Kezzie to go out that first day the other girl had visited, nor the day after that, or the day after that. Nevertheless, Ethel made a point of calling at the shop every day. Whenever she did, in the street beyond the open door, a collective band of bedraggled children waited in the street, an assortment of hoops, sticks, and stones gripped in their hands as they waited for their friend to make her daily pilgrimage.

Each time, Ada gave a polite smile but shook her head.

Kezzie knew that any amount of pleading and stamping her feet would not affect her mother. Kezzie would watch the children wander off, their attention already moving on. Then she would get on with her work.

One evening, as the grey fog rolled heavily along the street outside the shop, the bell tinkled. Without looking up, Ada announced that the shop was closing.

"Ada."

Kezzie turned mid-step and saw Rose standing in the doorway.

"Please," Rose said patiently, "I miss my friend. Can we forgive one another and move past this?"

For a moment, the two friends stared at one another. Then the front door was locked, and Kezzie was sent upstairs.

The next day, it seemed all was normal once again in Doyle's apothecary.

Rose arrived early at the shop with three finger buns from the bakery and returned to work. Ada was lighter, her smile given more freely than on the days when she didn't have her best friend by her side. And then, when Ethel made her daily visit, Kezzie was astonished when Ada agreed that she could go into the street and play, provided she stayed on East Alley where her mother could see her.

At first, Kezzie stood on the other side of the road, watching the group playing. Their laughter echoed, floating through the cool air, and bouncing off the dingy brick walls. She observed the game, the children quickly adapting to the rules of having to stay in front of the apothecary store.

When it was her turn, her movements were not as practised as theirs, yet they cheered as she awkwardly hopped around, clapping and shouting their encouragement. They returned the next day, a raggedy crew standing out on the street, led by their leader Ethel.

Again, Ada let her join in with them.

And so it was that Kezzie formed friendships with these urchins in threadbare clothing. From hopscotch, where they'd scratched a grid into the pavement, to playing marbles with stones rather than pretty glass balls, it seemed to Kezzie that they never had the right equipment, yet that never stopped their imagination.

The weeks rolled by, and her confidence in being outside and playing with the children began to grow. Kezzie stuck to the rules, only playing as far as the end of East Alley. Beyond felt like a whole new world. At the end of every meet-up, she watched the children scatter into the alleys when she waved goodbye to them.

As her confidence grew, so did her mother's trust. Kezzie was allowed to venture to the next road, which opened up a whole new world of more children playing in the dingy gutters of the streets.

Kezzie was still out of breath from playing when she let herself into the shop. The bell tinkled. Ada and Rose looked up from their place at the counter. A row of green bottles had been arranged on the countertop in front of them, and the air was pungent with rosemary. Cheeks flushed from the cool air, Kezzie began to tug off her mittens.

"What are you doing?" Ada questioned her.

Kezzie paused, eying her mother as if she'd taken leave of her senses. "I'm going to hang up my coat and then go back to dusting the shelves in the back, Mama."

Ada waved her hand, rounding the edge of the counter. She handed her back her gloves. "No time for that."

Kezzie frowned at her gloves, the expression deepening when she noticed Rose's smirk from behind Ada. "Mama?"

Ada twisted and pushed the basket, now brimming with potions and herbs, along the counter. She tapped the piece of paper resting atop. "Three places. This one here is in a little alley off Nelson Street. If you pass the tanners, you've gone too far."

Kezzie wondered if perhaps she was dreaming. "Mama? You mean I can make the deliveries?"

Ada pressed her hands together in supplication. "Yes, Kezurah. But you come straight back here, please. I worry. I know you think you're growing up," Ada cupped her rosy cheeks, and lifted her chin, "but you'll always be my baby girl."

Kezzie threw her arms around her mother. "Thank you, Mama! Thank you!"

"Straight back, Kezzie."

Kezzie jammed her hands into her gloves, hefting the

weighty basket, tossing over her shoulder a quick smile, "Yes, Mama, I will."

∼

Ada Doyle watched her daughter striding along the street. Her heart filled with unbridled joy. Golden curls bouncing about the edges of her bonnet, her small stature quickly swallowed by the sea of people out on Brewer Street.

Fear, akin to a panic, drove her to want to run after her. To scoop up her baby and shield her from the evil of this world.

She wasn't ready for it.

She would never be ready for the cruelty of this city.

"You've done the right thing in letting her go," Rose commented behind her.

Ada hadn't even heard her approach, though she didn't take her eyes off where she'd last seen Kezzie. "I'm not sure."

She wanted to believe Rose. She truly did. They'd butted heads over this for almost a year… ever since Kezzie had started asking to make the deliveries by herself.

Rose appeared in her peripheral view and looked through the window. "You can't stop the sands of time, Ada. None of us can."

A small smile curved her mouth. "That's true enough."

"And that means you'll have to tell her the truth at some point."

Ada could ignore her, as she always did whenever the subject came up. Instead, she met Rose's gaze. "I will."

"When?"

Ada resolutely shook her head, her mouth firming into a flat line. "Not yet. I told you. I'll do it in my own time." She turned from the window, wrapping her arms around her slender waist.

"The girl isn't stupid, Ada. She's already asking questions. Someone will tell her before you get the chance if you leave it much longer."

Ada rounded on her friend. Her trusted advisor. The one person who knew her better than she knew herself. Still, she let the annoyance flash into her tone, "I know, Rose. I know that my time is running out, but can I not just let her be a child for a little while longer?" Ada blinked at the sudden hot sting of tears. "Every time I look at her, it's like I hear the countdown in my mind. I lie in bed at night, and I picture each day of her life. I want to keep her safe for as long as I can."

Rose sighed. She crossed the room to where she stood and rubbed the tops of her arms soothingly. "I understand why, Ada. I do. I love that girl like my own."

"Kezzie will know the truth one day. She will know all about her history and where she came from. For now, let me keep her tucked safely away from that world."

Rose gave a slow nod. "Very well."

CHAPTER 6

The fire crackled in the hearth of the sitting room above the apothecary shop, pressing back the chill of the winter morning. Snow piled up on the window ledge beyond the glass.

Ethel stood by the window, her breath blooming on the glass as she watched the snow flurries dance beyond the pane.

"Can we get back to work now?" Kezzie prompted gently, glancing up at her friend from where she sat on the floor in front of the hearth. "These letters won't write themselves."

"Sorry," Ethel murmured, tearing her gaze from the window. "It's just… You can't see the snow from my windows."

Kezzie wondered about Ethel's house. She knew where her friend lived, but Ethel had always seemed reluctant to share more of her life and had never once let her step inside. She knew that Ethel still had both parents and that she shared her room with several siblings, mostly brothers, from what she had gathered. Kezzie couldn't imagine life in such a large family.

They spent the morning practising Ethel's letters. Ethel had proved to be a good student, catching on quickly to the task. She was able to form the shapes with ease and was keen to move on to paper. However, Ada hadn't been too pleased about this. Paper was expensive, and she had made sure that Kezzie kept Ethel working on a slate until Ethel's writing had improved significantly.

"It's so peaceful up here," Ethel said, breaking the silence.

Kezzie set down her chalk piece on top of the slate. She rose and crossed to the window, joining her friend. "Everything looks so different from up here," she mused.

"Do you ever wonder what life will be like when we're grown up?"

"Of course," Kezzie replied. Below, the fresh snowfall had blanketed the streets, alleys, roofs, and shingles. Covering the world they looked out on with a deceptive calm. By tomorrow, it would be blackened by the city's fog, but for now, the pristine white almost hurt her eyes. "I will be here, no doubt working alongside my mother for years to come."

She eyed Ethel carefully. "Can I tell you a secret?"

Ethel's eyes shone. "What are friends for?"

"I want to train to be a doctor," Kezzie whispered, her eyes sliding towards the door in case her mother might be listening.

"Isn't that what you do now?" Ethel asked, puzzled.

"Yes, in a way, I suppose," Kezzie acknowledged, "but it's risky. We're not supposed to perform any surgeries here, but we do, as you know."

Ethel had been hanging around with Kezzie long enough to see the types of injuries that erupted through the door. The local people knew that Ada was the better choice when they couldn't afford a surgeon or a doctor.

"If I were a doctor, it would be different. I wouldn't be watching the front door of the shop, waiting for the police to storm through and cart me away to jail. It would be official. It would mean that I could help more people and make more of a difference in this life," Kezzie continued.

Ethel spoke softly, her gaze sliding back to the glass. "It must be wonderful to have such a clear path. I don't know what I want to be."

Kezzie smiled. "You have some time to work it out. Who knows what will happen once we get you reading and writing? You could work in any factory in the country."

"I'm sure you can do anything you choose to, Kezzie. You're already so brave," Ethel said, her eyes on the snowy vista outside.

Kezzie smiled at her friend, shaking her head. "I wish I was as brave as you. You are fearless, Ethel. You are out on the streets every day, looking for work and helping others. You saved me from Mad Mable, too."

Ethel shrugged modestly. "I don't have much choice in the matter. Ma and Pa need my help with the little ones, so that's what I have to do." Her gaze drifted across the white expanse below them. "I'm just surprised that you will be able to leave the shop. I thought that the curse…" Her voice trailed off, leaving an unsettling silence in the room that was punctuated only by the crackling fire.

"The what?"

"You know, the Doyle curse?"

Her brows knitted together in confusion. "I don't know what you mean. What curse?"

Ethel's eyes widened, and she hurried away from the window, returning to her seat and picking up her slate with nervous hands. "Never mind," she said quickly. "How does my 'b' look?"

Kezzie wasn't to be diverted.

She had heard the whispering, caught the unnerving stares… remembered the ravings of Mad Mable that shimmered constantly around the edges of her mind. She stomped across the floor, and fisted her hands on her hips. "You tell me right now, Ethel Mooney," she demanded in a firm voice, "or I won't help you ever again."

Ethel looked as close to tears as Kezzie had ever seen her, and this was the girl who wasn't scared of anything. "I'm sorry. I thought you knew. Please... Please don't curse me."

Kezzie didn't know whether to laugh or shout. "And how am I supposed to curse you?"

"Because you're a witch."

Kezzie sat down next to her friend, trying to puzzle her way through those words. "I might very well be, but as I know only herbal medicine, not magical spells, it's unlikely. But," she tilted her head, "is that what you really think of me?"

Slowly, Ethel shook her head.

"Why would you think it, then?"

Ethel began to recite the words that had haunted the edges of Kezzie's life.

> *"The name of Doyle, the seer did tell.*
> *Wealth plenty, but the death toll knell*
> *For every man, a Doyle holds dear,*
> *Will meet his doom before they're wed a year.*
> *The Doyle line, no sons shall be born.*
> *Only one daughter, her life forlorn.*
> *She walks alone, to wither and fade,*
> *An heiress of solitude, living in perpetual shade.*
> *Blessed by beauty and gold in lieu*
> *Of love's eternal kiss, the Doyle's curse holds true."*

Ethel's words hung in the air as Kezzie's heart tripped over in her chest.

Ethel continued in a whisper, "You're a Doyle. Your dad died before you were one, didn't he?"

Kezzie nodded. Her mind reeled as her heart raced.

This was it. This was what her mother had tiptoed around for all these years.

"The Doyle women only have one daughter. The husbands die soon after their first child is born. The Doyle women die early, leaving the child orphaned. It's happened ever since the Doyles have lived here. Everybody knows it."

Ethel's words dropped like bricks into a puddle in Kezzie's mind. She had heard snippets of such tales before but had never heard the full weight of the legend laid out so plainly. "Is that why people look at me so strangely?"

"Your witch's eyes," Ethel pointed to her own eyes. "They're afraid. They think if they get too close to you, they'll be cursed too."

Kezzie focused on her friend. "Is that what you believe too?"

Slowly, Ethel shook her head. "It's just what everyone says."

"But that night, you chased off Mad Mable. You helped me that night. Did you know who I was then?"

"Not at first, but when I listened to the ravings of Mad Mable, I realised who you were."

Kezzie lowered herself to the floor as the wailing epithet of Mad Mable drifted through her mind. "Mable was right. She knew who I was."

"People say she's a see but Mad Mable is just that, mad. She raves about many things, most of them nonsense," Ethel told her.

"But what if it's true? I don't have any powers to curse anyone…" Kezzie's thoughts trailed off as she considered her family history. Her mother had raised her alone, constantly avoiding talking about her father and anything to do with her past.

It all made sense to her now.

"If it helps, I'm not scared of you anymore," Ethel offered.

Kezzie squeezed her friend's hand. Her only friend. No wonder people had been avoiding her all these years if they believed that she was cursed. "That's all that matters then," she sniffed. "Thank you for telling me."

"I meant what I said," Ethel pressed. "I think you'll make a wonderful doctor."

Kezzie forced out a smile. "Thank you. Come on. Let's focus on your letters for today. Who knows, maybe you'll become a teacher too one day."

They resumed their practice, the crackling fire in the hearth and the falling snow beyond the window cocooning them in their own world. She waited patiently as Ethel scratched the letters onto the slate, forming words and making the other girl smile. All the while, her mind was whirling.

Despite the dark whispers and the old tales, Kezzie decided that she would change her fate. She would be the one to end the cycle.

If she didn't fall in love, the man wouldn't die young.

If she didn't fall in love. she wouldn't have a child.

She would break this curse, not with magic, but with logic. She would carve her own path with kindness and strength, and she would do it with the unwavering bond of true friendship.

CHAPTER 7

Whitechapel, London

1878

It wasn't that she didn't notice the people loitering in the doorways of the dilapidated buildings. Or the remnants of humanity that hovered around the edges of the heaving city as she cut her way through the busy streets: how the skinny children, their legs curved from rickets, eyed her with hungry curiosity.

She saw them when she knew that they were simply ignored by many folks. She had no concerns about being attacked or robbed. The basket hooked over her arm didn't contain meat or bread. She was confident that the Doyle name was well known enough in this part of London. It was this notoriety that meant she could walk without fear.

The church clock heralded the middle of the day though the mantle of dense fog kept the sun at bay, dimming the light to a pale glow and casting a luminous haze over the city.

Kezzie skirted around the edge of an overturned cart where an old horse had collapsed in a dead heap, leaving the owner to defend his cargo against opportunists who might think otherwise. She ducked under the waving arms of two men outside The Vine Tavern – the only pub on Mile End Road – as they argued voraciously with the pot man, both unhappy about being tossed out of the pub when they had beer left still.

Up ahead, through the murkiness of coal smoke and the stench of the unwashed masses, the jangling melody of an organ grinder filled the air. Here, the barefooted urchins danced a jig in the middle of the road, their faces lit with joy and laughter, forgetting their poverty for a moment.

She passed by Lycett Chapel, a hulking building which stood at the corner of Whitehorse Lane, its long stained-glass windows dull against the grey. Horse-drawn trams rolled along the road with a rumble, the driver's horn whistle being used to keep the horses moving forward.

The cacophony of a city that was divided by the haves and the have-nots.

Hands were pressed towards her, begging for alms, haunted women drifting along the street. She gave what she could when she had it, but today her purse remained empty. She offered a smile and a blessing, her stride full of purpose when she turned into Bull Yard. Down here, the ground was slimy, blackened by the filth that ran off the chinked roofs.

It opened up into a small courtyard where clumps of rubbish had collected in the corners. Overhead, lines of dank washing were strung between the broken windows, crisscrossing like a dusty cobweb.

A gaggle of washerwomen huddled on the stone steps, and it was only then that Kezzie's steps faltered as she swiftly assessed who was outside. Almost everyone was welcoming to her in this building, although there were those who didn't trust the healers of the community, believing that the Doyle women were cursed, their unnatural health-giving skills marked by their strikingly pale blue eyes.

But today, she saw that none of the crones who would spit and curse at her were sitting on the steps. Laughter and camaraderie filled the echoing space like a melody from a different world.

It was Maud Fishwick who first spotted her. "Hello, Kezzie, love. How's your mother?"

"Well, thank you for asking, Maud," Kezzie replied as she approached the group. Although the Doyle women were neither wealthy nor educated, Kezzie knew herself to be touched by fortune's hand. Never in her life had she worried about whether she would eat that day. She knew the gentle touch of a loving mother, slept in a clean bed, in a warm room, under a dry roof and had an endless supply of candles.

"Remind me to her, love," Maud nudged the others back to allow Kezzie through. "She saved my George's life. Mine, too. She's a miracle worker, no doubt about that."

Kezzie thanked her, slipping through the narrow door and into the begrimed hallway beyond. She climbed the stairs with the sure-footedness of one well acquainted with the treachery of the foul stairway, having learned which planks were softened with rot as she climbed three flights of stairs. The scurrying black creatures that darted into holes in the wall up ahead did not faze her, and as she climbed higher, she heard the echoing cries of the mess of life that filled this rotting building to bursting point.

She paused when she reached the top landing, the air stale and stinking.

The O'Malleys were a family of nine, Maggie and John, with a flock of children who shared a single room with another family of five. It was understood that they were crammed into the tiny space through necessity rather than choice.

Even before she knocked, she could smell the taint of disease through the open splits in the door.

The room was a tiny stifling space that barely pushed back the deep shadows with the stubby candles flickering in either corner of the room.

"Thank the Lord!" John O'Malley exclaimed as she stepped inside. "It's the young 'un," he indicated the unmoving bundle that she could see lying in a cardboard box on top of the unsteady table.

"She ain't made a squawk in a little while but she's fine. Can you help her?" Jane O'Malley beckoned her across the room. Jane was only a few months younger than Kezzie yet noticeably shorter. Ada Doyle had once explained this difference to Kezzie; that many people in this city simply couldn't afford to eat the right food. It was why some children's legs bowed like they'd been born ready to fit perfectly onto a horse.

Kezzie offered a smile at Jane, but she quickly looked away. She had long ago let go of the hope that she could become friends with the children in this building. Other than Ethel and her group of characters, her strangely vivid eyes often meant that friendship was repelled, dismissed in a sea of wary glances.

"Let's have a look, shall we?" Kezzie set the basket on the table. She reached into the box and peeled back the thin, worn sheet. Her hand flickered only slightly as she observed the child's white, waxen complexion. She knew that no tincture could remedy this.

She met John's eyes and he nodded slightly, knowing what Kezzie didn't want to say out loud. "Over 'ere, Kezzie. Come see to Maggie, will you?"

"But Pa–"

"Leave it, Jane," her father snapped at his child.

Kezzie carefully picked her way across the littered floor, gently nudging her way through the assortment of materials used in making matchboxes, the piecework that kept the roof over everyone's heads in this tiny room. Kezzie knew the work to be tedious and paid a pittance, but she was careful not to knock anything over as she crossed to the thin straw mattress that covered the floor in the corner.

Maggie O'Malley was only a young woman, yet today she looked dazed, exhausted beyond her years. Her head lolled against the soiled wall behind her, her grimy dress blending with the dirty bedding. A bone-white shoulder, the collarbone showing sharply through the skin, poked out of her tunic. She held a tiny, unmoving bundle to her empty breast. The two other O'Malley children sat next to their mother and stared vacantly up at Kezzie.

Kezzie longed for her mother's unfazed guidance right at that moment. The sight was so pitiful that Kezzie was at a loss for words, but she knew that Ada Doyle would calmly cover up the exposed shoulder and offer some practical advice to Maggie.

"Four days ago, I had seven children," Maggie's voice was worn, the sadness of the words not aligning with the practicality of her tone.

"You still have three to watch over, Maggie," John intoned gently. He stood up heavily and crossed to the rickety chest by the wall that held the blackened window. "I'm waiting for the parish to come and collect them," he opened the bottom drawer and revealed two more tightly wrapped bundles inside. "At least they didn't die alone."

Kezzie, unable to stop the tears of desperation that slipped past her eyelids, said, "I'm so sorry, I could have got here sooner but…"

John nudged the drawer closed with his boot. "I'm not sure that would've helped. But we still have more mouths to feed. And I need Jane to be back at work. Maggie, too. I can't leave the youngsters to fend for themselves as I go out looking for work. And she's got boxes to make, haven't you, Jane?"

Spurred on to try and help this family the only way she knew how: Kezzie set to work. She quickly handed the blue glass bottles to John, pointing out the labels though she understood that he couldn't read.

She wished she could do more to help the community here, learn how to work as a pharmacist or train and become a doctor. She knew that that wouldn't be possible, just as much as she knew that the Doyle curse would end with her.

She set to work.

After the O'Malley's place, she went down a floor to the Garrett's. Then across to the McMurty's.

On and on, family after family.

Slum building and alms house.

She dished out the tinctures and salves, bathing the sores and applying the blends. For now, she'd do the charitable work that she knew she could do to help, as her mother sold the remedies in the shop which meant they could do this kind of work for free.

Some days, she loved the work. But on days like today, when she saw life at the other end of the spectrum, it made her so incredibly heartbroken for those that she simply could not save.

CHAPTER 8

"What is it, girl?" Rose Donovan asked her.

Kezzie slowly closed the book she was reading, marking her page with a piece of yellow ribbon. "Nothing," she replied carefully.

Rose scoffed, folding her arms as her brow curved. "Pull the other one, Kezurah Doyle. It has bells on it."

Kezzie couldn't help a snuffle of laughter at Rose's humour. "I'm sad," she admitted after a moment or two. She gave Rose a brief rundown of her experience at the O'Malley's, the start to what was quite a difficult day for her.

Rose's brown eyes softened in sympathy.

She settled onto the side of Kezzie's small bed, leaning forward, and clasping one of her hands. "I'm sorry that you had such a trying day. You have a good heart, Kezzie. It comes from a long line of good hearts who are put on this earth to heal. Though the vagaries of life mean that sometimes, it is just our time to leave this place."

Kezzie searched Rose's face. Questions raced through her mind. Her mother was often reluctant to talk about things that pained her personally, much preferring the safety of the world of healing and herbs instead. "Do you think that my father could've been saved? When he was sick, I mean?"

She wished that she could remember her father. She had no recollection of him. He'd died when she was an infant. She was told all the time that she looked like her mother, so even when she looked in the looking glass, she couldn't be sure which of her features were his. She never told her mother this. Ada refused to engage in conversations about him. Kezzie wondered if it was because it was too painful for her.

"If anyone could have saved him, it would have been your mother. In the end, well, it was his time to go."

A line formed between Kezzie's brows. "That's not what I was asking. I meant...the curse."

She saw rather than felt the way Rose stilled. "What do you mean 'curse'?"

Kezzie waited for the denial. She didn't say anything more. She just looked at Rose and waited.

She pulled her hand away from Kezzie. "So, you've heard then." Kezzie remained mute. Rose clicked her tongue. "I know that you are curious about your history but you mustn't take any credence in what people say."

"You don't believe that the Doyle women are cursed?" Kezzie asked.

Rose managed to look prim and amused all at once. "Your father died of influenza. It wasn't part of a curse. We had a doctor come out to the house. Nothing helped. Not the herbs I pounded, nor the tonic the doctor swore blind would bring him back. Ada loved him very much, Kezzie. If that was all it took, she would have saved him."

Kezzie had heard the story many times. It never changed. "What about my grandfather?"

Rose's mouth twitched as she searched Kezzie's open, honest expression. "Where are all these questions coming from?"

Kezzie broke the starch look that Rose was giving her, pleating the sheet that covered her legs instead. She longed to ask for reassurance that their misfortune – where every man in the family died before their child turned one, where only daughters were born to the women – was nothing but bad luck that seemed to run in their family. After all, every Doyle woman had only been able to bear one child – a daughter. Every man they had chosen to spend their lives with, pledged to love for all eternity, died an early death. The women were strong, of strong blood and pure hearts, but the luck of each woman did not run into love or family.

Kezzie shrugged. "Mama won't talk about it."

"There's nothing to talk about," Rose reassured her softly. "There is no curse on the Doyle family. Your mother loves you very much. Your father passed far too young, and it was illness, not fate, that took his life. You will find a handsome young man and you will fall deeply in love with him."

"And only be able to give him a daughter?" Kezzie whispered.

Rose sighed, exasperated at the way Kezzie refused to be placated. "And what if you only have a daughter? What's wrong with that? You'll love her. You'll teach her the ways of healing, just like your mother did for you, and her mother did for her.

"A long line of clever, brilliant, beautiful Doyle women will continue the legacy. You'll grow old in the shop downstairs, safe in the knowledge that your great-grandfather's legacy will hold fast and true for you. You have so much luck in your life, Kezzie. Stop looking for shadows and doubts where there are none." Rose reached forward and drew the bed covers higher up the bed. "It's time you went to sleep."

Kezzie pushed the blanket straight back down, reminded too much of the sight of Maggie O'Malley earlier that day. She wasn't sure she would ever get that image out of her mind.

"Aren't you asleep yet?" Ada Doyle stepped into the

room. Instantly, Kezzie felt the tight ball of angst and upset ease.

Her mother was indeed a beautiful woman. Her hair, the colour of spun gold, was wound into an intricate pleat that she'd pinned up at the back of her head. The Doyle eyes, striking pale blue, matched Kezzie's identically.

Rose smiled kindly at Kezzie, pausing in the doorway to murmur something to her mother.

Ada's expression didn't change. But her smile held a tinge of sadness. The bed dipped as she sat at the end. For a moment, she watched Kezzie. She reached out and placed a hand on the bump where Kezzie's foot rested under the eiderdown. "When you got back earlier, you didn't mention Maggie."

Kezzie's eyes dropped to her hands. She picked at her nails, trying to hold back the tears. "It was fine… just…"

The bed shifted as Ada repositioned herself high enough along the bed to gather her daughter in her arms. "It's alright. Let it out now."

That permission broke the dam of emotions that had clogged her chest all afternoon. The bleak and desolate faces of families trying to scrape together enough to barely survive. Thinking of the O'Malley's having to bury their tiny infant children in graves that didn't have a marker on because they couldn't afford more than just a pauper burial for them.

Ada rocked her slowly, patting her back rhythmically until the sobs had subsided. Kezzie felt spent and allowed Ada to press her gently into the pillows.

"Better?" Ada's fingers brushed the fine hairs away from Kezzie's face.

Kezzie nodded, filled with such love for her mother. "Thank you, Mama. For everything. I knew I was lucky but when I see how much we have compared to those who don't have anything, I feel ever so grateful to you and to all the other Doyle's."

Ada's smile wobbled and her eyes became a little

misty. "There, now, you're setting me off," she laughed softly.

"I mean it," Kezzie laid a hand on her mother's cheek. "I knew that doing what we do here is important but being out, making deliveries to those who couldn't have even the slimmest chance if we didn't help? I see it now."

Ada searched her face. "My sweet girl," She kissed her forehead and cupped her face. "How I wish I could bottle this up for you so that when your beliefs wobble as you get older, you could take a sip and replenish it."

Kezzie longed to ask her now about the curse. It seemed like the right time. To see what her mother felt about the rumours that swirled about the family name. But it felt like she was always arguing with her mother these days. She didn't want to ruin this moment by seeing the pain shimmer in her mother's eyes, nor hear the remote tone when she assured Kezzie that she would tell her one day in the future when she was old enough to understand.

She was old enough now.

But she knew that Ada would smile at the words.

So, she stayed mute. She accepted the goodnight kiss.

She would bide her time.

One day, she would find out the truth.

CHAPTER 9

Sunday was Kezzie's favourite day of the week.

After Saturday's rush, always the busiest day in the apothecary shop when Ada and Rose started their work when it was still dark, Sunday was the day that Kezzie spent foraging for the items that they couldn't grow in their tiny garden at the back of the shop.

Kezzie rose early, setting out a basket for each of them. Inside each one, she placed a pair of topiary shears and a trowel for digging at roots, whilst Ada wrapped up chunks of cheese, meat and a flask of cider.

Early morning mists clung to the buildings, draping the cobbles as they wound their way along half-made pavements and muddy streets that had been churned by milk carts and drays, out making their deliveries. Hawkers bellowed into the damp air, proudly selling trotters and muffins, their barrows jostling for space alongside the market stalls piled high with tin plates and fresh fish.

They caught the omnibus from Aldgate and, by the time they drove past Victoria Park, the morning sun had broken through the clouds. The air changed as they neared the marshes, a more earthy scent carried on the wafting breezes. Crows and pigeons winged on the warmer air drafts, gliding over emerald fields that stretched as far as the eye could see. The air here was cleaner, sweetened by the scent of grasses and blossoms.

Kezzie hopped down from the wagon at the White Hart Inn, at the end of Temple Mills Lane.

"Ready?" Ada asked her.

Kezzie nodded enthusiastically.

The city's constant calamitous energy had been replaced with nature's gentle melodies. Kezzie tipped her face to the sunlight, enjoying the warmth of it on her skin. Winds whispered through the leaves, and weeping willows dipped their drooping fingers into the river that dribbled through the marshes. Where the waterways puddled into ponds, ducks and moorhens hid amongst the tall reeds that skirted them. Bursts of vibrant yellow marsh marigolds stood out against the deep green and brown of the marshland.

A cluster of caravans, striking with their curved roofs and bright colours, was parked up along the edge of the river, the chunky cobs hobbled under the shade of a nearby tree. The Romany gipsies watched their progress from beside their campfire.

The shade of the forest was a welcome relief. Carpets of wild garlic showed up stark white against the dense carpets of vivid green. Deeper into the forest they ventured, pausing to dig for herbs and roots, pulling up clumps of fennel and garlic, and digging for the roots of Marsh Mallow that would be dried and then ground into powder. Their baskets became heavy with the bounty as they meandered through fields and marshes.

Kezzie loved to feel the cool soil under her fingers and the sun warming her back. There was a joy in pulling plants and shaking off damp clumps of soil from the roots. They played a game of identifying the plant and naming the ailments the plants could help with.

They stopped for their picnic on the side of the riverbank, nibbling on the bread and cheese and washing it all down with the tart cider.

"Did you come here with your mother?" Kezzie asked, distracted by the chaotic path of a speckled wood butterfly as it spiralled through the air with its mate.

Ada's smile was wistful. "I did, yes. And she came here with her grandmother before that."

"You didn't all come together?"

Her expression turned melancholy. "Alas, no. As you know, my Mama was no longer in my life by the time you came along. My grandmother passed when my mother was still young."

Kezzie shielded her eyes, trying to study her mother, recalling how upset she'd become with her whenever she'd tried to ask about the past. She knew what others said about the Doyle women and them dying young – hadn't Ethel made that much clear to her?

Still, Kezzie hated the thought of losing her mother and she couldn't help but ask, "How old were you when your mother died?"

Ada stood, dusting off her skirts. "We ought to start making our way back soon."

Kezzie tried not to let her disappointment show. This steadfast refusal to talk about the women in the family frustrated her. "A little longer, please, Mama."

Ada's mouth firmed as she gazed at her daughter, letting out a long breath through her nose. "Kezzie…"

The word was drawn out though Kezzie grinned, knowing when her mother was about to capitulate.

She bent down for the basket and skipped towards the treeline that bordered the edge of the field.

By the time they packed their tools and hoisted their laden baskets over the last stile, the sun was already dipping lower, bathing the marshlands in hues of golden light. Kezzie had to trot to keep up with Ada's quick pace back the way they came. The White Hart was doing a bustling trade with farmhands and labourers, washing down the dust of the warm day with a pint of ale. Kezzie knew even before they'd stepped into the yard that they'd missed the last wagon of the day.

"Never mind," Ada said brightly, guiding Kezzie out of the enclosure and onto the road once again. "The walk will do you good."

Kezzie knew better than to complain to her mother that her feet were burning as they walked the four miles back, or that she was tired. It was her fault that they'd missed the omnibus, and she didn't need her mother to remind her. Twilight had embraced the familiar landscape of the city, wrapping them in a blanket of fog that slid in off the river by the time they were passing Bethnal Green, the globes of the gas lights flickering dimly between the long dark shadows.

Ada grasped Kezzie's hand, squeezing it reassuringly. "Almost there. I bet Rose has left us some of her stew out. How does that sound?"

"I'm starving," Kezzie admitted tiredly.

The hectic London streets became shadowy corridors, though her mother didn't slow her pace as she led them down the network of alleys, as sure-footed as a mountain goat. When they popped out onto the street, Ada almost collided with the group of men strolling along the pavement.

"Steady on, love!" The biggest one reached out to balance Ada, grasping her by the shoulders. A long scar rippled his face from brow to jaw, showing up white against a tanned face. The stench of rotten fish wafted from their oilcloth clothing, cloaking them as the men congregated closer to them both. Dread shot through Kezzie's belly. "Oh-ho, look what I caught meself, lads!"

"I'm so sorry, sir," Ada said quickly, trying to sidestep the group. Bleary-eyed and staggering, the group of men leered closer to her mother.

"Landed right in your arms, Rigger! Seen it wiv' me own eyes!"

"Please," Ada moved to one side, then the other "I'm just trying to get home. Can you let me by?"

"Where's 'ome, love?" The ringleader edged closer, his breath laced with the smell of alcohol. He reached out to tug the coil of gold hair that had come loose and lay over Ada's shoulder. "You got yourself an 'usband waiting in bed for you? Or do you want a real man?"

"A sailor! That's what you need!" The taunt was followed by a drunken guffaw.

"Just let me by. Please, sir," Ada continued moving side to side, trying to avoid confrontation until the big one gripped her by the shoulders.

The men, reeking enough to make Kezzie's eyes water, clustered around her mother.

"'Sir'!" Another cackled in mockery, prodding Ada hard enough that she stumbled, and she had to let go of Kezzie's hand. "You ever 'ear the likes of it, Bill? She thinks you're a '*sir*'!"

"Must have got ourselves one of those posh bits of skirt," Bill growled, grappling with Ada.

"You look like you need some company," Rigger ducked closer to Ada, twisting her by the hips to manoeuvre her closer to him.

In the low light, his puckered skin twisted his face into a grotesque mask. Ada turned her face, only for him to wrench her back around to face him. Whatever he was about to say died on his lips, and Ada whimpered as he turned her face more into the light.

"Look here, lads," his lips peeled back, green teeth flashing, "look at her eyes!"

Kezzie mewled in terror as her mother was engulfed by the group, each of them with shaggy dark hair and thick beards.

The grunting grew in intensity.

"Always fancied myself a witch!"

"Enough!" Ada raised her voice, shoving the one they'd called Rigger back. "You let me go–"

Rigger grabbed her up, holding her face in one hand and licking her cheek.

"You let my Mama go!" Kezzie yelled, glaring at Rigger.

As though they'd forgotten about her, the group turned in unison. Kezzie lifted her chin even as her belly turned to water.

"A miniature witch," Bill tilted his head. "Fresh and ripe for the plucking."

"Kezzie, run!" Ada pulled her face free of the sailor's clasp.

Kezzie hesitated just a second, but she was too late. A hand snaked around her middle, plucking her up so that her feet cycled the air. She opened her mouth, but her screams were cut off by a filthy hand. She writhed and thrashed; basket forgotten as she clawed at the hand over her face.

Rigger released Ada, holding her still with one hand as he beckoned her captor closer, "Fetch her here, Tom. Let me take a closer look."

"Please, please," Ada struggled against the sailor's hold. "Let her go. It's me you want."

"You've changed your tune," he sneered.

No sooner had Tom reached Rigger when Kezzie sank her teeth into his palm, biting until she tasted blood. Her ears filled with screaming, and pain shot through her feet as she was promptly dropped to the ground. She scrambled upright, though was caught again. This time, black eyes stared at her, hidden under heavy brows. He hefted her under one arm and marched her over to Rigger once again.

With everyone's attention on Kezzie, no one saw the dull glint of steel until it was too late.

Everything then became a blur.

Her mother yelled at her to run, to keep running; Rigger bellowing like an angry bull, the rounded handle of her mother's shears poking out of his thigh. There was scuffling and howling in the confusion, but Kezzie didn't wait. She shot down the alleyway, her ears filled with the pounding of her heart, her breath sawing in and out of her chest until she thought her lungs would burst.

"Run, Kezzie! Run! Run and don't look back!"

Her mother's words became a mantra, sobs choking her, animal-like. Down the next alley, out the other side. She knew these alleys now. She raced ahead. Rats and people, scattered before her until finally, the welcoming glow of the apothecary shop came into view in the street up ahead.

Relief made her so weak that she tripped. Heat burned into her hands when she slid over the damp cobbles. She didn't stop until she reached the doorway.

She slid down the wall, panting, her body on fire. Slowly, her breathing eased, and Kezzie realised two things at once.

She was safely back home.

Her mother wasn't behind her.

CHAPTER 10

"You stay here, Kezzie!" Rose's voice was tight with panic, but Kezzie didn't wait. When Ada hadn't followed Kezzie, she'd gone to the only person she trusted enough to help.

Rose had been awake, her surprise quickly sliding to horror when she held her oil lamp higher to cast more light through the narrow doorway onto a bloody and bedraggled Kezzie standing on her doorstep.

The lamp that Rose held aloft to light their way swung wildly, matching her harried steps as she tried to keep up with Kezzie. "I told you to wait at the shop."

"You don't know where to look," Kezzie reasoned.

"Your mother will be furious to know I've let you out at night again."

"I don't care, Rose."

"It isn't safe out here, child. Kezzie! Slow down!"

"There's no time!" Kezzie's dogged steps retraced her way back through the dark alleys.

Rose yanked Kezzie round by the arm. The older woman scanned her face, softening when she saw the horror in her eyes. "Commercial Street police station is just over there. We're going to get a policeman. He'll help us."

Kezzie followed Rose, eyes over her shoulder as she was led through the streets. They stuck to the illuminated route, though the gas lights didn't reach into the shadowy recesses of the doorways.

Kezzie knew these streets by day. She'd walked them alone often enough to feel as if she belonged. The white eyes that peered at them from the shadows held hidden dangers tonight.

Kezzie stayed close to Rose's skirts.

Every minute it took for the policeman, a spindly man named Sedgewick, to be convinced that there had been an incident, urgency pressed in on Kezzie like a thousand slices of glass to her skin. His suspicious expression turned dubious when he realised that it was a young girl was making the report of an attack. Before he could make any salacious remarks about why Ada and Kezzie were walking the streets in the dark, Rose scalded him until his cheeks reddened and he followed them like a docile lamb along the cobbles.

Kezzie kept walking, trying not to let the fear choke her. Coughs and shouts drifted through the fog, echoing along the labyrinthine heart of the city.

She shouldn't have run.

Why hadn't her mother followed her?

Had she run in a different direction to lead the men away?

She slowed as she neared Kinder Street, trepidation etching a layer of vigilance into her mind. She paused, struggling to hear anything over her heartbeat.

"Is it here?" Rose, sensing the fear rolling off Kezzie, whispered from behind her.

Wide-eyed, Kezzie lay a finger over her lips and nodded. She then pointed her finger right, indicating.

Sedgewick drew himself up by his britches. "Step to the side, young miss. Let me deal with this."

Rose's mouth flattened and she squeezed Kezzie's shoulder and then followed the police officer into the thick fog. "Wait here."

But Kezzie didn't wait.

The tang of the river wafted in the winds that teased her messy hair. The rumbling of activity from the nearby docks resonated along the street. Kezzie didn't pay any heed to any of it. Alarm drummed against her ribs so that she felt like she was fighting to catch her breath.

Her attention was fixed to the pool of light that puddled on the muddy street just ahead of them. Two wicker baskets upended and forgotten lay in the road.

Sedgewick, full of his own self-importance, nudged one of the baskets. He turned slowly in the circle of light. Kezzie didn't miss the way the policeman paused, nor did she hear his words of warning as he held out a hand for Rose to stay where she was. Short, sharp, shrill blasts of his whistle filled her ears.

Kezzie was younger and nimbler than Rose. She ducked under the grasping hand and sprinted towards the clearing.

She saw the edge of her mother's cloak as she ran. Her eyes tracked the black material to the indistinct mound that was sprawled just beyond the light. In the shadow, her mother's flesh showed up luminous white. Lifeless eyes stared up at the night sky.

Whimpering, Kezzie fell upon her mother's still form, muted sobs tearing from her open mouth. She knelt, uncaring of the dark, sticky mess that seeped through her clothing and chilled her knees.

And kissed her cold cheek goodbye.

CHAPTER 11

"Rose?"

The older woman stood at the window, staring out at the dreary grey sky. It seemed as if the light had been extinguished in Rose's eyes ever since her best friend had gone. Her light dresses had been swapped for black, which suited her sombre mood perfectly.

Kezzie couldn't tell how many days had passed since her mother's murder. Each day merged into the next, a series of indistinguishable and empty hours.

She had tried to care for a grieving Kezzie as best she could, but it felt like they were both stumbling around in the dark. Rose had moved into the shop but she knew that Rose was struggling with the business; she had never had a head for it, yet somehow, she managed to keep things running.

But today, the apothecary would remain closed.

"We should go," Kezzie said quietly from the door. "They're waiting for us down the street."

Rose's mouth trembled, and she nodded.

They made their way down the stairs and out onto the street. Up ahead, the hearse waited, the six jet-black horses prancing impatiently.

They walked slowly behind the hearse, their heads

bowed. The day was shrouded in a bleak grey fog, fine raindrops gathering on Kezzie's black woollen coat. They turned into the graveyard between the wide stone pillars and made their way along the gravelled pathway. Kezzie clenched her teeth when she saw the black grave yawning in the ground ahead of them. As the vicar's voice droned under the oppressive sky, Kezzie's heart grew heavier. She stood next to Rose, each holding the other's hand, feeling as if the world had been drained of colour and sound, leaving only the dull ache of loss.

Her gaze drifted around at the small gathering of mourners clustered around the graveside. Among them, she recognised one of the policemen as the one who had tugged down her mother's skirt to try and preserve her modesty.

Jenkinson—the name leapt out from her memory.

Despite this small act of kindness, the police still had no leads on her mother's murderers. From her detailed description, Inspector Sedgewick believed that the men were sailors. He claimed that as London was full of sailors and that the docks were among the busiest in the world, with ships and cargo from all over the globe passing through every day, he believed that her mother's killers could already have left the country. Kezzie was convinced that Sedgewick had already given up trying to find them.

Rose was furious that the police didn't seem to care. More than once, Rose had clashed with Sedgewick, insisting that he let go of his prejudices. Ada was an apothecary, a good and decent businesswoman, not a common prostitute. Neither she nor her daughter had been selling their bodies that night. But it seemed the police—Sedgewick, at least—believed Ada had gotten what she deserved.

Kezzie hadn't shed a tear yet.

She had observed from the sidelines. She had given several statements to Sedgewick and Jenkinson, talking in detail about every little thing she could remember of that night.

But she had left the scene and hadn't seen whether the men had remained in the street after she'd fled. A terrible scene that had played over and over in her mind.

Her dreams were filled with the blackest eyes and green teeth, with long claws chasing her through the endless labyrinth of streets at night.

Following the actions of others, Kezzie went through the ceremony to bury her mother. She dropped the mud onto the casket, the sound hollow and empty. Rose's gentle sobs echoed over the graveside.

Afterwards, she allowed Rose to lead her back to the apothecary. She spooned the stew into her mouth. She washed her face and said her prayers. She went through the motions and climbed into her bed. She obediently closed her eyes, opening them as soon as Rose had closed her door.

She lay in bed, staring through the window. When the church clock struck twelve, Kezzie slipped from her bed, tiptoeing out of her room, across the landing, and into her mother's bed. Here, surrounded by the familiar smells of lavender and chamomile, of her mother, Kezzie drifted off to sleep.

∼

Rose had seemed reluctant to open the shop once more, but Kezzie was determined that her mother's efforts would not be in vain.

The next day, whilst news of Ada's death had shocked the community, it seemed just a fleeting blow that was quickly swallowed by the city's relentless tide of daily tragedies. Everyone knew the kind-hearted apothecary who had dedicated her life to helping others. The palpable void she'd left behind was evident, judging by the stream of customers who called the shop. The atmosphere inside was thick with grief and uncertainty.

Kezzie found the list of deliveries that Ada had written the day before she died. Seeing her mother's neat, careful handwriting filled her with a deep melancholy. She would never again hear her mother's voice. Never again would she feel the warmth of her embrace or the reassurance of her presence. As that realisation crashed over her, the urge to lock the door and hide away was almost too much to bear.

It was Rose's squeeze on her shoulder that grounded her.

She squared her shoulders and finished packing up the basket with what was needed.

Leaving Rose to manage the shop and chat with the customers, Kezzie set out into the cold, grey morning to make the deliveries.

The streets were beginning to stir, with carriages and cabs filling the streets alongside drays and the wagons of the delivery men.

She had walked these streets so often, but everything seemed so very different to her now. Rather than hope and potential, she saw danger and death, shimmering at the periphery of the street corners. Decay and rot permeated the air and the buildings she passed.

She knocked on each door, bracing herself for the commiseration that showered her. Hearing the memories of her mother brought back some of her purpose in the work she was doing. There was a need for this, a pointed purpose to help those who couldn't help themselves. Ada would want her to continue, of that, she was sure.

She noticed that the last delivery to be made was in Ethel's building. She realised she hadn't seen her friend since before her mother had died. Filled with a sudden longing to see her, she decided to call on Ethel before making her last delivery. She hoped that her friend was home so that she could find some comfort in her company.

She climbed the steps to the first floor and knocked on the door. Once, then again. She almost gave up and left when she heard shuffling behind the door.

It cracked open, and time seemed to stand still.

She was dreaming. She had to be.

She stared up into the black eyes, the same black eyes that she'd seen on the street the Sunday before last. Only that time those black eyes had green teeth under them, leering at her and laughing maniacally.

Tom.

Panic surged through her. As if standing in molasses, she turned slowly and tried to run. She stumbled down the stairs, her foot catching on the edge of a step, sending her sprawling to the bottom. She landed heavily. She lay there, dazed and breathless. Shouts echoed above her head, and Kezzie curled into a tight ball, waiting for the grasping hands to come once more.

But it was Ethel's voice, filled with concern, that reached out to her. Kezzie peered up at her friend, blinking, her heart thundering in her chest.

"Kezzie, are you alright?"

Kezzie's vision cleared. She realised that this wasn't another dream. Her eyes darted to the top of the stairs. The man still stood there, lurking, watching her. In the daylight, he looked different but was unmistakable.

"Who is that man?" she whimpered.

Ethel frowned up the stairs. "That's my brother, Tom."

A knot formed in Kezzie's stomach. She quickly scrambled to her feet, pain shooting up from her ankle. She backed away towards the door, staring up at those soulless black eyes. "I have to go. I have to go to the police right now."

Ethel's face folded in confusion. "The police? What for? What are you talking about?"

Shaking her head, trembling as hysteria bubbled up

within her, Kezzie cried, "It was him. He was there that night. He was with the other men that killed my mother. I must tell the police!"

Ethel's expression switched from confusion to horror. She slapped Kezzie across the face. "My brother is not a killer. You take that back!"

Kezzie reeled from the blow, her hand pressed to her flaming cheek, tears filling her eyes. "How can you say that? I know what I saw. Your brother was there, Ethel. He was there."

"Shut up, Kezzie! Shut up!

Kezzie stared at her friend. "Ethel, I know it was him. He was there that night."

"No, he wasn't!"

Their voices echoed up the stairwell.

"Ethel, please. You must believe me. I wouldn't lie about something like this."

Ethel's face twisted with fury. "Everyone knows what your mother was doing out on the streets that late. Don't you dare blame my innocent brother."

"He isn't innocent–"

"You're just as crazy as your mother was! I should never have believed you were a nice person," Ethel spat, her eyes blazing with anger. "Get out, witch! Just get out."

Kezzie turned for the door, a yelp ripping from her throat as her basket hit her square in the back. "Don't you bother coming back here!" Ethel bellowed after her.

Kezzie fled, streaking through the filthy streets that twisted ahead of her. The world around her was a blur of noise and movement, but all she could think about was the look on Ethel's face, the accusation in her voice.

She ran as fast as she could, bursting through the door of the Commercial Street police station. The policeman looked up, his face creasing with annoyance.

"Please, you must help me! Thomas Mooney—he was one of the men who hurt my mother. You have to go there now. He lives on Black Bull Yard. It's him, do you hear me? It's him!"

Inspector Sedgewick called upon several of his colleagues, including Mr Jenkinson. They refused to allow Kezzie to accompany them, and she waited outside the police station, uncaring of the chilly air or relentless drizzle. She wasn't sure how long it was before Inspector Sedgewick returned.

She only had to take one look at his face to know what he was about to say.

"Tommy Mooney hasn't been in the city for over a year. His father said as much. And you can't go around accusing just anyone with your preposterous notions. Take yourself home and stop bothering me, girl. I have real work to do."

"But–"

"Home!" He jabbed a finger at the air around him. "Go home. Right this minute."

Kezzie left the police station, her mind a cyclone of anger and confusion.

She was certain it had been him. How could he have left already?

Unless Ethel had told him who she was.

Unless Ethel had told her brother to run.

And betrayed her friend in the worst way. Either way, not only had she lost her mother, but she had also lost her only friend as well.

PART II

CHAPTER 12

Whitechapel,
London

1888

The jingling of the little brass bell over the door startled Kezzie out of her quiet musings. From her vantage point atop the short, wooden ladder, she swivelled, eyes widening at the sight of the first customer in hours.

Instead of a familiar face braving the rain for her remedies, a stranger stood at the threshold. Water dripped from her umbrella as she shook it out. Kezzie noted the fine lilac dress and the glints of gems at her ears and throat, and Kezzie wondered what a tourist was doing venturing into these parts on a day like today.

The day had stretched long and dull, forcing Kezzie to invent tasks to pass the time.

"Good afternoon," Kezzie greeted, descending the ladder and setting aside her dusting cloth.

"Hello," the woman replied, shaking more droplets from her umbrella, and positioning it by the door, where it quickly formed a puddle. By the time she managed to close the door against the storm, more raindrops had blown into the open doorway. Pointing through the glass, she remarked, "What a day!"

Outside, rainwater cascaded from the eaves in continuous streams, rivulets travelling down the windowpanes. The usually bustling lane beyond the door was eerily deserted. The relentless torrent had filled the crevices and cracks of the cobbles, forming a narrow stream that swirled around the iron grates.

The sky, a dreary blanket of grey, had deterred any passing trade, which made the woman's visit even more peculiar.

Still, business was money, as Rose had had to remind her over the years. Her mouth curved in a welcoming smile, catching the woman's profile as she peered through the glass. The woman was older than Kezzie, though she had taken great care to disguise her age with meticulously applied makeup. Her dress was elegant, made of a fine fabric that hinted at luxury.

"You're my first customer this afternoon," Kezzie said. "The weather has chased everyone inside."

As if aware of Kezzie's shrewd inspection, the woman delicately touched the coiffed hair at the back of her head. "I think I chose the wrong day to come looking for your shop."

Kezzie's eyebrows arched involuntarily, a wave of unease stirring in the pit of her stomach.

Doyle's shop was hidden from the main thoroughfares, nestled in a quiet corner where the clamour of the city scarcely reached. Her customers were rarely those who deliberately sought out her shop, nor were they ones who stumbled across it.

They came because they knew she was here.

This seclusion suited her just fine.

Preferring the company of her remedies to that of people, Kezzie embraced her solitude, crafting her potions and tinctures undisturbed by the outside world. Though by now, she understood that the renown of Doyle's apothecary had expanded far beyond the boundaries of her mother's time.

The woman's accent was silky, a stark contrast to the rough, guttural intonations that she was used to.

Kezzie masked her rising apprehension about the stranger's distinguished presence with practised ease. "It's quite the storm. Is there something specific you were looking for?"

Brown eyes, sparkling with curiosity, briefly met Kezzie's before she turned to take in the interior. "Actually, yes. My mother used to bring me to a place just like this when I was little," she reminisced as she trailed her gloved fingers along the teak counter that bore scars from years of use. "The truth is that these modern medicines just aren't as effective on me," the woman stated. " Mama swore by the old ways, you know," she paused in her perusal of the shop to look at Kezzie, wrinkling her nose conspiratorially, "The traditional ways."

Kezzie nodded with understanding. "Of course."

"These days, druggists only sell what they want to you, rather than what you need. When I said as much to my maid, she told me about this place." A gloved hand waved in the air, and she was on the move again, touching as she went.

Maids frequently ran errands to Doyle's, usually to procure items their employers wished to keep confidential. They navigated the quieter back streets to avoid recognition. Which meant it was highly unusual for an employer to appear here.

The woman gave her a sidelong look. "Perhaps you know her? She claims she used to live near here."

"What's her name?"

"Janie Thompson."

Kezzie hadn't heard that name in years. The last time she had seen her, Janie had been standing in amongst a crowd of women, laughing and jeering as Kezzie hurried away from Bone Lane.

The girl was spiteful and mean.

But she had managed to get out of the slums, and so there was something to be said for that. Thinking of Janie made her think of Ethel, another who'd managed to claw her way to a better life.

Kezzie shut down her line of thinking. It would do her no good to linger on the past. Ethel had avoided her ever since that day in the stairwell of her dilapidated building. The Mooney's had moved away not long afterwards and another family had taken over their rooms.

Kezzie's smile was brittle. "How is Janie? I haven't seen hide nor hair of her for years."

The woman shrugged, disinterested in the welfare of one of her servants. "She's waiting at the end of the street. She refused point-blank to get out of the cab and show me where this place was. Perhaps she thinks she's going to melt in this rain," she grumbled. "Wretched girl. I had to carry my own umbrella."

Kezzie knew full well why Janie had remained in the carriage. She had grown up in the same building as Ethel. What puzzled her the most was why Janie would send her employer to her in the first place.

"That was very kind of her to recommend my shop," Kezzie responded though she suspected that Janie's employer's discontent would be reflected in her next wage envelope.

The woman came to a stop a few feet away from her. "You own this shop?" The astonishment seemed genuine.

Kezzie nodded, gazing about her with pride. "It's been in my family for three generations."

"Well, it's perfectly charming," she said, her eyes travelling around the rustic interior, where earthenware jars and coloured-glass bottles lined the shelves. Some of the labels still bore the careful script of her great-grandfather.

She knew the interior wasn't as pleasant as some of

the new chemist shops that had sprung up over the city in the last decade, but people came because they trusted a Doyle to help them.

"Thank you. I'm Kezzie, Kezzie Doyle."

"Oh, where are my manners!" she gushed. "My name is Eunice Joy. My husband is Arthur Joy, you may have heard of him?"

Kezzie's expression remained passive, and she shook her head. "I'm afraid I haven't. Though owning a place like this means I rarely get time to keep up with the local happenings. My work here keeps me busy. That also means that I rarely step foot out of Whitechapel."

Eunice examined her. Instinctively, Kezzie averted her gaze. She had grown weary of being observed and judged, especially as a Doyle. Compared to the affluent woman's opulent lilac dress and meticulously styled hair, Kezzie's felt decidedly shabby.

"But you're so young to be hiding away here in this back alley."

Kezzie bit back the smile. Eunice sounded a little like Rose. "I like what I do. There is no time for anything else in my life."

Eunice sighed reminiscently. "Your youth will pass you by without notice. You should be going out, enjoying yourself. Are you married, at least?"

Kezzie shook her head. "No."

"But Kezzie," Eunice tilted her head, shaking it. "A woman is nothing without a husband. Don't you want a family to pass on your knowledge? You need to marry, have a family, and continue with this delightful little place so that future generations can access these medicines!"

Years of practice meant that Kezzie no longer flinched whenever a comment like that was made. "How can I help you, Mrs Joy?"

Eunice sighed in exasperation, seemingly oblivious to Kezzie changing the subject. "I can't sleep."

The wandering had finally halted.

Eunice pressed her gloved hands together in supplication. "My mother always swore by a concoction that had lavender and something else in it, though everyone I speak to about this tells me that I'm making it all up."

"Of course," Kezzie replied, walking towards the shelf where she kept the sleep aids. She selected a brown jar filled with powder. "My grandfather used to make a blend of lavender and chamomile. His secret ingredient was to add a hint of valerian root in it, too. My grandmother was the one who used to steep it in tea for insomnia." She lifted the jar and tapped the lid twice.

"This blend is very effective. You steep a teaspoon of it in hot water for 20 minutes so it's warm, not hot. If you drink it around half an hour before you wish to retire for the evening, you'll find that you should get a good night's sleep."

"I'll take two drachms," Eunice said.

Kezzie was amused that Eunice hadn't even inquired about the price of the powder. Apparently, she was unaccustomed to fretting over the cost of such items. Kezzie wondered what Arthur Joy did for a living.

Kezzie walked around the back of the counter to the equal-arm scales. She set the two small drachm weights, shaped like gold coins, that were the standard measurement for purchases.

The weights were set on one side of the scales, and she carefully measured the powder into the opposite brass dish. Precise measurements of some powders could be a matter of life and death, and Kezzie carefully ensured that the weights were accurate, even as Eunice made small talk behind her.

She tipped the measured powder into a jar that bore the embossed 'D' symbol, pressing the cork stopper into the top.

Eunice continued with her exploration of the shop's contents. The tall shelves lined the walls, cabinets filled the back wall. Each shelf was packed with bottles, vials, and jars.

Towards the front of the store, the only change Kezzie had agreed to was a fancy display arranged in the shop window to entice passing trade.

Tiny glass vials filled with essential oils; Parisian perfume bottles tucked up behind jars of honey. Beeswax candles and bundles of dried flowers meant to ward off the ill spirits of the night.

Eunice selected a small bottle of rose oil and some wintergreen soap. Kezzie wrote them in her sales ledger, recording the name and date, before she carefully wrapped them all into a brown paper parcel, securing the lot with twine that Eunice had called 'twee'.

Eunice thanked her profusely and promised that she would be back soon. She collected her umbrella from by the door, and Kezzie held the door open, bidding her goodbye.

Eunice stepped into the pouring rain; the parcel clutched close to her chest. The woman hurried, leaping over the muddy puddles on the tips of her toes. Kezzie shut the door, drawn to the contrast of the elegantly dressed woman against the grimy backdrop of East Alley.

Perhaps it was because she was naturally suspicious.

Maybe years of living in the shadows, hiding away from the probing looks and cruel whispers had made her this way.

But she couldn't help but think that Eunice's visit today was more than just a shopping trip.

Kezzie felt as if she'd been put through a test, only she wasn't privy to the results.

CHAPTER 13

Bobby

BOBBY LUCKETT SAT HUNCHED under the windowsill, immersed in the pages of her book. The walls were damp and cold to lean against, but, in this spot, the trade-off for light in the dingy little bed chamber was worth it.

She read quickly, snatching a few moments of joy in the thin pages before her day began. Her brother's hurried footsteps across the bare landing floor interrupted the quiet. Their muffled quarrels drifted through the walls as the boys fought to be first down the stairs, driven by the hope of an extra slice of bread with their breakfast.

Below her bedroom window, she could already hear the clink and scrape of hobnailed boots moving along the streets. The world was waking up, yet Bobby would do anything to be able to spend the day cocooned in the world between the pages of her book.

The door erupted inwards. Startled, Bobby tried and failed to conceal the book. A malevolent look gleamed in her younger sister's eyes as her gaze fell upon what was in Bobby's hands.

"Pa says if you're reading that blasted book again, I'm to take it downstairs for him to burn it."

Her heart lurched yet outwardly, she clambered off the floor with a nonchalant air. "And who's going to tell him, Lydia? Not you, that's for certain."

Her sister, younger by only a year, folded her arms. "What Pa says goes 'round 'ere."

Bobby wrapped her arms around the book, hugging it to her chest. Her father ruled the house with brawn and belt, but Bobby was used to her sister's one-upmanship and held her ground. "That's right. But I'll have to tell him you just swore, and then we'll both be in for the belt."

Lydia's fair brows crunched. "I did no such 'fing!"

Bobby shrugged, enjoying the shame on her sibling's face. "You did. Now, run along. I'll be down shortly."

"But–"

"Go away, Lydia!" Bobby raised her voice, glaring at her sister for good measure.

As soon as the door clicked shut, she swiftly pried up the loose floorboard in the corner of the room. Bobby had grown accustomed to hiding her book under the mattress that lay directly on the bare floor—the wooden bed frame had been surrendered for firewood two winters ago. However, with her sister in a particularly troublesome mood, she couldn't risk leaving her most cherished possession in such an obvious spot.

Her father's temper had become increasingly volatile each year, and she had no desire to provoke his wrath. His threats to burn her beloved book were all too real, and Bobby knew better than to test his resolve.

She set the rotten plank back into place and rushed down the stairs. As she descended, she could hear the familiar argument that had erupted between the boys. Sure enough, as she rounded the door jamb, they were grappling for the last piece of bread scraps left over by their father.

Bobby knew that if she or either of her sisters made such a ruckus in the house, they'd each feel the sting of their father's belt. George Luckett made no secret that boys were prized in this household. He'd kept Mary Luckett pregnant until she'd successfully birthed one, losing two other children in the process.

Rather than be cross with them, George Luckett watched his sons, a proud smile on his face. The smile dimmed as Bobby walked into the room.

"Half the day has gone, Bobby," he muttered, pushing his plate back with a shove. "You better not have been reading again, my girl."

Bobby felt the eyes of her siblings. She bowed her head as she took her seat. He'd resisted sending his children to school for any longer than necessary, pushing them to work as soon as they were old enough. "No, Pa."

"Lydia?"

Her sister froze mid-chew under the weight of her father's beady-eyed stare. Bobby held her breath, hoping that her sister wouldn't betray her.

"Was she reading again?"

Lydia swallowed audibly and shook her head. "No, Pa. She was praying."

That seemed to satisfy George. He leaned back with a nod. "Fair enough, though I don't know what you're asking the Lord for. You just need to get your skinny backside to the factory."

"Father?" Percy interrupted the beginnings of the lecture, hungrily eying the remnants of their father's breakfast. "Can I?"

George's expression visibly softened, and he pushed the chipped plate towards the boys. "Eat up, my lad. Put hairs on your chest, that will!"

"I asked first," Percy slapped at Jack's hands that snaked out and snatched up the rabbit bones.

"I'm the eldest boy!" Jack crowed, holding the food morsel out of his brother's reach. "Percy the slow poke!"

"Ma! Tell him!"

Mary Luckett stood at the stove, her shoulders hunched with exhaustion. She was adding carrot tops and peelings to the pan that held the leftovers of a stew.

"You share nicely now," she murmured over a shoulder. "Bobby, come and get yourself some breakfast, love."

Bobby studied her mother. She looked paler than usual, a sheen of moisture on her forehead. The familiar furore of her brother's bickering slid to the back of her mind as she joined her mother next to the stove.

"You okay, Ma?"

Mary bussed her cheek with a kiss as she handed her half a slice of bread. "Just fine. Get that in you."

George stood up, shaking off his breakfast crumbs onto the floor. "Get this mess cleaned up, Mary. No wonder we have rats running through here. This place is a pigsty!"

"Yes, George," Mary replied by rote.

"Mind you all get to work on time," he snatched up his coat and plopped his black cap on his head. He swung a finger at the three girls. "I don't want any of you being fined today. Do I make myself clear?"

"Yes, Pa," they all chimed obediently.

Bobby bit back the argument that sprang to her lips, knowing all too well that she could never hope to win in a confrontation with her father. The factory where they all toiled was notorious for the fines it imposed on its workforce.

It was a rare occasion for any of the workers in the match factory to take home a full wage. The foremen were infamous for levying arbitrary fines against the workers.

Thruppence forfeited for an untidy workbench or for talking at work, the same for having dirty feet, though hardly any of the children could afford shoes. If they dared to be late, they'd lose five pence; a shilling for having a burnt match on the workbench. Last month, poor Sarah Charlton had lost sixpence from her wage packet when she'd dropped a tray of matches.

The women and girls also had to buy brushes and glue out of their own pockets and pay the boys who brought them the frames of matches from the drying ovens.

But George Luckett didn't care about these injustices. He only cared about how much coin was in his pocket come Friday night down at The Talbot Inn.

Without another word, he stalked out of the room. The front door shut firmly behind him, the sound echoing through the small house. Bobby watched from the window as her father's shadow passed by, merging with the stream of navvies trudging towards the city. They were bound for another gruelling day of digging trenches, labouring tirelessly for a world that remained indifferent to their suffering.

The silence didn't last long. The boys began to tussle once more.

"Pack it in!" Gertie, the youngest of the girls, bellowed.

Bobby caught her mother's wince. Gently, she touched her arm. "Ma?" She spoke softly, only just heard through the squabbling of her siblings. "What is it?"

Mary's smile was forced. "It's nothing, love," she patted her daughter's hands and returned to stirring the watery mix in the pan on the stove. "I'm alright."

Bobby wasn't to be put off. A lick of horror streaked through her. Mary Luckett worked in the dipping room at the matchstick factory, handling the dangerous phosphorus that gave the matchsticks their flammable white tips.

Phossy jaw was a real fear amongst the workers. She had seen the disfigurements of the women who survived the damage that the disease could cause. Many of the workers had had to have teeth removed and pus-filled cavities drained out of their lower jaw bones. Many more died. Headaches and toothaches were the first signs, but her mother shook her head.

"Do you have a headache?"

"I'm fine," Mary reiterated, cupping her daughter's face between her hands. "Help me clear up and let's get to work."

Bobby rounded up her siblings, ensuring that her brothers pulled their weight by clearing away the breakfast things and sweeping the floor, straightening the house before they all set off for work.

The walk to the factory was a familiar one. The cobbled streets flowed with other workers just like them, trudging towards the factories. The daylight barely reached through the murky smoke that clung to the buildings. Percy and Jack, with youthful energy no doubt from having a belly full of food, raced ahead, a stark contrast to the trudging steps of the adults.

The blackened factory buildings appeared through the mists ahead, swallowing the sea of workers relentlessly.

Thirteen-hour days stood in the grimy factory.

Bobby hated her work, hated that it was eroding her mother away before their eyes. Maybe her brothers were excited to get to work because they knew they would not always be chained to the workbench at the match factory.

They could find a job at the docks, or aboard a ship and sail around the world. They could work outside alongside their father or find work on any of the rivers in this fair land, but Bobby knew that her prospects were limited even though she longed for a life far from soot and squalor. Her only hope was to marry a kind man who treated her better than her father treated her mother.

Her job as a match machinist involved inserting the phosphorus-tipped sticks into matchboxes, a task that stained her fingers and made them perpetually sore. Lydia and Gertie were packers, placing the finished boxes into the crates before they were ready to be shipped out. The boys were runners, carrying the materials between the different sections of the factory.

The factory was dark, filled with the pungent smell of chemicals and dust. She took her place at the workbench, another cog in the relentless machine of labour in the city. As the engines roared to life around her, drowning out her thoughts, she let out a sigh.

Hours to wait until she could hide away for a few minutes once again in the pages of her book.

CHAPTER 14

Kezzie

"There she is, my favourite girl in the whole of East London!"

Kezzie instantly recognised the voice so when she turned, an amused smile tipped up the edges of her mouth. "There he is," she leaned on her broom, "the most persistent boy in all of East London."

The rains had subsided, leaving behind a sludge which kept getting tracked into the shop each time someone walked inside. The streets were once again filled with the sounds of street vendors hawking fresh fruit, bread, and other wares. The clattering of horse hooves echoed off the narrow buildings. The distant chime of church bells and the hum of conversation drifted through the air, scented with cooking meat and wood smoke.

She'd spent much of the afternoon trying to clear the door stoop.

Archie Clapper's grin was wide as he approached her. His thick chestnut hair was so voluminous that his cap perched on top, barely covering the brown frizz. Archie's clothes were smudged with a day's labour; a canvas bag slung over his shoulder, he wore woollen trousers that were too short for his long legs and his dark wool coat was missing all its buttons.

"Is today the day that you're going to make me happy and say you'll let me take you out?"

Resuming sweeping the doorstep, she replied, "You don't give up, do you, Archie?"

"I keep telling you, and you keep breaking my heart. One day I'm going to marry you, Kezzie Doyle. You mark my words!"

She snorted, pretending to chase him with the end of the broom. "Get away with you. Your mum will be wondering where you are, and I'll get the blame again for keeping you busy."

Archie chuckled, trotting just out of reach of the filthy brush bristles. He stood in the middle of the cobbled lane and clutched his chest. "You break my heart every day, Kezzie. One of these days, you'll see that I'm the man for you and you'll become my wife."

For too long, she'd kept Archie at arm's length. He was a hard worker. His mother, Mary Clapper, had raised him to be honest and polite. His endearing charm and infectious smile made him almost irresistible. She guessed that in different circumstances, Archie could probably make her happy.

"See you tomorrow, Archie!" She called out, returning to the doorway.

"He's not wrong," Rose spoke directly behind her, jolting her. She had been so focused on her task that she'd almost forgotten Rose was at the shop today.

Kezzie treated the woman like a precious piece of blown glass.

If not for Rose's care after her mother's murder, Kezzie would surely have ended up at Mile End, digging in the mud for bones to boil for broth with the rest of the orphans.

Instead, Rose had taken over everything.

She'd been the one to pressure the police for answers, even though nothing ever came of it.

She'd been the one to comfort Kezzie when she awoke screaming, her mind filled with black-eyed monsters and gnashing green teeth.

She'd been the one to take over the shop until Kezzie could legally take ownership.

The woman had a heart of gold and a spine of steel. Too often, she'd chased off ruthless men seeking to usurp the lone women and take the building for themselves.

Age had reduced Rose slightly; these days, she walked with a small stoop and was slower as she moved around the corner between the shop and her little box house.

For a short time, Kezzie had resided there, too. The brick house was modest, a one-up-one-down building that overlooked the stoned yard of the neighbours.

Rose had maintained the apothecary shop, somehow using the knowledge that she'd gleaned across the years from Ada to keep the wolf from their door. The income had been enough for them both to live on. Eventually, though, Kezzie had wanted to move back into the rooms upstairs.

Just as she had in the aftermath of her mother's death, she had continued with her mother's legacy. She took alms to those who couldn't afford medicine into places where the doctors wouldn't tread. She had faced the accusation and the condemnation of those slum dwellers who believed she was evil, chasing her out of the street. People still crossed the street when they saw her coming, too scared of her witch's eyes.

She was determined to persevere through the judgment and rumours, continuing the healing work that had defined her mother's life, even in the shadow of such profound loss.

Kezzie ensured that any hours Rose spent at the shop now were only when the older woman was up to it. She tired quickly. Her bones had twisted with age, her sight not what it once was. Rose was the last connection she had to her mother, and that made her priceless.

"He's not wrong about what?"

"Archie is the man for you."

Kezzie rolled her eyes and gently shooed the woman back into the shop, shutting the door firmly. She waited for the bell to quieten before she added, "I'm not getting into this argument again."

Rose held her hands up in surrender. "Who's arguing?"

Kezzie stored the broom in the back of the shop, resuming her position behind the counter next to Rose.

Ingredients were scattered across the back bench. Wide-neck bottles with their stoppers removed waited for their contents to be added in. Rose didn't even require the recipe books; she knew the potions and concoctions by heart, having made them often enough in the past.

"Have you almost finished?" Kezzie wafted her hand across the array of herbs. "I made a stew this morning. We can have that and then I can walk you back before it gets dark."

"Kezzie..." Rose's brown eyes had yellowed with age. In them, Kezzie saw the melancholy she'd carried in the decade since her mother's death.

"No, Rose," Kezzie replied resolutely.

She knew that look.

She knew where it would lead to – heated words and frustration on both sides.

"We are not talking about how I need to find a husband, nor how Mama would have wanted me to experience the joy of bringing a child into the world."

Rose made a soft sound of disappointment and shook her head.

Kezzie let loose a sigh. She used the edge of her hands to sweep up most of the loose herb fragments and brushed them into the bucket by their feet, working to keep her patience.

Rose lay a hand over Kezzie's forearm to still the movement. Kezzie resisted the urge to give in to her irritation and snatch her arm away.

"You have such a kind heart, Kezzie," Rose explained gently.

Kezzie lifted her gaze and found a look of understanding in her friend's expression that squeezed her throat.

"Ada–"

Kezzie twisted her head away. "No, Rose–"

"Please, let me just say this one thing," Rose insisted. When Kezzie remained silent, she continued, "Ada would have been proud of you."

Kezzie stilled then, her breath catching in her throat. Too much for words.

"The work you've been doing around the community, continuing with it all, despite… well, despite everything that happened."

Kezzie lifted a shoulder in dismissal. "It is what she would have wanted, I'm sure."

Rose smiled wistfully. "Kezzie–"

The chime of the brass doorbell interrupted the solemn atmosphere.

With practised ease, Kezzie quickly schooled her expression, masking the storm of emotions inside. Any talk around her mother evoked deep-seated feelings that she tried to keep under careful control.

Ivy West, one of the local maids, burst through the door, her words tumbling out in a frantic rush. As the frazzled maid explained the events of her day – how the scullery maid had knocked over her employer's favourite perfume that morning – Kezzie sank into her refuge.

Her work was familiar, and there was comfort in that.

She understood why Rose kept nudging her towards romance, believing that companionship was the remedy for her grief. After all, she didn't want Kezzie to be left alone in this world after she'd gone.

Yet she failed to grasp the depth of Kezzie's resolve.

Her mother had died young. Her father had died young.

She didn't care how many times Rose told her any different – the curse had taken her parents and made her an orphan. She wouldn't do that to her child.

She wasn't going to fall in love.

By avoiding love and foregoing a child, she could spare her future daughter the same legacy of loss and heartache that she'd endured.

As far as she was concerned, the Doyle curse was going to end with her.

CHAPTER 15

Kezzie

Night had claimed the daylight by the time Kezzie was making her way back to the apothecary.

The fog rolled in off the river, draping the buildings and turning the narrow lanes of Whitechapel into a shadowy maze. Kezzie walked with purpose, her booted heels echoing between the too-narrow buildings.

Rose often took care of deliveries on a Friday, but Kezzie had sent the older woman home earlier that day with a flea in her ear about resting. Although she insisted that this recent bout of illness wasn't as bad as it sounded, Kezzie was worried.

She could tell it had taken its toll on her frail body. The persistent cough hinted at a lingering weakness. There was a tight coil of dread in her belly because she wasn't sure what she would do once Rose passed away. She was her only connection to Ada. After Rose died, Kezzie would truly be on her own.

With Rose hopefully recuperating in her tiny home, Kezzie's workload had increased. She had hoped to complete the deliveries earlier in the day, but without an extra set of hands, she'd left the shop later in the day and had spent her afternoon hurrying from rickety door to broken window, tending to the sick at dusk.

Perhaps Rose was right, and the time was coming for her to find an assistant to help in the shop. The thought of letting somebody into her sanctuary frightened her; after all, how many people around here would want to work with a Doyle? The ones who knew her secret were too afraid that she was going to curse them, too.

Distant shouts and rattles of wheels striking cobbles drifted through the fog, the sounds of a city that boiled with humanity and never slept.

It was these sounds of an underbelly that unsettled her. She quickened her steps.

Drizzle had driven all but the desperate inside; cobbles shone in the intermittent pools of gaslight. Kezzie pulled her shawl tighter around her shoulders, shrugging off the permeating damp. She turned into East Alley, the soft glow from the apothecary windows up ahead a comfort on this soggy night, penetrating the gloom like a beacon of safety.

She reached into the basket hooked over her arm to find the shop key and was almost at the door when she froze. Through the gloom, she could just about make out a pair of legs stretching out into the lane, from right in front of her doorway.

Her blood ran cold.

The legs were immobile, the feet lying at a strange angle.

Senses on high alert, she glanced back along the alleyway to the lighter end of the street, with vivid memories of another night flashing through her mind.

Unable to quite slow her breathing, her breath formed puffs in the air as she deliberated.

She could run back along the alley and out to the street, find a policeman to help her. But a body lying in the street was not an unusual occurrence here in Whitechapel.

The destitute and the slum dwellers often expired in the street, with people stepping over them as if they were nothing.

A policeman would laugh at her, no doubt. They'd certainly been no help when she'd needed them all those years ago. Their mockery was still etched into her memory.

The alley was deathly quiet.

Rather than her shop key, her fingers curved around the knife hilt. You didn't walk the streets of Whitechapel at night unarmed.

Slowly, cautiously, she drew the knife out and approached the shape. Peering through the gloom, she made out the shape slumped across her threshold.

It was a man.

From here, in the faint glow from the shop windows, she could tell that he was injured.

"Sir?" Her voice was high, and she cleared her throat and tried again. "Hello, sir? Are you awake?"

She edged closer.

He'd been beaten, his face cut and bloodied. He appeared to have crumpled in her doorway.

She wondered if he had chosen this doorway because he'd been seeking refuge, or perhaps he was seeking something medicinal to help his current situation.

Perhaps he'd been dumped here.

She didn't recognise him as local, though she'd wager that his mother would have a hard time picking him out in a crowd right now.

Her heart pounded louder as she deliberated on what to do.

She could step over him, go around the corner to Rose's, and find comfort in having another person to talk to whilst she helped the injured man.

She immediately rejected the thought. In Rose's weakened state, bringing her out on a damp night like this wouldn't help her condition. Nor could the older woman be any match for a man his size.

Judging by the breadth of his shoulders, he was tall and stocky.

Taking a deep breath, she steeled herself. She stretched out her toes, pressing gently on his leg. "*Oi!* Are you alright?"

He didn't move.

Guardedly, she leaned in towards him. She could just about make out in the dim light that he was breathing.

Unconscious, but alive.

"Sir! Can you hear me?"

There was still no response.

Kezzie pondered as she glanced down the alley once more; the shadows seemed to close in on her as she realised that his assailants could still be nearby, waiting for her to let them into her shop.

On the other hand, she was a healer. She'd sworn an apothecary's oath, an ancient promise to help, to do no harm. She couldn't leave him here, not in this state.

She had seen enough injuries during her time in Whitechapel to know that his beating was severe. She carefully stepped around him with a determined sigh, unlocking the door.

As the door swung open, he flopped further into the interior, causing the door to swing wide.

She waited almost half a minute for the unseen assailant waiting in the street to rush upon her, but the street remained still and silent.

She set the basket on top of the counter and placed the knife and heavy iron door key next to it. The damp air curled into the warm shop, and she moved quickly to light several lamps.

In the glow from the lamp that she held over him, she saw just how badly his face had been battered. A nasty gash over his eye was oozing, trickling blood into his hair.

One eye was already swollen shut, and he had a bruise that exploded from the edge of a bloody mouth along his jaw.

She tried again to revive him, but his eyes stayed closed.

Placing the lamp on the floor, she summoned her strength. The man was a deadweight, and it took several attempts to get her hands under his shoulders. In the end, it was easier to grip the collar of his coat and haul him inside that way.

Progress was slow. Several times, she had to stop, needing to take off her cloak and her shawl.

Perhaps it was because she was used to hefting around large sacks of ingredients that she was able to manoeuvre him. Still, by the time his feet were far enough inside where she could shut and lock the door, she was breathless. Pulling him to the back room took longer. When she finished, she had a light sheen of sweat on her brow.

Kezzie cast a quick assessing eye over him. She guessed that this might have been a robbery. His knuckles were scuffed, showing signs he'd at least fought back. His clothes were well-tailored—a fine wool jacket over an expensive-looking suit, now tattered and torn, his white dress shirt turned pink from blood.

In the pale lamplight, his battered face was illuminated. The rain had turned his hair dark and plastered it onto his skin. A wet and bloody streak trailed from the door to his feet. She could only guess how long he'd been out there.

Lacking the strength to lift him onto the bed, she made a makeshift bed on the floor, cushioning his head with her cloak and covering him with a heavy wool blanket.

Confident that he was safe for now, she crossed to the squat iron stove in the corner of the room. He would need warmth so that his body could get to work on healing. The flame caught the sticks and coal, heating up the small room quickly.

She filled a copper pan and set it on the stove to boil. She gathered her supplies as it did. Carbolic soap to clean the skin and hold off infection, compresses and rags to mop up the blood. Comfrey and rosemary to apply to the wounds, honey for after she'd cleaned them.

The man didn't make a peep as she worked, washing his face and bathing his lacerations. She worked swiftly, her hands steady despite her racing heart. He had a deep puncture wound on his side that she was worried about. She estimated he had at least four broken ribs. As she worked, she spoke to him softly, the words calming herself more than trying to reach his unconscious mind.

Her black cat, Delphi, roused by the commotion, wound his way around her knees before settling himself on the patient's midriff.

"We have a guest," she shooed the cat away, a brief smile breaking through her worry. "Guest doesn't mean a bed."

Delphi settled on a nearby chair, watching intently as she worked. The clock struck a late hour when she began clearing up, picking up the strips of cloth that she had cut from his body to clean him properly.

He was still unconscious, but his breathing sounded much more evenly now.

Kezzie set the kettle on the stove, heating herself some tea and cleaning up the debris of her work, checking on him several times.

In the flickering light, she studied him. With such a strong face, it was difficult to put an age on him, and she wondered what a man of his apparent fine standing was doing in an alley in this part of town.

Gambling dens, pubs, dockland dealings… the kind of business enterprises that attracted both businessmen and ne'er-do-wells.

She washed her hands and heated some stew, then fed

the cat, all the while keeping an eye on her guest. Tonight, he lay at rest. However, Kezzie knew that infection posed the greatest risk for the body.

Carbolic soap might clean the skin, yet the deep gash in his side harboured unseen perils.

Settling into the worn armchair beside the stove, ready to spend the night keeping vigil, Kezzie understood that infection was the least of her worries.

She wondered what trouble this stranger would be bringing to her door when he woke.

CHAPTER 16

Kezzie

The loud knocking roused Kezzie.

Blurrily, she blinked around the room. Her brow wrinkled. Instead of looking at the walls of her bedroom, or the familiar view of the rooms in the building across the lane, she was in the back room. She grimaced as she tried to sit up. The room had grown chilly, with the fire reduced to a heap of ashy embers. Silence enveloped the space, broken only by the faint ticking of a clock on the wall. The familiar scent of herbs and the faint tang of carbolic lingered in the air, but it was the unconscious man by her feet that brought her memories flooding back.

More knocking again, and she realised the sound was coming from the front door. It grew louder, more insistent. She carefully stepped around her patient and crept to the curtain, parting it slightly to peek into the shop's interior and beyond.

Her alarm eased a little when it was Rose's face that she saw peering back at her through the glass.

She hurriedly unlocked the door, beckoning Rose inside.

"Where were you?" Rose exclaimed, huffing at her. "Half the day has gone, and the doors are locked!"

Kezzie stepped out to check the street. All appeared to be normal on the streets with no lingering people watching the doorway. Still, she shut the door and turned the key, re-locking it.

"Kezzie?"

Kezzie laid her finger against her lips. "Quiet," she murmured.

Rose's eyes widened, darting between the locked door and Kezzie's face. "What's going on?"

"There's a…," she paused, unsure where to start. Rose wasn't going to like what she'd done. "This way," she beckoned her to follow into the back room.

She brushed aside the heavy curtain, revealing the man lying on the floor.

In the cold light of morning, he looked even worse—pale and bruised, his supine figure wrapped in blankets.

Rose gasped, her hand flying to her mouth. "Is he...?"

"No," Kezzie said quickly. "He's alive. He has a concussion though. He hasn't woken yet."

"Why do you have a man in here? How did you get him *in* here?"

"I dragged him in," Kezzie said, reaching for her shawl. She wrapped it around herself, all the while staring at him. He'd not moved. The bruising had gotten worse, but the bleeding appeared to have stopped.

"Who is he?" Rose asked.

Kezzie lifted a shoulder and let it drop in a shrug. "I don't recognise him. He was in the doorway when I got back from deliveries last night. He's been like this through the night."

Rose bustled past her, setting about reviving the fire in the stove. "You mean to tell me you were locked inside all night with a man you don't even know? He could be dangerous. We could be locked inside with a madman right now."

Kezzie shook her head, a flicker of amusement at the corner of her mouth over the contrary actions. Rose didn't seem particularly concerned about the dangers of the unconscious man lying beside her as she busied herself around the grate and coaxed the fire back to life.

"What else could I have done?" Kezzie said. "I couldn't leave him outside all night. It was pouring rain and freezing cold. He is badly injured. I don't know if he was left here or if he found his way here looking for help."

Rose paused, turning to look back at the unmoving figure on the floor. "Is that the shirt he was wearing last night? What's left of it, anyway?"

Kezzie nodded. "He has a nasty laceration to his left side. I cut the shirt from him because I needed to find the source of the blood and stop the bleeding."

"Look at the detail along the edge," Rose remarked after she inspected the fabric for herself. "A dress shirt. The kind you'd wear to a fancy dinner." Rose did some more gentle exploration behind him. "This coat is from a tailor on Savile Row."

Kezzie had deduced that he was wealthy; he lacked the callouses from manual labour and the grubby fingers of those accustomed to digging in the mud. It was clear he came from money. A Savile Row coat confirmed it. It hadn't even occurred to her to check his pockets, as Rose was doing now. She'd only been focused on stopping the bleeding.

Rose gently teased back the edge of the blanket. "No cufflinks. No pocket watch."

"I wondered if it was a robbery. He certainly fought back because his knuckles were bleeding last night."

Rose tugged the blanket gingerly back over him, tucking it around his shoulders. "It only begs the question: what is a man in a quality tailored suit doing in the East End? Up to no good, I'd wager."

Kezzie wasn't sure why, but she almost defended the man. She didn't know him or what he was like. There were plenty of reasons why men came to Whitechapel, and not all of them were ones she wanted to think about.

The quick succession of sharp raps on the front door startled them both. Their eyes met, Kezzie's heart pounding.

Rose was the first to recover. "You have a business to run."

Kezzie ignored the reminder. "What about him?"

"What about him? Your mother had plenty of people recuperating in here whilst she worked. He'll be fine. I shall make us all some tea."

"I don't think people should know he's here. Why else would someone come to a back-alley apothecary that no one knows about unless you want to remain hidden."

Rose fisted her hands on her hips, looking every inch the force of nature she was. "You said yourself that you must take care of the people of Whitechapel, Kezzie. To do that, the door must be open," Rose nudged her towards the curtain.

Kezzie hesitated, not moving when the door rapped again.

"It's daylight now. We can get one of the local boys to put him in a cart and take him up to the hospital."

Kezzie acknowledged that this would be a sensible thing to do, and yet she still dithered. "Let me wait until he's at least awake, and then I know that I've done as much as I can before I turn him over to one of the surgeons."

"How do you mean to serve your customers and take care of him, too? You have but one pair of hands. He looks like he can afford a proper doctor, judging by his clothing."

"I don't know how," Kezzie replied honestly. "I just know that I need to."

The door knocked again, more insistently this time.

"They're not giving up," Rose gestured towards the shop interior. "That must mean it's urgent."

Kezzie sighed. "Stay here. Stay quiet, just in case. I'll handle it."

Rose waved her through the curtain, drawing it closed behind her to conceal the injured man.

Kezzie composed herself as she crossed the interior.

Eunice Joy stood on the threshold, her smile warm and friendly. "Good morning, Kezzie! Did I wake you?"

Her sweeping gaze reminded Kezzie that she'd not yet freshened herself up for the day. No doubt she looked like a drowned rat, her hair dishevelled, her dress wrinkled from being slept in.

"I'm so sorry, Mrs. Joy. Come on in. I'm afraid I had a late night tending to someone."

Eunice's eyes widened, her brows rising slightly as she noted the clutter strewn across the floor and the counter from the night before. "Goodness," she breathed. "I do hope everything is alright?"

Kezzie quickly lit some of the lamps in the interior of the shop. The morning light pushed against the heavy fog, casting a ghostly pallor across the streets outside. The weak morning light barely filtered through the windows.

"How can I help you today?" she said, neatly sidestepping the question.

If Eunice noticed the subject change, she didn't seem overly concerned. Today she wore a rich, emerald dress, adorned with sparkling stones of jet and garnet shining at her throat. Kezzie wondered about a woman who would wander the streets of Whitechapel with such trinkets on show, unafraid of having them taken from her, even in broad daylight.

"Nettle hair rinse and cold cream," Eunice replied briskly. "Do you sell them?"

"Indeed," Kezzie replied, trying to suppress her testiness at the woman's blasé attitude.

She'd been hammering on the door for items that could be purchased anywhere in the city.

Eunice pressed gloved hands together. "Of course, I usually buy these items in Knightsbridge, but I thought I might give your products a try. I was so delighted with what I had the other day, and as you know, I'm a great fan of herbal products."

Kezzie murmured the required response, quickly locating the items on the shelves. She pulled out her ledger and carefully wrote in the date and made the entry. All the while, her attention drifted to the back room. She wasn't sure why she needed to keep the man hidden, she just knew she did, at least for now.

"You look a little under the weather, Kezzie. Are you sure that you're alright?"

"Actually, I'm just recovering from a cold," Kezzie lied, her voice as steady as she could make it under the woman's avid inspection. "But I do thank you for your concern."

Eunice looked at her with an almost motherly concern. "Well now, I just feel awful. You should be resting, not racing around here, waiting on me. Don't you have a shop assistant? What happened to the other lady that was in here?"

Kezzie set the two items and a piece of paper on the counter, expertly rolling them into a parcel. "That's Rose, she's not been well either."

"And it's just the two of you running this whole place? Well, no wonder you're exhausted," she clucked at Kezzie's nod. "You need a shop assistant. Someone who can manage it whilst you go off and do some shopping, or while you go for a long walk through one of the parks to take in some fresh air. My mother always swore by fresh air. You surround yourself all day with these herbs and tinctures and yet there must be a miasma if you're getting sick from people in here all day."

Kezzie tried not to let the irascibility show, her smile

stiff as she handed over the parcel. Lack of sleep was making her irritable, and it wasn't Eunice's fault. "You're right, of course. It probably is about time that I find myself a young shop assistant."

Eunice nodded enthusiastically. "Someone younger with a strong back whom you can mould and train for the future. At least until you have had a child of your own to pass things onto."

"Will that be all today, Mrs Joy?" Kezzie asked tightly.

"For today, yes. Although I will certainly be back for some of your perfume. I've had nothing but compliments at all the dinner parties. The smell is positively intoxicating."

Kezzie took payment, thanking the woman for her visit. Eunice chatted as she crossed to the door. Kezzie waved her off, watching once more as Eunice made her way over the cobbles, stepping over the rags and debris of the street. She wondered if she'd left her maid in the carriage again today.

She shook her head, reminding herself that it was none of her concern.

To be certain they would be alone, she turned the key in the lock. She wasn't going to close the shop but at least it would stop people from bursting in unexpectedly, and she could be sure that the man was concealed for now.

No doubt Rose had heard Eunice's comments about finding a shop assistant to help her, at least so she wouldn't be alone after Rose had died. She understood that Rose's comments came from a place of concern, but she'd never met anybody quite so forthright about the subject.

Sweeping the curtain back, she was almost ready to defend herself against Rose's smugness.

Instead, she found Rose kneeling beside the man, a look of deep concern on her face. But it wasn't Rose's expression that held her attention.

It was the stormy grey eyes staring up at her from the floor.

CHAPTER 17

Bobby

"What's wrong with you, lad?" George Luckett barked across the quiet table, startling them all.

All eyes moved to a subdued Percy. His thin shoulders slumped forward, his chin touching his chest. "Nothing, Pa…"

"Is the food on this table not good enough for you now?"

Mary lightly touched his forehead with the back of her hand. "Oh, poor love," she murmured. "You're burning up."

George snorted derisively. "There's nothing wrong with him, Mary. He said so himself. You fuss them all too much," he rested an elbow on the table and poked the air towards his youngest boy, "Don't think you're going to be lazing around this house all day. You earn your keep under my roof, boy."

Percy's head remained down, and the sniffling signalled that he was holding back tears. "I'm not sick, Pa. I'm just…"

"Maybe we should fetch the doctor, George," Mary ventured as boldly as she dared. "There's a sickness going round, and he—"

"You heard him," George interrupted her. "There's nothing wrong with him. Get that food eaten, Percy, lad. If not, Jack will eat it, won't you, Jack?"

Bobby frowned as her other brother seemed less enthusiastic to mop up the extra morsels of food with his usual vigour.

He nodded timidly. "I would, but I'm full up myself this morning, Pa."

Bobby exchanged a look of concern with her mother. "Do you feel alright, Jack?"

Jack shrugged. "I'm fine," he murmured, his gaze moving anywhere else in the room that avoided his father's stern look.

"Am I the only one in this household fit enough to work?" George pulled a disgusted face. "You're all lazy, good-for-nothings! You all have a job to do to keep the wolf from my door."

Mary moved from Percy to Jack, performing the same action by checking his forehead. "They feel clammy, George. Will you let me fetch the doc—"

"Do you think I've got money that grows on trees, woman?" he exploded. "I don't have time to waste money on a quack! I'm not sending good money after bad when neither of them are sick. Quit your moaning and get this house cleaned up. I work my fingers to the bone, Mary. I don't need a lazy wife. Look at the state of this place – it's like living in a pit."

Mary flinched with every syllable of George's words, and Bobby placed herself in front of her mother. She was used to hearing her parents quarrel, used to the complaining her father made when there wasn't enough money at the end of the week. She was also used to hearing her mother's pain-filled cries when her father's temper ignited this way.

"I could call by the apothecary on my way home from work, Father."

She'd seen the apothecary, with her pale blonde hair and strange blue eyes walking through Mile End as she made her deliveries to those less fortunate, to the needy and the sick.

"And waste money on a witch?" George rose to his feet, sending the chair toppling as he did so. "I'd rather throw money in the river than give it to a Doyle witch."

"They will help for free. I know people who have–"

"I will not have a Doyle witch step over this threshold!" He roared.

"I will go there," Bobby tried again.

"I won't have their poison under this roof, Roberta!"

Bobby paused; brows drawn over the rising panic in her father's voice. She wondered if it was indeed fear that drove him to refuse help. She was well aware of what the locals said about the Doyle women, the whispers of curses and spells to enchant men into their webs so they could cook them and feast on their flesh.

George flushed, surging to his feet. "I've lost my appetite now, thanks to you ungrateful sods." He snatched up his coat and black cap, slamming his way out of the house.

Behind her, Mary drew in a shuddering breath. "Best do as your father says, love. Help me clean up and get to work."

By the time they were ready to leave for work, Percy had laid his head atop the table, his eyes half-closed. Damp curls of hair clung to his forehead. Bobby had Lydia lift him onto her back so she could carry him along the street. His small body next to hers felt as if a furnace had wrapped itself around her back.

They merged with the seam of brown and black that filled the streets, their mood even more sombre than normal. Jack stumbled alongside Gertie, clinging to her hand.

"Ma," Bobby turned to her mother, "They're not well. Jack can barely stand. They need a doctor or the Doyle woman. Please, Ma. I can call by there on my way home tonight."

Mary dragged her eyes up. Bobby could see the anguish in them though her tone was flat, "Your father says they're fine."

Bobby bit back the sigh.

She wanted to remind her mother that George Luckett wasn't a kind man, but to speak out against her father was disrespectful. Her musings were interrupted by Liam Byrne.

As a dipper, Liam was one of the few men employed in the match factory. He mixed the chemicals that the slivers of wood were dipped into. He had a quick smile, lively green eyes, and a thick thatch of brown hair.

"What about yer?" he asked Bobby, his Irish lilt singsonging through the sombre atmosphere and the plodding boots on the stones.

"Hello, Liam," Bobby smiled, ignoring the pointed look that Lydia was giving her. Liam made no bones about the fact that he was interested in Bobby romantically, though she'd never encouraged it.

"Will I be seein' yer at the dance hall tomorrow night, Bobby?"

The Paragon Music Hall was a popular spot for all the match girls looking to have a little fun and a good time. Most nights it was packed with match girls seeking husbands, but the weekends became raucous when the dock workers and sailors joined the fray. Liam was handsome enough, but she knew her father would never agree to letting her out to enjoy her youth. He wouldn't agree to her finding a husband. Not because he cared about where his firstborn was, but because he could ill afford to lose her wages coming into his household.

Anyway, Friday night was George Luckett's favourite night of the week

Bobby shook her head, her usual rebuttal. Percy's head lolled against her shoulder—the rocking motion of her walking seemed to have lulled him to sleep.

"You know he's asleep up there, don'cha?"

"He's sick," Bobby muttered, her worry for Percy putting out thoughts of finding an excuse not to meet up with Liam.

"Here, let me take him," Liam offered.

Gratefully, Bobby passed her brother over to Liam, stretching out her shoulders.

"He's hot enough to cook an egg on," Liam exclaimed.

"If he's sick, he needs a doctor, not a shift in that hellhole," Charlie, Liam's friend, nodded at the hulking factory building that loomed in the road ahead of them.

"I know, but my father…" Bobby's voice trailed off. She could see in their expressions that she needn't explain it any further. They, too, understood that the men in their lives ruled the roost and that fighting against their word usually resulted in a beating.

Bobby caught the smile that Charlie exchanged with Lydia but she didn't have time to comment on it as Liam said, "How about I keep an eye on him today for you, Mrs Luckett?"

Mary quickly accepted his kind suggestion, but Bobby frowned. "How do you intend to do that? Your foreman is the same as mine, and he has eyes and ears like a dirt house rat. Percy needs to work or else we'll all be docked!"

Charlie sniggered at Bobby's vulgarity; Liam's eyes gleaming with amusement as he jostled a limp Percy into a more comfortable position. "I can hide him under me table," Liam suggested. "I'm sure with a bit of rest and some of me sandwich, he'll perk up a bit."

Bobby eyed him dubiously.

Lydia slid her arm through her sister's, tilting her head at the men. "Would you do that for us?"

Bobby rolled her eyes at her sister's coquettish hair pat.

"I'll cover for him as much as I can," Liam offered.

Bobby looked to Mary, seeking her input, though her mother stared listlessly at the floor.

"What do you say, Bobby?" Gertie nudged her.

The prompt reminded her that Liam was taking a risk by offering to help, even though she wasn't convinced he was going to pull it off. Still, as the flow of workers poured into the factory gates, it showed her that no one else seemed concerned about Percy.

"Very well, but don't blame me if you end up in trouble."

"There you go, worrying about me," he winked.

Bobby laughed at him, even though the last thing she felt like was laughing.

"We'll get him through this, don't you worry. You'll see, by teatime, he'll be back to his usual self - under me feet and scavenging in the lunch pails for leftovers."

With a nod of thanks, Bobby watched as Liam and Charlie took Percy away from the main belly of the factory, towards the dipping shed on the other side of the yard.

She turned back to Lydia, who was still watching Charlie with interest.

"What?" Bobby asked, raising an eyebrow.

"Nothing," Lydia said quickly, looking away. "We'd better get to work."

Mary trailed behind them, her steps shuffling, as if the worries of the world pressed her into the ground. They joined the stream of matchmaker girls that flowed into the factory, stepping into the dusty interior. The machines clattered, cacophonous roar filling the air that reeked of pungent garlic and chemicals.

She took her place at the workbench and began her work though she couldn't shake the unease that had settled in her chest. She remembered her mother losing the other infants, remembered that melancholy that crushed her then.

Percy was in good hands, she told herself, determined to get through the day. Liam would make sure he got the care he needed. If she left the factory as soon as the bell went, she could stop by the apothecary shop before her father was any the wiser. She didn't know how she would explain away having any medicine in the house but surely her father would come round to her helping her brother if it hadn't cost him a penny.

She saw the commotion rather than heard it.

The day was late, judging by the dull ache in her back and the way her feet throbbed from standing all day.

As soon as she saw Liam and Charlie, her heart dropped into her boots. Workbench forgotten, matchsticks dropped, her attention was on the barrow that Liam rolled towards them.

No, not the barrow.

The small, unmoving form that filled it.

CHAPTER 18

Kezzie

"Where am I?"

His voice was raspy, gravelly from lack of use. His brow furrowed, trying to clear the cloud of confusion in his eyes.

"You're safe," Kezzie crossed to him, crouching down close to him. "You've been injured. You were in the doorway of my shop last night."

His frown deepened, his mouth moving before any sound came out. "Water."

She took the cup that Rose handed to her. She gingerly slipped her hand under his head, bringing the cup to his mouth. Rivulets ran down either side as she poured too much, and he coughed, crying out in pain. "My head. What happened?"

"We were hoping you could tell us that," Rose muttered but the man had already faded, eyes his closed, his face slack. Kezzie relaxed as she noted his breathing had returned to the same rhythmic movement he had maintained throughout the night. Rose's eyes met hers above him. "One thing's for certain," she said dryly. "That ain't no East End accent."

Kezzie gave a slight shake of her head. His accent had been rounded, enunciated through education, no doubt. His face had continued to swell from his injuries. She dabbed at the wetness around his mouth.

Rose straightened up, dusting off her knees. "But he's awake now, just as you wanted. I shall go and fetch one of the Rogers' boys. I'm sure one of them can find a cart somewhere and take him up to the nearest hospital."

"Absolutely not," Kezzie said.

Rose paused, a thin brow arching. "But he's awake."

The fire crackled in the stove, yet his face remained very pale. She knew from experience that head injuries could be troublesome. He'd given them no information of substance.

"He isn't cognizant, though. I want to see this through," she spoke with her head bowed.

"He's awake," Rose stated again. When Kezzie didn't reply, she added, "You can't mean to keep a man here in the shop. We don't know him from Adam. It's too dangerous."

"He's injured. I don't know how deep that wound is on his side–"

"Exactly!" Rose crowed. "He needs a surgeon and as good as you are, Kezzie Doyle, you are not a surgeon."

"I know that, Rose. But he's staying put until he can at least stay awake longer than a few seconds."

"You cannot possibly think it's right to keep him here," Rose scoffed with incredulity. "What if he dies here? What, then? You think the police won't hesitate to blame you? They'll brand you a murderer and hang you, Kezzie."

The harsh words sent cold dread sliding down her spine. Dread because they were true. Kezzie spread her hands, indicating the man lying between them. "He's not fit to be moved. He has a terrible head injury and a wound on his side. He's my patient, and I'll say when he's moved."

Rose huffed in exasperation. "The older you get, the more like your mother you are. She would never listen to reason, either."

"That may be," Kezzie said as she crouched down next to him. "But I know Mama wouldn't have turfed him out in his present condition."

Rose huffed out her objection. She prepared a broth for him, complaining the whole time. Once that was simmering away on the stove, she stomped out of the shop, announcing that she was going to fetch meat for a stew.

Kezzie ignored her grumblings, focusing on the tasks at hand. The day dragged on, each moment stretching into an eternity. Every knock on the door sent Kezzie's heart leaping into her throat.

Each time, it was a familiar face, a regular customer, or a curious neighbour, asking to be let in.

"Why is the door locked, Kezzie?" each one asked, their eyes filled with curiosity and concern. "Are you sick?"

She sidestepped the subject each time, weaving intricate verbal dances to deflect their questions. "Just taking some precautions," she replied with a forced smile. "It's been a strange few days."

Rose refused to leave her alone with the mysterious man. *Just in case*, she insisted. But Kezzie could see that the day's activities had taken its toll on her.

"He has been unconscious all day," Kezzie had pointed out. "With his head injury, he won't be getting up any time soon. Other than dying on me, he is no threat."

"You don't know anything about him or his dealings," Rose confirmed, even as Kezzie draped her mantle around her shoulders. "His accomplices could be waiting along the street. They could come back tonight to finish the job they started."

Kezzie brushed a kiss across the older woman's soft

cheek and steered her towards the door. "I'll be careful. I promise."

Reluctantly, Rose left, though not without a final grumble of concern.

The apothecary shop fell silent once more. The back room was dimly lit by the flickering light of an oil lamp, casting long shadows on the walls. Kezzie filled a bowl with Rose's stew and sat on the narrow seat next to the makeshift bed where the stranger lay to eat it.

The hearty meal settled her jittery nerves somewhat.

She opened a book, wanting to give her mind something else to do other than flinch each time she heard a noise from beyond the walls. Her mind wandered often, though she managed to work her way through several pages when a soft groan emitted from down by her feet.

His lashes fluttered. Blinking once, twice, his one good eye slowly travelled around the room, before finally settling on her. This time, he studied her silently, as if trying to commit her face to memory.

"It's you," he murmured, his voice weak but clear. "You're here."

A smile brushed her lips. "Where else would I be? I live here."

"Do I know you?"

She set her book on the floor. "No, I don't think so."

"Where am I?"

"Doyle's Apothecary."

The line between his brows deepened. "Where?"

"An apothecary shop," she carefully helped him take a sip of water, her touch gentle.

"Thank you," he breathed, eyes closing once again, though he didn't fall back to sleep.

"How do you feel?" she asked him.

He thought for a moment, wincing as he shifted slightly. He met her gaze. "Dreadful. My side... it's on fire. I... don't remember what happened."

Kezzie nodded, her expression sympathetic. "You have

a wound on your side. Possibly from a knife. It's quite deep–"

"I was stabbed?" Alarm shone in the one open eye that stared at her. He twisted to see his injury better.

"Yes, now lie still because you're causing the wound to open again," she gently pressed him back down. "I can give you something for the pain if you like. It will make you sleepy."

He frowned. "Are you a doctor?"

"Better," she replied with a small smile. "I'm an apothecary."

Beads of sweat popped out on his temples from his effort. She used a damp cloth to try and soothe him.

His breathing was laboured. His good eye was staring upwards. "Why can't I remember anything?"

"I've seen it often," she murmured, testing his skin temperature with the back of her hand. "You've been badly assaulted, sir."

His investigating fingers travelled upwards, wincing as he touched the split and swollen skin.

"Do I look a mess?"

Kezzie searched his face, the edges of her mouth curling up to soften her words. "The body is an incredible thing. You will heal, though unless you get that cut over your eye stitched properly, I'm afraid that you will be left with a significant scar."

"Can you do it?"

"Yes, but…" She folded her hands into her lap. "I've stitched as best as I could. However, it's your face and a more skilled physician will probably do a better job."

"I'm sure you've done a perfectly adequate job," he spoke succinctly.

"I can fetch a cab for you, but you'll have to walk to the end of the road. I can take you to your over physician, now you're awake."

"No," he said quickly, eye widening.

"It's okay," she said softly. "I will help you walk there–"

"No," the word was expelled on a gust of air. "No... that is, not yet."

Kezzie made a task out of folding the rag she'd used on his forehead, concern rippling through her as Rose's dire warnings sang in her head.

She was alone in a room with a man she didn't know. Surely, he ought to want to return to a place where he felt more comfortable, rather than the floor of an apothecary shop.

"Please," he said again. "I'm certain you're more than capable of dealing with whatever ails me."

"But I'm not your doctor," she said.

Fear, stark and real, flashed in his gaze. "I can't explain it... at least, that is, I don't know why I shouldn't go to a doctor except... I can't tell you who my doctor is. Please, let me stay a little longer."

Kezzie tilted her head to meet his gaze, studying his face in the dim light. He was incapacitated right now, she reasoned. Nothing stopped her from standing up right then and running to fetch a policeman. Would placing her trust in this stranger bring about her death?

Questions pounded through her mind, begging to be let loose.

"What's your name?" she asked, hoping to piece together a little of his identity.

His mouth parted, though the blank stare he gave her confirmed he wasn't pretending. "I don't know that, either."

CHAPTER 19

Kezzie

"I don't trust the fellow," Rose whispered, her eyes sliding towards the drawn curtain as if he might hear her, though Kezzie knew the man was still fast asleep. "He's skimalink."

"Do you mean he's pretending?" Kezzie whispered back.

Rose shrugged her reply.

Kezzie frowned. "Why would he pretend to forget his *name?*"

Rose's lips pursed. "It wouldn't be the first time a man had tried it on with a pretty young girl now, would it? He could be looking to hide out in here for a while from whatever dangers did that beat him up in the first place."

Kezzie's thoughts raced as she pushed the stoppers into the bottles she had arranged on the countertop, sealing in the tonic they'd prepared that morning. She thought about the man's confusion from the night before. She believed that the fear she had seen shining in his eyes was real and that he had no recollection of the answers to her questions.

His agitation at her cautiously probing where he was from or if he could remember a family name had grown with each of her questions. Not wanting to exacerbate his condition any further, she had remained quiet until he'd fallen into an uneasy sleep.

She had maintained her vigil over him through the night, waking herself up every so often to check on him. This morning, her body ached from having not rested properly for the last few nights. He hadn't roused enough since last night to put himself up on the bed, although at least when he was on the floor, he couldn't roll off and injure himself further by falling off the bed.

"You can't keep him back there indefinitely," Rose muttered, disapproval rolling off her in waves.

A lick of annoyance flickered, making Kezzie's tone sharp. "I have no intention of allowing him to stay here any longer than necessary. I'm certain that his memory will return. I've seen this kind of thing many times, mostly when someone's taken a hefty knock to the head. More often than not, their memory returns in full, but it can take time. Sometimes months."

Rose's eyes climbed up her forehead. "He is not staying here—"

Kezzie thumped a stopper into the bottle with unnecessary force. "Of course not! I'm just telling you what the recovery rate could be."

She collected several bottles and wound her way around the counter to place the items in the gap on the shelf.

"What if your healing services are needed whilst he's in there? Your mother always kept the room free for this very reason. Although what she would make of her only daughter–"

"Rose, please!" Kezzie curled her fingers on the shelf, trying to curb her temper. The soft sigh of the other woman pricked guiltily at her conscience. Kezzie set the rest of the bottles on the shelf and then turned. "I'm sorry. I don't mean to be sharp with you. I'm exhausted," she avoided the hurt look Rose gave her, making her way back behind the counter.

She gathered up the remaining bottles, filling up the shelf, needlessly rearranging their neighbours as the atmosphere seemed to pulse unpleasantly around her.

"Are you hungry?" Rose asked, her movements erratic, betraying her inner turmoil. "Would you like something to eat?"

Kezzie could see the tightness in her shoulders and heard the tremor in her voice. It was painfully clear that her brusque tone had upset the other woman, and it left a palpable tension in the air.

"I would, yes, please."

"I'll go see what Nellie Wilson has on her barrow today," Rose jerked her head, stalking past Kezzie. "I need some fresh air anyway," she added as she opened the door.

The jingling bell mocked her, the door closing firmly behind her. The silence that followed was deafening. Kezzie sighed, a sharp pang of guilt stabbing through her as she watched Rose's retreating form hobbling across the cobbles.

She couldn't help snapping at her. Any time her mother's name was used in an argument, it sparked a visceral reaction inside, one that she couldn't quite explain away. She was unable to control the bitterness that had welled up within her.

Perhaps it was the deep-seated feeling of responsibility she kept hidden away.

She run, just as Ada had told her to. But she'd left her mother alone with those ruffians. And none of them had ever been held accountable for that life they'd snuffed out.

She sighed, turning away from the door to clean up the counter, trying to chase away the remorse that gnawed at her. The mundane task provided little distraction from the weight of her thoughts.

A few minutes later, the doorbell tinkled again, its sound jarring in the quiet. Kezzie looked up, expecting to see Rose, but instead, Eunice Joy stepped in.

Kezzie forced up a smile. "Hello, Mrs Joy. Back so soon?"

Today, Eunice looked splendid in a fine midnight blue dress. It perfectly complemented her creamy complexion and her auburn hair. The fitted bodice with the tiny pearl buttons down the front and lace-trimmed neckline looked as out of place here as Kezzie would look standing in a palace in her plain brown dress.

Her hat was decorated with silk ribbons, pinned to the coiffed hairstyle.

Kezzie noted the unusually subdued demeanour and tilted her head to study Eunice more closely. In her experience, the other woman had been a bluster of energy, vivaciously confident. Now, she appeared... fragmented.

"Hello, Kezzie," Eunice said, her voice trembling slightly. "How are you?" The smile didn't quite reach her eyes, which shimmered with unshed tears.

"I'm well, thank you for asking... Forgive me for asking but are you alright, Mrs Joy?"

"I just—" Eunice blinked rapidly, and Kezzie's heart ached at the sight of the tears threatening to spill over. "I'll be fine." Eunice retrieved a lace handkerchief from her bag, dabbing delicately at her eyes. "I'm just... please, don't mind me. I'm just being silly."

Concern etched her features. "I doubt that's true. Would you like to sit a moment?"

Eunice shook her head, tucking the handkerchief back in her bag. "Thank you, no." She fanned her cheeks with a lace-gloved hand. She gave herself a little shake and exhaled noisily, giving Kezzie a quick, watery smile.

Kezzie dredged up a smile, setting aside the last few days' events, glad of something else to focus on. She hoped that her worries weren't as evident as Eunice's. "What brings you by today?"

Eunice glanced towards the door, a flicker of anxiety crossing her face. "Are we alone?"

Kezzie nodded, keeping her gaze steady even as her heart skipped a beat at the small lie. Her house guest was still sleeping off the effects of the laudanum she'd administered earlier. "Quite alone," she assured her, confident that he wouldn't hear them.

"Good," Eunice breathed a sigh of relief, her shoulders relaxing slightly. "I... I needed to talk to someone. Someone I trust."

Kezzie stepped closer, her concern deepening. "Rose will be back soon."

Eunice hesitated, her eyes filling with tears once more. "I could come back another time..."

"Please," Kezzie prompted her. "Tell me what's wrong."

Eunice took a deep breath as if gathering the courage to continue. "I... I don't know quite where to begin. Nor who to tell. You'll probably think me a ninny–"

"Eunice," Kezzie spoke firmly, interrupting the rambling.

"My husband..." She whispered, fresh tears spilling over her lids. "He's a... a cruel man." She drew back her sleeve, revealing a bracelet of bruises around her wrist.

Kezzie gasped, gently cradling her hand to examine them. "He did this?"

Eunice sniffed and nodded, dabbing at her eyes. "He was a good man, or so I believed but... he's quick to anger over the most frivolous of things."

Kezzie frowned. The bruises, in the shape of fingertips, seemed small. Though perhaps Arthur Joy was a slight man. "I don't think it's broken–"

The jangling bell exploded into the tense silence.

"Nellie wasn't there, so I – oh, hello, Mrs Joy!"

Eunice snatched her hand out of Kezzie's grasp, and in a flurry of midnight blue satin and rushed excuses, she was out of the door and away along the street in a flash.

Rose and Kezzie watched her leave.

"What was that about?"

Kezzie turned to Rose, a smile propping up one side of her mouth. "Just another reason why I'll never get married."

CHAPTER 20

Bobby

THE HEAVENS WEPT, matching the grief that hung heavily over the ragged group gathered in the graveyard. The matching dark mounds piled next to the gaping holes in the ground. The rhythmic patter of the downpour was broken only by the dull thuds of soil tumbling from the shovels of the gravediggers.

Gertie and Lydia huddled together, shivering under a shared blanket, heads touching in solace.

Nearby, Mary stood apart from them, isolated in her grief. The downpour matted her hair to her face, mingling with the tears that streaked her cheeks. The insurance money had paid for the grave plots, but it could never heal the wounds of a mother who had lost both her sons within a week. Every clod of soil that thumped onto the coffins made Mary wince.

Even to Bobby, the boxes seemed so small. She didn't feel the cold from the rain, only the grief that encompassed her mother.

"Come on, Ma," Bobby had had enough of the flinching. "Let's get you home in the dry, hmm?"

"My boys," Mary whispered, her voice trembling, as Bobby gently tried to steer her away from the graves. "I let them down."

"No, Ma," Bobby squeezed her shoulders, her voice firm despite the lump in her throat. "It wasn't your fault."

She knew the weight of her mother's guilt. She'd heard the ferocity of her father's insults after Jack had passed. She'd cried over how George had blamed Mary for giving him sons too weak to survive.

"I can't leave them," Mary whimpered. "They'll not like being left here alone."

"It's fine, Ma," Bobby murmured. "We can visit them whenever you like. You can't stay out here, though. You're not well yourself."

Mary twisted to look back at the graves, releasing a low keening sound.

"Come now," Bobby coaxed her.

"Your father will be waiting, won't he?" Mary acquiesced after Bobby agreed.

The bruise along her mother's cheek, yellowed from age, was a stark reminder of the man who had driven himself into a stupor at the Talbot Inn, leaving his family to fend for themselves in their darkest hour.

She'd never known hate like it, until now.

They stepped through the black iron gates of the graveyard, and Bobby was surprised to see Liam and Charlie standing on the other side of the street. They had the caps pulled low; their collars turned up against the rain. Each was too superstitious to venture into the graveyard. The deluge distorted their features, but Bobby could see the sorrow on their faces.

"I'm sorry, Mrs Luckett," Liam said, his voice barely audible over the rain. There was nothing more to say to a woman who had buried two children in one day.

Mary either didn't hear him or chose to ignore him.

Bobby acknowledged Liam's sentiment with a nod, then continued to guide her mother down the street. The walk back to their house was long and silent, the rain soaking through their shoes, their footsteps heavy with the burden of loss.

Charlie held an umbrella up over the girls. Bobby was aware of Liam behind them, and was grateful for his company, even though no one spoke.

She sent him a grateful smile as she guided her mother into the gloomy house. They waited until the door was shut before leaving the girls to it.

The hearth was cold which made it impossible to warm up. Mary stood at the stove, oblivious to the damp, lost in grief. Bobby gently nudged her back, taking a lucifer match to light the stove. She needed to feed them all, had to take the chill off the room.

The house was eerily quiet without the boys. Their laughter, their bickering, the sound of their feet racing across the floorboards—all gone. Gertie coughed weakly, breaking the silence. Bobby examined her little sister more closely. She was deathly pale and listless, and she realised now how quiet she'd been all morning.

"Gertie? What's wrong?"

"I don't feel so good," the young girl whispered.

Bobby's heart clenched. She couldn't stand by and watch another sibling slip away. She crossed to the chair, using the back of her hand to check her sister's skin. Clammy and hot, even as chills shivered throughout her body.

"Come sit by the stove, it'll warm you up," Bobby urged, but Gertie protested.

"Lemme sleep," she moaned, turning into Lydia on the threadbare sofa.

"Is she going to die, too, Bobby?" Lydia asked in a whisper.

Helplessly, Bobby looked to Mary, but she watched

her three remaining children without a flicker of emotion, her eyes hollow.

She knew she couldn't do this alone. She could go and find their father, but George was at the Talbot Inn, drowning his sorrows in a bottle, even though he still had three children who needed him.

She'd been made to stand by and watch this fever claim her brothers. She was sick of waiting, of watching.

"Not if I can help it," Bobby pulled a dry shawl off the back of the chair and tied it around her shoulders. "Keep the stove lit. Reheat some of that stew. Get Ma to eat it, then put her to bed. Oh, and don't let Gertie sleep."

"Where are you going?" Lydia cried out.

Bobby turned in the open doorway, the deluge battering the street behind her. "Father might be scared of witches, but I'm not."

CHAPTER 21

*B*obby

EAST ALLEY WASN'T REALLY an alley.

Too narrow to be a street, too wide to be a lane, it had once bustled with the vitality of a main thoroughfare to those wanting to cut through the buildings from the busy Commercial Road to the housing clustered beyond.

The cobbles, many worn down to smooth nubs, formed an undulating and uneven path between the tall, narrow buildings.

The blackened building facades hid the intricate patterns hewn into the stonework, buried under decades of smoke damage and city grime. For those who dared to look up, faded shop signs jutted out, showing where there had once been a cobbler, a butcher, a chandler.

Several of the shops looked to be more like homes now, the only signs of life were the threadbare curtains hanging limply in the dirty windows. Two old women stood on one of the door stoops, watching as Bobby made her way along the alley. Other than that, the lane was quiet.

The apothecary shop looked in much better condition than its neighbours. Although the windows were still coated in city dust, there was a pretty arrangement of items displayed for sale in the window. The doorstep was dipped in the middle, worn away by countless boots over the years.

For just a moment, Bobby hesitated. Whispers and dire warnings, rumours of cauldrons and dungeons, almost made her turn around until she thought about Gertie needing her, about how she'd stood at the side of her brothers' graves that morning.

She pushed through the front door, the brass bell clanging loudly overhead. Inside, her eyes went wide as she took in the array of pots, coloured glass bottles, and tin boxes lining the shelves. Strange smells assaulted her senses, a potent mix of herbs, spices, and something indefinably medicinal.

Not unpleasant, just different.

In the corner, barrels and crates were stacked neatly. The displays set out along the wide wooden counter were meticulously arranged.

But Bobby's attention was focused on the young woman standing in the middle of the shop floor. She tried not to stare at her vividly piercing eyes.

Kezzie Doyle.

Her smile was warm and welcoming as she said, "Welcome to Doyle's. Can I help you with anything?"

Bobby hesitated, knowing that her being here would bring down her father's wrath on all their heads. She glanced nervously towards the door, seeking an escape.

"I don't bite," the woman joked. "At least, not during the daylight."

Despite herself, Bobby smiled, albeit briefly. "It's my sister," she mumbled. "She's sick."

"I'm so sorry," Kezzie's mouth turned down at the edges. "Can you give me some more details? Is she vomiting? A fever? A rash?" She clarified when Bobby gave a little shrug.

"She's hot to the touch," Bobby explained, blinking against the sudden rush of tears.

"How long has she been ill?" the woman asked, her eyes soft with understanding.

"Just this afternoon," Bobby replied, thinking how she'd been stood out in the torrential rain. "But that's how it was with my brothers. It comes on so fast," she rolled her lips inwards, trying not to cry. "My brothers... they died of the same. It happened really quickly and I... I'm scared."

She nodded sympathetically. "Does your sister have a cough?"

Bobby shook her head, swiping at her wet cheeks.

"Did your brothers?"

Again, she shook her head, sniffing as she used her sleeve to wipe her face. She hesitated when the woman with the strange eyes handed her a white handkerchief.

"Thank you."

"I'm sorry about your brothers," Kezzie said when Bobby met her gaze once more.

"They lost their appetite, at first," Bobby's breath hitched. "They went really hot. Both just went to sleepy and then... it's like they couldn't wake up, no matter how much we tried to rouse them." She dried her wet cheeks, trying to compose herself.

"That's really helpful," Kezzie nodded. "If there was a cough, we might try something with angelica in it, but we'll start with something to bring the fever down," She moved to one of the shelves and pulled down a jar filled with a mixture of dried herbs. "This is *hemp agrimony*," she reached under the counter for a smaller empty bottle that was embossed with a symbol. "It's good for–"

The strange sound interrupted Kezzie mid-sentence. Her eyes popped wide as she stared at Bobby, as if checking that she'd heard it too. Bobby watched her closely, noting how Kezzie's movements suddenly grew hesitant, her attention fixed on whatever had made the sound. When it came again, Bobby recognised it as a cough, followed by a long, drawn-out moan.

Kezzie froze, staring at the paraphernalia she'd just set out on the counter.

"Excuse me a moment," she said, setting the jar and measuring spoon down before disappearing behind the heavy velvet curtain along the back wall.

Bobby blinked, her eyes flitting between the medicine and the curtain, ears straining into the silence. She could take the medicine now, though she wouldn't have a clue how to use it.

She glanced at the shop door, the pressure of knowing that her father could return home at any moment gnawing at her. Her mother was in no fit state to defend herself once he flew into one of his tempers, and then there was Gertie. Worry filled her as Gertie's pale face drifted through her mind. Poor Gertie was younger than the boys, smaller and weaker.

Bobby whimpered, urgency driving her across to the curtain. The sporadic coughing and moaning beyond it continued, and she could hear the soothing tones of the apothecary as she spoke in a low volume to whoever else was behind there.

Inspired, Bobby quickly began to scan the shelves. She picked up the jar marked 'Angelica'.

"Hello," Bobby called out, "please, miss, I know you have someone else but my sister, she's very sick and my brothers—"

The curtain was snatched back. At once, Bobby's eyes moved beyond the apothecary's stern expression. In amongst the pile of blankets and cloth spread out on the floor was a man. He writhed; his battered face visibly damp.

Bobby held out the jar. "For the cough. You said *angelica* helps."

THE CURSE OF THE WHITECHAPEL ORPHAN

The bright blue eyes darted between the jar and Bobby's face, the worry swimming in them stark. "You can read?"

Bobby nodded, unable to drag her eyes from the man on the floor. "Please, will you help me?" she asked, desperation creeping into her voice.

Kezzie sighed. "Very well." She brushed past Bobby, though instead of making the medicine for Gertie, she only locked the door. The mild panic at being locked inside with a witch abated when she hurried through the curtain and into the back room again. "I'll help you, but I need you to help me first."

"Me?"

"Of course, you," she said briskly.

"I-I don't know anything about caring for people."

Kezzie snorted and gestured for Bobby to come closer. "Yes, you do. You have younger siblings, don't you? This is the same. Do you know how to build a fire?"

"Y-yes, miss."

"Good. Do that, and then come and help me give him this medicine."

The coughing and writhing continued. Bobby did as she was told, working as quickly as possible as the apothecary pulled down jars, mixing a concoction of powders in a pan of water that simmered on the stove.

Kezzie handed her a small cloth. "Press this to his forehead. He'll move, but you are not hurting him. The coolness will feel good against his skin," she instructed, then turned back to her shelves.

Bobby stepped closer, her heart pounding as she knelt beside him. His skin felt like he was on fire, just as Percy and Jack had. He moaned softly, his eyes fluttering open and then closing again.

Bobby glanced up at Kezzie, who was decanting the mixture into a vial with practised efficiency. "What's wrong with him?"

"He's been badly hurt and the wound's become infected," Kezzie explained, not looking up from her work. "We need to bring his fever down. I have more honey for the wound but it's upstairs," she paused, turned her head to eye Bobby. "What's your name?"

"Roberta Luckett," she replied. "Everyone calls me Bobby."

The apothecary watched her for a moment. "You know who I am, don't you?"

Bobby nodded.

"I don't eat children, nor do I boil men for fun, contrary to all the legends around these parts. So, please stop eying me like I'm going to grow an extra head," Kezzie muttered, dusting off her hands. "Dip the cloth to make it cold again. I'm just going to get the honey," she paused, the curtain held aside as she looked back. "Please, try not to rob me blind whilst I'm gone."

"Yes, miss," Bobby nodded, focusing on her task.

It might have been only a few minutes, but it felt much longer. Kezzie hurried back into the room. She collected up the small vial, then set it and the honey jar on the floor before she knelt on the opposite side to Bobby.

"Will-will it be much longer?" Bobby stammered, "Only my father... he'll be back at any time. He won't like it if I'm not there and..."

Kezzie's eyes met hers briefly, then focused on the vial she held up. She poured the bright green liquid into a spoon. "Hold his head up for me," she said. "This part is just quicker with two people." Bobby carefully tilted his head. Kezzie thumbed open his jaw, moving quickly to tip the liquid into his mouth, even as he twisted and moaned.

He coughed but almost instantly, he quietened, his distress easing.

Bobby stared. "Is he...?"

"Dead?" Kezzie queried, then shook his head. "No. Sleep is a great healer for your body." She moved quickly, peeling back the blankets to reveal the angry-looking gash on his side.

Bobby gasped, rearing back.

Kezzie glanced at her, her attention switching to the wound. "Does this make you feel sick?"

"N-no, but it's just... I mean, I've seen injuries like it in the factory."

Kezzie took a clean knife, using the blade to scoop out a glob of honey. "What factory?"

"I work in Bow," Bobby watched what she was doing, at the careful yet efficient way she applied the gloopy stuff. "One of the match factories."

Kezzie set the knife aside and wrapped the wound up once more. "Do you like it?"

It was Bobby's turn to look at her as if she was ready for the asylum. "Does anyone enjoy that place? I should be there now. My father will skin me alive knowing that I've taken the day off."

"You buried your brothers today, yes?"

"That's right."

"Then you have a good enough reason not to work, don't you?"

Bobby's nose wrinkled as Kezzie rose to her feet. "He doesn't see it that way."

Kezzie dealt with the utensils, then stepped back into the shop. She set the curtain back to conceal the room, then returned to the counter, resuming the preparation she'd started. Just like she had with the man, she worked quickly and efficiently, her hands deftly measuring and mixing.

"This has bear's breech and peppermint in it, with the hemp. Mix it with cooled boiled water. Be sure to give a dose every hour on the hour for half a day. Spoon it into her mouth like I did in there," she pressed a stubby cork into the opening of the green bottle, tapped it into place, before expertly rolling it in paper.

"It will help with the fever, but you must keep her hydrated." She slid the package across the counter. "A bone broth will do. Small sips. If you can keep her head cool but not cold, that will ease her discomfort."

Bobby reached for the package, though Kezzie kept her fingers on top of it as she said, "You did very well today. I won't charge you for this. Thank you for your help, but I have another favour to ask of you."

"Miss?"

Kezzie's eyes were serious as she searched Bobby's face. "Please don't tell anyone about what you saw today. Not what I did nor... that there is a man in the back room."

Bobby nodded, taking the small bottle, and clutching it to her chest. "I promise."

The apothecary seemed to relax slightly. She smiled, her eyes kind despite the worry etched into her features "Thank you." She stretched across the counter and gently squeezed Bobby's shoulder. "You're a brave girl, coming here. Your sister is lucky to have you."

A smile wobbled across her mouth, fear bubbling in her belly. "I just want her to be okay."

"I know," Kezzie said softly. "Please come back if you need more help."

CHAPTER 22

𝓑obby

THE WALK HOME FELT INTERMINABLE.

The earlier downpour had made the cobbles slick and treacherous. She trotted along the narrow lanes and alley ways, clutching the glass bottle to her chest, her mind focused on the desperate hope that little Gertie would be alright.

Puddles of stagnant water collected in the indentations of the uneven road, the edges slick with mud formed by dust from the smoky fog. The houses were packed tightly along the road, their once-neat facades now cracked and flaking. The mortar had fallen away from bricks in places, forming yawning holes in the structures.

Wisps of smoke drifted out of several begrimed chimney pots towards the bruised-looking sky. Bobby hurried past the skinny children in their tattered clothing and ignored the weary women who called to her from the crooked doorways.

She reached the Luckett's front door, pausing to

steady herself with a deep breath. The burden of the past few hours clung to her, but she pushed the door open, ready to face whatever awaited her inside.

Mary stood listlessly at the kitchen window; her vacant gaze fixed on the rain-slicked bricked yard out the back. Gertie lay on the couch, shivering under a threadbare blanket, her face ghost-like against the dirty upholstery. The stove emitted a faint warm glow, but the rest of the house was swallowed in darkness.

"Where were you?" Lydia hissed as she jumped up, her eyes bright with hysteria.

"Sorry," Bobby shed her damp shawl. Her eyes were on Gertie, whose breathing was shallow and laboured, her small body drenched in sweat. "I had to..." Bobby trailed off, struggling to find an explanation that would appease Lydia's worry. Instead, she held out the green bottle. "I got her some medicine. We need to boil some water. Keep her cool. Try to get her to drink something."

Lydia, though fraught with anxiety, sprang into action, setting a pot of water on the stove. Bobby moved to her mother, gently coaxing her into a chair. Mary's eyes fluttered closed, and Bobby's heart ached at the sight of her mother's almost catatonic state. She wondered if the apothecary might have something to help ease her mother's overwhelming grief.

"Where's Pa?" Bobby asked though she dreaded the answer.

"Not back yet," Lydia replied absently as she watched Bobby add the powder to the boiling water.

Knowing that their father was still out was a familiar but no less worrying concern, especially with the rent due soon. Bobby shoved the thought aside, focusing on the task at hand. She carefully dispensed the mixture to Gertie, as Kezzie had instructed.

Gertie looked so small and fragile under the blankets, her chest rising and falling with effort. "Please, let this work," Bobby whispered, pressing a gentle kiss to Gertie's damp forehead.

Night came, plunging the house into a deeper darkness. Bobby kept a vigilant watch over her family, her thoughts a flurry of fear and determination.

The hours dragged by.

The fever seemed to tighten its grip. She couldn't bear the thought of losing her sweet Gertie, not after all they had already lost. She gave her two more doses of the strange mixture.

Just as the first light of dawn began to brighten the room, Bobby was jolted from her light doze by the sound of the front door crashing open.

George Luckett stumbled in, reeking of alcohol. His bloodshot gaze swept the room. "Why is it so bloody hot in here?" he bellowed, his fury palpable.

Bobby could feel the damp morning air from the open door rapidly cooling the room. She jumped out of her chair, worriedly looking at Gertie, who was pale but still breathing. "Gertie's sick," she muttered, trying to keep her voice steady.

"I don't care," George roared. "I don't have money to waste."

"Pa, please," Bobby pressed a hand to Gertie, relieved to feel dry, not damp skin. "I don't want to lose another sibling."

George slumped against the wall, dragging his hands down his face. "You should be getting ready for work, not lazing around like Lady Muck!"

"We're going, Pa," Lydia said, rubbing the sleepiness from her eyes, her voice small and frightened.

Mary was still sitting in the chair, her eyes distant and filled with sorrow. "The boys died, George," she said forlornly.

George's eyes narrowed; his face twisted with rage. He stormed across the floor, yanking Mary out of her seat and shaking her like a rag doll. "Get up and get to work, you lazy cow!" He roared in her face. He turned on Gertie, yanking the blankets off her small form. "All of you, get! Just because there are fewer mouths to feed, don't think you can all laze about here. I'm sick of the lot of you!"

Bobby rushed forward to help her little sister. "No, Pa," she shouted, trying to shield Gertie with her own body. "She's got what the boys had."

George knocked Bobby back then his eyes fell on the green bottle. Bobby lunged for it, but George was quicker, snatching it up and holding the bottle up to the light. The 'D' stood proud of the shiny surface. "What is this?"

"M-medicine," Bobby stammered.

George's eyes narrowed on Bobby. "You brought witches brew in this house? When I told you not to?"

"I had to try–"

With a roar of anger, he hurled the bottle across the room. It exploded against the wall, sending shards of coloured glass scattering everywhere.

"No!" Bobby lost her temper, the fear and frustration of the past days boiling over. She flew at her father, her small fists pounding against his chest. "I'm trying to save her!"

The backhanded blow sent Bobby sprawling. Pain bit into her where the glass pieces pierced her skin.

"I don't care a fig," George spat. "If I'm to be saddled with women, then you need to earn your keep, else you'll be out on your ear. I don't need you wasting time and money on lost causes."

Bobby scowled at her father, her face throbbing from where he'd struck her. Disbelief and despair flooded her senses. Mary stared at the floor; her arms wrapped around her middle as if trying to keep from shattering like the glass bottle. Lydia watched with wide, fearful eyes, too scared to move.

Satisfied that he had made his point, George turned and stumbled towards the door. "Get to work," he barked over his shoulder. "Or there'll be hell to pay."

CHAPTER 23

Bobby

Bobby was sick with nerves by the time she stepped back into the apothecary shop. Strange smells filled the space like the day before, a heady mix of herbs and concoctions.

An older lady stood behind the counter today, her demeanour calm and a little curious. Her kind eyes crinkled in the corners as she smiled at Bobby.

Bobby felt both cheeky and shy under the woman's attentive gaze.

"Please, miss, is Kezzie here?" she asked.

The older woman nodded kindly. "One moment."

She stepped over to the curtain, brushing it aside and murmuring something softly. Moments later, Kezzie appeared around the edge of the curtain, her frown softening into a smile when she spotted Bobby.

"You're back," she said, stepping further into the shop. "Did the tonic help?"

"I-I'm not sure," Bobby stammered. "That is, I had to leave Gertie at home this morning. I have to work, you see," she explained, wringing her hands nervously as she remembered the image of little Gertie hidden in the back room upstairs.

All day packing matches, the nagging worry that her father had returned and would fly into a rage knowing that one of his family members was not pulling their weight churned her stomach. Gertie would be no match for her father's fury, even if she were at full strength.

She drew some comfort from the knowledge that Gertie had appeared to perk up a little before they left, whereas the boys hadn't woken at all. Bobby had made Lydia clean up the glittering glass as she'd tried to coax food into a reluctant Mary.

"She was too sick to work but my father..." Bobby's voice trailed off, her eyes growing glassy with tears.

"Did you give her the medicine through the night?" Kezzie asked gently.

"Oh yes," Bobby nodded. "She survived the night. She seemed a little brighter this morning except..." Now came the difficult part, having to explain that her father had destroyed Kezzie's kind gift. "I need more medicine."

Kezzie's eyes widened in surprise. "You've used it all already?"

"No, no," Bobby said quickly, hesitating as she chose her next words carefully. She needn't have worried.

The long-drawn-out sigh from Kezzie indicated she understood. "Your father found the bottle, didn't he?"

Bobby blinked, "Yes, miss, but how did you know?"

Kezzie rounded the end of the counter. "You're not the first woman in here looking for a replacement because a man believed in some superstitious nonsense."

Bobby couldn't tell if the apothecary was offended or annoyed as she took down the same jars from the previous day.

"I'm so sorry, miss," Bobby said quickly. "I can pay you for this one." She reached into a pocket and held out a single coin.

She had taken it from the tin her mother kept on top

of the cupboard in the kitchen, knowing that her father would be apoplectic with rage if he knew.

Kezzie's gaze swept over her attire, her mouth firming when it settled on the angry red mark on the left side of Bobby's face. "Keep your money, Bobby, though I thank you for the offer."

"Miss?" Bobby said uncertainly.

"I still owe you for your help yesterday," Kezzie replied briskly.

"How is your…guest?"

Kezzie and the older lady exchanged a peculiar look. Kezzie quickly explained to Bobby how she came to know that there was someone behind the curtain.

"Bobby was quite the helpful hand, you see. This is Rose," Kezzie nodded towards the other woman. "She was my mother's friend. She is like my aunt, only better." That compliment seemed to appease the older woman as Kezzie said, "Bobby won't say a word, will you, Bobby?"

"No, miss, definitely not."

"He's improved a little," Kezzie said. "Thanks in part to your help."

The doorbell chimed, cutting off any further conversation.

Bobby's mouth went dry when two policemen entered, their spiffy navy uniforms and shiny silver buttons adding to their intimidating presence. The atmosphere in the shop chilled instantly as the men surveyed the shop with blatant curiosity.

Kezzie didn't miss a beat, continuing to mix the powders for Bobby as she sent the two stern-looking men a winsome smile. "Welcome to Doyle's, gentlemen. How can we help you?"

The older one of the two stepped forward, addressing Rose in a formal tone. "Are you the owner of this establishment?"

Bobby wanted to make herself as small and inconspicuous as possible. The second office's gaze skimmed over her before he began to inspect the shop, his movements slow and deliberate.

"That would be me," Kezzie replied, dusting off her hands and holding one out in greeting. "I'm Kezurah Doyle." He stared at her hand as if waiting for it to bite him.

Kezzie lowered her hand, her mouth tightening. "What do you want?"

He drew himself up, peering down his nose at her, his lips twisting in distaste. "We are looking for someone. A man. He isn't local, but we have reason to believe he's in the area."

Kezzie held his gaze steadily. "What does this have to do with me?"

He inhaled sharply through his nose, though his colleague stepped forward, "Our guv'nor has the whole force out looking for this chap. We tried the local hotels, public houses, that sort of thing first. The next step is contacting the shop owners and the like who might have seen something untoward that could help us find him."

"This is Whitechapel," Kezzie countered. "Everything around here looks untoward."

Taken aback, he huffed out a chuckle. "Well, I couldn't comment about that. In truth, we didn't know you were down here."

"Doyle's been here for over a hundred years," Kezzie didn't pause in her pressing the powder.

"The man seems to have disappeared," the policeman said.

"The docklands are not too far away," Kezzie pointed out. "You can get anywhere in the world from there, I'm told."

"Checked ship manifests," he replied, admiration lighting his eyes. "You're out of the way along here, and you help people who are sick. Anything you've seen in the past week?"

"What's he done?" Rose blurted out. "This man – is he dangerous? I mean, we're two women very often here unaccompanied and it's a worry for me, being that Kezzie lives alone upstairs," she added when the taller man's gaze sharpened on her.

The younger one patted the air. "He isn't dangerous, miss. We just need to find him."

"What's his name?"

"Elias Turner."

Kezzie's expression remained neutral. A pin could be heard dropping in the silence that followed. "Can't say I've seen anything that looked out of place, can you, Rose?"

Rose dropped her gaze, feigning interest in the cork stoppers. "Just the same old faces I see almost every day."

Kezzie paused in her pounding, her face a mask of polite concern. "Why are you looking for him if he's done nothing wrong?"

"He has–"

"We don't have time for idle chitchat," the taller man snapped, annoyed at the flirtation. He pivoted, his eyes alighting on Bobby. Twin spots of pink bloomed on her cheeks as she studied her boots harder. "What about you, girl?"

"M-me?"

"Where are you from?"

"M-mile End," she muttered, heart pounding until she felt lightheaded.

"Have you seen anything suspicious?"

Bobby shook her head vigorously.

"He has dark hair. He'll be the same height as me. He'll be better dressed than you are, no doubt."

"I've seen nothing, sir," Bobby said timidly. "I just came to get some medicine for my sister."

"Her sister has a very contagious disease," Kezzie

spoke up. "I wouldn't get too close to her as she's very sick, indeed."

The obnoxious man visibly recoiled. The younger one held the door open for his associate who hurried through it, then with one last friendly look at Kezzie, he said, "If you see or hear anything, let us know immediately."

"Of course," Kezzie said smoothly. "Thank you, sir."

"You can find me at Leman Street station. Good day."

The door closed, the doorbell chiming their exit. The tension in the room lingered on until after the policemen had exited the mouth of East Alley.

Bobby let out a breath she didn't realise she'd been holding.

"Oh, my giddy aunt," Rose seemed to deflate. "Oh, what have we done? Kezzie, do you realise what you have just made us do – this young girl, too?"

Kezzie serenely tapped the cork into the bottle, rolling the bottle into the paper and securing it with string, as Rose's hysterical words tripped out of her mouth.

"We've lied to the police! Oh! Oh, what will happen to us?"

"It's fine, Rose," Kezzie said evenly.

"How can it be fine, girl? We lied! You've just implicated yourself in a crime by lying. You don't even know him – he's a stranger to you, and you've incriminated yourself!"

Kezzie calmly held the bottle out to Bobby. "Are you alright?"

Bobby stepped forward on rubbery legs.

She didn't know who the man behind the curtain was, or if he was still there, nor did she understand why Kezzie Doyle seemed to be hiding him. She had more important things to focus on. She needed to get home before her father did, to make sure that her sisters and mother were safe.

"Thank you. Are you certain you won't take any money from me?"

Kezzie smiled warmly. "Quite certain," she said, her vivid blue eyes scanning Bobby's face with understanding. She turned and handed Bobby another package from the countertop. "This has comfrey in it. Dissolve two spoonfuls into a cup of cold water. Soak a rag in it and hold it to your face. It will help the bruising heal faster."

Bobby felt a flush of mortification at Kezzie's knowing look. She reminded herself that Kezzie was a native of the area and likely accustomed to seeing such things as a child who'd taken a beating. That was probably why she had something so specific on hand.

"Thank you," she murmured gratefully.

Kezzie nodded, her expression softening. "Take good care of yourself, Bobby. You've saved my bacon yet again. If you need anything else, don't hesitate to come back."

Bobby thanked her and left the shop. She hurried across the cobbles, leaping over puddles and weaving in between the carts that clattered down the road, urgency nipping at her heels.

She tucked the green bottle safely away, determined that her father wouldn't be able to get his hands on this one.

She only prayed that she wasn't too late.

CHAPTER 24

Kezzie

"Why are the police looking for you?" Kezzie's voice vibrated with anger, her eyes blazing with temper.

She could tell by the look on his face that Elias had heard the conversation from behind the curtain. He was sitting up and leaning back against the wall, a hand clutching his rib cage. His face was pinched with pain, the healing cuts on his face stark against his pale skin.

"I don't know," he said.

"Is your name Elias?"

He hesitated, his face screwing up into a shrug.

"What did you do?" She threw her hands in the air. "Why would they come here, of all places, looking for you? No one official in the city even knows this shop exists."

"I don't know what to say to you," he replied, wincing as he moved.

"I've had to send Rose out for food. She was about to have kittens when those policemen walked in." She watched as he tried again to move. "What are you doing?"

"I will go," he muttered, frustration clear in his tone.

"Go where?"

"Somewhere else. I don't want to bring trouble to your door."

"It's a bit late for that, isn't it?" she grumbled.

His breath caught as he got his foot under him, a pain-filled gasp hissing out between his clenched teeth.

Kezzie tutted loudly. She glanced behind the curtain to check on the shop, her concern for his pain overriding her anger.

"Just sit still, for pity's sake," she told him as she crossed the room. She took down a bottle of laudanum from the shelf.

"I have already caused you enough problems, Miss Doyle." His foot slid out from under him, and he dropped back to the floor. He was panting; sweat beading on his skin.

"Yes, you have," she took the stopper off the bottle. "Yet you can barely stand, so for the love of God, sit still. You're going to open up that wound again, else."

Elias flopped back against the wall, scowling at her. "That stuff makes me feel groggy," he grumbled.

"But it helps with the pain, doesn't it?"

He bobbed his head. "I've already inconvenienced you enough. If I fall back asleep, then that could endanger you all further by my being here."

"I told you that sleep is good, that your body needs to rest," she pointed out.

Elias mulled over her words.

"If you can stand to be in such pain, you don't have to take the ruddy stuff," She stared down at him, spoon in hand, "but there are no awards for bravery in this place."

He held her gaze steadily, his expression troubled. She wished she could know the thoughts turning in his mind. That way she could be sure that his amnesia wasn't a pretence, that he wasn't really a criminal hiding out here.

"I'm sorry," he muttered, "for bringing trouble to your

door. I have no recollection of how I ended up here. My mind is a blur." He rolled his free hand in the air, squeezed his eyes shut tight, and a sound of vexation escaped him. Then he rubbed the top of his head with the same hand, trying to bring back his clarity. "My father…"

He stilled.

His eyes shot up to meet hers, a look of wonder brightening his face. "I have a father! My name…Yes, yes, I'm Elias. My father's name is… it's Albert Turner. He's a…," he paused, eyes searching, waiting for another memory to surface. He squeezed his eyes shut, groaning. "Blast! It's just there yet I… I can't remember any more."

"That's good," she nodded encouragingly.

He looked up, his voice laden with desperation. "Why can't I remember more? Why is it only coming back in pieces?"

She could only shake her head. "I don't know," she replied softly. "I just know that this is normal."

He shoved his hands through his hair, cradling his skull. Her heart ached a little at the pitiful sight. He was starting to come back to himself, but that also meant their time together would be coming to an end. Perhaps a bit of Rose's hysteria had seeped into her mind as well because she realised that she almost didn't want him to leave.

Which was madness.

She didn't know him.

She had sworn to never fall in love.

Yet she found herself wondering about his father. His life.

Who Elias Turner really was.

She believed him to be a good and kind man, though this might all be in her mind. She still knew nothing about him. Trusting her instincts didn't mean he wasn't a bad person in a different life, that hadn't ended up in her doorway because he'd crossed the wrong person.

"I can go and get the police now that we have a name,

and that we know someone is looking for you. I'm sure your father is worried sick."

"What if we don't get on?" he said defeatedly. "What if I was hiding from him? I…" A wry smile hooked his mouth. "I feel safe here."

"I don't think your father would have the entire police force searching high and low to find you if he didn't care."

He studied her face with the same intensity that he had the first time he woke up. Only this time, it felt different for her. This time, she felt the swirl of something instinctual deep inside.

"Have you always been such a reasonable and logical woman?"

She broke the look, suppressing the urge to touch her hair, to check her appearance. "I suppose I have."

"Your father must be proud."

"I don't remember my father."

"Your mother then," Elias murmured.

Her heart ached with pain, stealing her breath. She cleared her throat. "My mother was murdered when I was twelve. I'm an orphan."

"Gosh, I'm so sorry. How awful for you."

She focused on the glass bottle in her hand, the way the light moved across the spoon, willing the tears back. Normally, she would speak about her mother with detachment. But his condolence sounded genuine, and it caught her off guard.

"It was a long time ago. I wasn't alone – I had Rose. That's why she's a little protective of me."

His brows knitted together. "Rose is your… your aunt?" he asked.

She shook her head. "My mother's best friend. She helped raise me after… after Mama died." She wasn't sure why she was sharing these details with him. She rarely opened up to other people.

He went back to studying her face.

"What do you want me to do?" She whispered.

"If it's as you say and my father is looking for me, then we shall have to go to the police," he whispered back, "but they will know that you lied to them here today."

Stormy grey eyes scrutinised her.

Memories of police derision and scorn swirled, kicking irritation into her so that her tone was sharper. "It won't be the first time a Doyle has bent the truth," she said, offering him the spoonful of laudanum. "Nor will it be the last."

Elias hesitated but then took the spoonful of medicine, grimacing as he swallowed. "Thank you," he said, his voice already growing groggy. "Tomorrow, we'll…go."

Kezzie put the stopper back in the bottle and then set it back on the shelf. As Elias's gentle snores filled the room, she braced herself against the dresser, slowly letting out a breath. Nerves fluttered in the pit of her stomach, the strange mix of emotions making her feel uneasy.

Kezzie knew then that she had taken on more than just an injured stranger; she had also taken on his troubles and his secrets.

And she knew she couldn't turn back now.

CHAPTER 25

Bobby

Bobby stepped into the dim interior of their shabby home, her eyes adjusting to the familiar gloom as she tried to get her ragged breathing under control. She needn't have been so worried, she realised, surveying the homely scene under the glow from the flickering oil lamp.

Lydia stood at the stove, stirring a pot of thin broth, while Mary sat in the chair, staring vacantly at the cold, unlit fire. Bobby's anxiety eased slightly when she saw Gertie peek from under the blanket on the sofa.

Pale and weak, but alive.

"How was your day?" Bobby asked, kneeling beside Gertie.

"I hid," Gertie replied with a quick grin. "Just like you told me to."

Bobby brushed back her sister's soft hair. "Where's Pa?"

"Not been home," Gertie whispered back, the smile fading.

She poured a dose of the tonic into a spoon and held it to Gertie's lips, wishing with all her heart that she'd gone to see Kezzie sooner.

When she voiced this regret, Lydia, without turning from the stove, said, "Father wouldn't have allowed his boys to take apothecary medicine, and definitely not from someone like a Doyle."

"But they both might still be alive," Bobby muttered, tucking the bottle safely behind the cabinet.

She replaced the coins she'd taken from the tin atop the cupboard, wishing that she could be as brave as Kezzie. The way she'd spoken to those policemen, without a tremor or a flicker in her voice, had been astonishing. She just wished her father could see how clever and kind she was, not just to her but towards a man she didn't even appear to know.

If she was a witch, like everyone else seemed to believe, well, Bobby wanted to be one, too.

Lydia served up the watery stew. Even Gertie managed to eat but Bobby's concern now turned to her mother.

"Please, Mama," Bobby coaxed. "You've hardly eaten a crumb in days."

"I'm not hungry," Mary said absently, brushing a stray hair back over her head. "You girls clean up. You know your father won't like it if the house is untidy." She took herself off to bed, her steps slow and weary.

"What's wrong with her?" Lydia asked quietly, watching their mother's retreating form.

Bobby glanced at the sofa where Gertie was already fast asleep, her breathing soft and even.

"She's heartbroken," Bobby replied, gathering the tin plates.

Lydia rose too, and together, the girls washed the dishes in silence, each lost in her own thoughts. Bobby wondered what would have happened if Mary had stood up to George, if she'd been outspoken like Kezzie and taken the unusual step of challenging her husband's authority.

Would their family still be so splintered?

As if reading her thoughts, Lydia asked, "Do you think Pa will come home tonight?"

"I don't know," Bobby replied softly.

"Then where is he, Bobby?"

Bobby suspected her father was at the Talbot Inn, drinking away his wages. But she didn't want to admit this out loud. "He'll be out working. You wait and see," she said, trying to sound confident, though she could hear the quiver in her voice.

"How will we pay the rent if something has happened to him?" Lydia's eyes filled with worried tears.

Bobby gathered Lydia into a comforting hug, rubbing her back as their mother used to do when they were upset or frightened. "We'll be alright. We have each other."

That night, as the house settled around them and the room was filled with the gentle snores of her siblings, Bobby tried to read her book in the soft lamplight, though her mind wouldn't settle into the words.

Instead, her thoughts raced.

Where was her father?

As cruel and repugnant as he was, Bobby was filled with uncertainty about their future without him at the helm. She knew what happened to the people who couldn't afford to pay for their homes. She couldn't allow her family to succumb to the workhouse.

She lay until the dawn light softened the sky. Then she rose, determined to start the day as if George was at home. She made breakfast for her siblings and managed to get a few mouthfuls of porridge into Mary. She was rewarded with a warm smile, her mother cupping her face and kissing both her cheeks.

"What would I do without you," she said, eyes crinkling in a rare smile. She was still pale though she could see the discomfort pinching her mother's face. Brows drawn, Bobby touched her mother's skin. She wasn't feverish like the boys and Gertie had been, but Bobby knew her mother wasn't quite right.

"Mama, let me take you to see Kezzie Doyle after work."

"I'll be fine," Mary patted her shoulder.

"She'll know just what to do. She didn't even charge me for Gertie's tonic."

Mary shook her head "I said I'm fine, Bobby. I have a bit of a headache but it's just from worrying about your father." Mary sighed at the crestfallen look. "I'll be okay, Bobby."

"Promise?" Lydia asked her.

Mary nodded, opening her arms to her children.

"I love you, Mama," Bobby hugged her mother fiercely, hoping that this might be the first step back to some form of normalcy.

"Come on," Mary sniffed. "We have work to do."

They walked to work, just like they always did.

The most welcome sight was Gertie, skipping ahead of the trio with carefree movements reminiscent of the days when the boys were still alive. Seeing her sister bright-eyed once more, racing ahead with the other children in the flow of people that poured into the factories, eased Bobby's troubled mind. It was a stark contrast to the frail, feverish girl she had been just days before.

Bobby made herself a promise to visit the apothecary shop and thank Kezzie in person, though she was certain she could never repay her properly.

Lydia waited until her mother got caught up in a conversation before she whispered to Bobby, "Do you think Pa's alright?"

There had been no sign of their father for three days. He had never been gone this long, and the uncertainty gnawed at her. She had half a mind to go looking for him at the Talbot Inn, but the thought of igniting his fury left her feeling nauseous.

Bobby tried to reassure her. "Mama says he's probably taken work to help us meet the rent. We'll be short this month and we need it."

Lydia nodded, though Bobby could tell that she wasn't convinced.

As they neared the factory, Bobby spotted Liam and Charlie up ahead. She hurried over to the charming Irishman, ignoring the fluttering in her stomach when he greeted her warmly, his eyes sparkling.

"Gertie looks better, to be sure," he indicated to her sister. His smile faltered a little when she only nodded.

"Have you by chance seen my father?" she asked him without preamble.

"George?" he clarified, his brow furrowing. "Not at all, why?"

"He's not been home in a few days," Bobby replied, keeping her voice low enough so that only he could hear her. "He drinks in the Talbot. Would you mind popping by there tonight? As a favour to me."

"A favour, you say? Hmm," Liam's forefinger and thumb framed his chin as he pretended to think, a twinkle in his eye. "What's it worth?"

"Please," she said. "I can't go in there now, can I?"

"Sounds like you'll be deep in my debt," Liam teased.

Bobby tilted her head, shaking it pityingly. "I don't have time for your shenanigans, Liam Byrne."

"He been saying how he wants to take you for a moonlit walk," Charlie cackled from behind Liam, earning a red-faced scowl for his trouble.

"Ignore him," Liam said, turning back to Bobby.

"Oh," Bobby couldn't help but smile, and it felt good to have something to be glad for. "And here I was thinking about saying yes."

Liam's grin widened. "I'll go to the Talbot this very night," he promised with a wink. He twisted the peak of his cap and sauntered off, sending her one last grin over his shoulder before he was swallowed up in the gloomy shed interior.

Throughout the day, Bobby found herself thinking about Liam, about what life might be like with a man who seemed so very different from her father. She imagined a life filled with kindness and warmth, a complete contrast to the volatile presence of George. The thought made her heart beat a little quicker. Maybe she could go for a walk with him, though not at night. Her father would never agree to such a thing. But thinking about a future with Liam Byrne gave her a small beacon of hope amidst the gloom and the dust.

As the end of the workday approached, John Simpson, the foreman came to fetch her. Normally a cruel and gruff man, today he seemed a little softer with her.

"Bobby! I need you to come with me," he said, his voice uncharacteristically gentle.

Fear clutched at her heart. "Did I do something wrong, sir?"

He didn't reply. He simply turned on his heel and she had no choice but to trot behind him.

Was she going to be fined? Or worse, sacked? She racked her mind. She hadn't dropped anything. She'd been on time.

She couldn't afford to get fired.

How would they meet the rent? They'd already lost Percy and Jack's meagre wage.

Her feet felt heavy as she followed him, her mind racing as she fretted about how her family would cope with the loss of another income.

But instead of taking her to the manager's office, the foreman led her to a small room where another man was waiting.

"This is Mr Townsend. He's a... he's one of the overseers," the foreman introduced, closing the door.

Mr Townsend's expression was grave, eyes soft with sympathy that did little to ease the panic clawing at her throat. "Bobby, I'm afraid I have some very bad news," he began, his voice gentle.

Bobby's eyes filled with tears. *Gertie's happy face…* she'd been fine just a few short hours ago.

"It's your mother," John Simpson said. "I'm afraid she's dead, Bobby."

CHAPTER 26

Kezzie

It was two days before Elias was well enough to leave the shop. Kezzie had to source him some clothes from the Salvation Army. He'd managed most of it himself but the act of dressing him seemed much more intimate than tending to his wounds, and they'd both been left flustered from the experience.

At least that's what she put his recalcitrance down to.

It was only a short walk from Doyle's to the Leman Street police station, but their progress was slow and difficult.

He leaned heavily on Kezzie, apologising constantly. Upright, he was a lot taller than she had guessed him to be. The bruising on his face had subsided enough for her to see just how greyish-blue his eyes were.

The clothes she had acquired for him were very worn and nowhere near the quality of the ones she had cut from him. The trousers were too short to cover his long legs, and the linen shirt was a very simple cloth, a far cry from the fine fabric she had disposed of because no amount of soaking in salt would get rid of those bloodstains.

The clothes were sufficient, if shabby. And they served a purpose for now. He was getting enough attention as it was, with the angry-looking cuts on his face drawing stares as they shuffled along the crowded pavement, without him being bare-chested too.

The day was mild enough, and the fog had lifted enough for it to seem only misty this morning. The streets were thronged with pedestrians, carriages, and carts, all filling the streets of a rousing city that ploughed on around them.

It seemed strange to Kezzie to be out on the street during the daylight with him, having spent so many hours hiding him, and wondering if the people who attacked him were going to come back and finish the job. Yet now it seemed he was simply the victim of a terrible assault.

Elias looked around him, his own curiosity blatant.

"Does anything look familiar to you?" she asked him.

"Not a jot," he replied.

He paused, staring as two scantily dressed women sauntered past them, loose curls dancing around their rouged cheeks. The women were young and pretty, eyeing Elias with knowing grins. Their tatty dresses left little to the imagination, the swell of their breasts rising from the narrow bodices made to do just that.

Kezzie was amused by the pink colour crawling up his neck. He seemed almost ashamed to see so much of their flesh on display this early in the morning.

"Goodness me," he exclaimed. "I don't think I've ever…" His voice trailed off when he met her laughing face.

"This is Whitechapel," Kezzie explained. "Women have to make money, and that is the oldest way known to man."

He stopped again, his brows sliding up his forehead as

he stared at her. "You mean you know what those women do for a living?"

"Indeed, I do. I have many visitors like that to my shop. They try and keep as healthy as they can."

He began shuffling forward again. "I don't I've ever known someone quite like you. Doesn't it bother you, knowing what they do?"

"Not really. Does it bother you?"

He appeared to think for a moment. "Well, no, but I'm a man. It's just I myself haven't ever…"

He blushed again.

"You must have led a sheltered life," she mused aloud.

"Who knows," he muttered, his ears reddening, too.

He fell quiet once more. All morning, he seemed touchy and distracted. More than once, she enquired if he was alright, if he remembered anything further that might explain his mood, but he assured her he was fine.

Perhaps it was the impending changes and returning to his old life that occupied his mind.

"You'll be glad to have your therapeutic room back, no doubt," he said as he hobbled along the pavement.

"Oh, I don't know," she replied teasingly, wanting to return his smile. "It's been rather fun beating you at cards."

They had whiled away the early hours of the last two evenings over the small table she set up in the back room. She had asked him into the private living quarters above the apothecary, but Elias, being the gentleman he was, had politely declined. It seemed he was unwilling to risk her reputation.

"I'm certain you cheated me somewhere."

She laughed, the sound fading when she spotted the police building ahead. The stone masonry had darkened, stained by the city smoke, and the Gothic exterior looked all the more austere with uniformed men standing outside, puffing on their pipes. Jet black horses hitched to the cabs dozed in their shiny harnesses at the side of the road.

She felt his body stiffen when he spotted the building, too. "I guess this is the place."

"Yes, that's the one up ahead."

He lifted his arm off her shoulder, and suddenly she felt chilled in more ways than one.

His gaze was unreadable as he studied the building and the men in front of it.

Then his gaze was on her, a hint of a smile softening his mouth. "Kezzie, I don't think I need to say—"

"You don't need to say anything at all," she interrupted, suddenly unwilling to hear his final words.

"But you see, I do." His lips parted, but he hesitated, searching her face, and she wondered what it was that he was going to say to her, before he changed his mind. "You've saved my life. I owe you more than a simple thank you. I have no idea how I could ever repay you."

"Your thanks is enough, Mr Turner."

The grin was quick, fleeting, before it faded. "I think we're past the formality now, Kezzie. You've seen enough of my naked skin to be able to call me Elias."

She coughed to cover the laugh that erupted. "Very well…Elias, then."

"And we shall part as friends."

Her stomach quivered thinking that she might not see him again. "You must get a proper physician to take a good look at you."

"I shall," he replied. "Thank you, Kezzie. For everything."

She clenched her fingers into her palm, resisting the urge to reach out and touch his face once more. "Take care of yourself, Elias."

A genial smile tugged at his lips. He hesitated a moment longer before he began shuffling along the pavement by himself.

She waited until several of the policemen had noticed his slow progress towards them. Only when two of them crossed to meet him did she turn and head back to the shop.

CHAPTER 27

*E*lias.

His name was Elias Turner.

He was twenty-six years old.

He'd been born in Northumberland. He had a sister called Alice who'd married an Army officer and had a gaggle of children in which she rarely showed any interest.

He'd been educated at Harrow. He remembered his childhood friends. His first pony was named Camelot. He had a dog called Seth.

He remembered. Not everything, but enough.

Just like opening the curtains to a sunny day, he'd woken that morning in the gloomy room in the back of Doyle's apothecary shop with names and places there whenever his mind called upon them.

The police had dispatched a messenger immediately to his father's townhouse in Belgrave Square, only for the boy to return shortly after with the news that Albert Turner was staying at his country estate. He carried a message that said the family doctor was expecting Elias at St. Thomas' Hospital.

Elias had been examined by the doctor, a stern man named Doctor Fenton, who'd been horrified by the extent of the beating Elias had sustained. Despite his obvious disdain for herbalist methods, the doctor had grudgingly admired the rapid rate at which Elias's body had started to heal. The doctor also concurred with Kezzie's diagnosis; Elias simply needed rest and time for recuperation. Given the rate at which his memory was returning, he was confident Elias would make a full recovery.

Elias lay back against the stiff pillows of the hospital bed. The room was a clinical white. The metallic tang of the hospital was a far cry from the herbal smells and chilly floor of the apothecary's back room.

The nurses at the hospital were polite but lacked the attentive nature of Kezzie. Her mesmerizing eyes and the way she had cared for him lingered in his mind.

He stared through the windows, at the smoky city and grime-covered buildings of the city beyond, wondering what she was doing.

Pain radiated from where he'd been stabbed in his side and around his back. It was acute enough to keep his thoughts from wandering too far.

His father would never approve of a strong and independent woman like her; someone who practised a calling steeped in the tradition of her forefathers. His father valued rank and status in society, not a woman who lived by her own rules and tended to the people whom society had forgotten.

Elias had responsibilities. A business to run and a family legacy of his own to uphold.

He squeezed his eyes shut, trying to quieten the racing thoughts, to relieve the constant poking into the clouds that shrouded his mind. There were still gaps there. A nagging need to draw back the veils. Still dark spaces in his memory.

Lethargy pulled on his limbs.

Finally, he gave in to sleep, his troubled mind easing as those brilliant eyes danced in his dreams.

∼

THE NEXT DAY, Albert Turner arrived.

The morning light glowed through the hospital windows, and Elias's attention was drawn to the loud and gusty demands of a man used to getting his own way that echoed along the corridors long before his father stepped into the hospital wing.

Elias summoned up a smile for his mother, though he was certain that she was only there because it was expected of her rather than out of genuine concern. She stood quietly behind her husband.

"There you are!" Albert stormed in, his voice rolling through the room, drawing disapproving looks from the matron. "Where the *devil* have you been?"

"Excuse me!" The nurse in charge of the ward hurried over. "We have sick people in this building," she said firmly. "Kindly keep your voice down."

"Don't shush me, woman," Albert blustered. "I'm here to see my son."

"That may be the case, sir," the matron huffed primly, "but unless you can conduct yourself *quietly*, you will have to leave."

"Look at the state of his face! Why aren't you doing your job and helping my son?"

"I assure you that I am fine," Elias said patiently, trying to calm the situation. "Please, Father, she is doing her job, rather well, in fact."

"Thank you, Mr Turner," Matron acknowledged.

"Well, you don't look it, Elias," Albert said, though his voice had lowered in deference to the scolding matron.

"I'll keep an eye on him, matron," Elias said to the nurse. "If I could trouble you for a drink of water."

The nurse briskly left, and Elias's gaze shifted between his parents.

"What happened to you?" Albert demanded.

"I don't remember the details," Elias replied honestly. His mind stubbornly remained a fog of disjointed images and sensations. "I believe I was robbed. My wallet and watch were taken. I was left for dead in the street."

"Robbed?" Elias nodded at his father's stunned face. "Then where have you been? I've had half the London police force out looking for you."

Elias nodded stiffly. "So, I gather." The policemen who greeted him at Leham Street police station made their disdain clear. From their demeanour, it was obvious they resented being used as a rescue party for what they assumed was a wealthy gentleman chasing street prostitutes. "I was taken in by a healer who found me in the street."

Albert scoffed, "Which street? What have you gotten yourself into, Elias?"

"Does that matter?" Elias asked, his voice weary.

Albert opened his mouth to argue further but then snapped it shut, conceding, "No, I suppose not."

Elias sighed inwardly, remembering the battles he had with his overbearing father over the years.

Albert held everyone up to high standards that were nearly impossible to meet. Standards far higher than he would hold himself to. Elias could sense the disapproval and frustration just below the surface.

Under the judgmental stare of Albert, Elias found himself longing for the sanctuary of Kezzie's apothecary shop.

Dr Fenton hurried into the room, ahead of the matron who was carrying a glass of water.

"Mr Turner," the doctor stretched out his hand, his obsequious bearing evident.

"Dr Fenton," Albert seemed to deflate in the man's presence. "Thank you for taking care of him."

Dr Fenton inclined his head slightly, turning a smile to Elias. "Actually, he has done most of the healing with the help of the woman who took him in."

Albert's eyebrows climbed. "What woman was this?"

"Just a healer," Elias said, trying to keep his voice even as a surge of protectiveness for Kezzie swelled within.

"Well, that makes more sense, the boy vanishing to spend time with a woman," his father's voice dripped with derision.

"No," Dr Fenton seemed to rush to her defence faster than Elias could. "I can assure you that your son sustained quite severe injuries.

"Whilst I might not agree with the antiquated methods, they've certainly been effective in returning your son to health as efficiently as they have. I would say that he's very lucky to have been found and treated by such a skilled healer."

His father looked dissatisfied, and Elias knew that he was in for further questioning once he got back home.

"I'm afraid I value modern science over any charlatan, Doctor Fenton. For all we know, this woman could've arranged the beating and taken my son's belongings for herself."

Doctor Fenton cleared his throat, clearly uncomfortable at the suggestion. He glanced at Elias and then turned back to his father. "He needs rest and relaxation. Complete bed rest, for at least a week."

Albert nodded. "He can get that at home. We have everything he needs there."

Doctor Fenton frowned. "The best place for him is here, where we can monitor his progress. His memory is not fully recovered and subjecting him to anything strenuous could hinder its return."

Albert's expression didn't soften, but he finally conceded with a curt nod. "When can he come home then?"

"I will monitor him personally and let you know when

it is safe for him to travel, though he must avoid any strenuous activity and get plenty of rest until he is completely healed. That includes anything business-related," he pointed out.

∼

THREE DAYS LATER, Elias found himself in a carriage heading for the family estate in Oxfordshire. Albert Turner sat next to him, quietly brooding after another telling-off from the hospital staff that morning.

The relationship between Elias and his father had often been strained. Even now, Elias knew that his father didn't approve of the news that the doctor had given him, that his memory of the attack might never return.

The questions had started almost as soon as the carriage door had closed. Elias knew that his father believed him to be faking his amnesia. When his questions had proved too much for Elias, Albert lapsed into a sulk.

The ride had been long and bumpy, repeatedly battering his already sore body. Elias rested his head against the back of the carriage, his head rolling with the movement, focusing only on the thought of getting out of this carriage and finally into a proper bed.

Elias's mind wandered back to Kezzie.

He couldn't help it.

His inert mind had been filled with wondering what she was doing. He wondered if perhaps he should've told her the truth the morning they'd parted—that he'd remembered more of his life than he had let on.

Those last few days when he'd been well enough to sit up and spend the evenings with her had been some of his favourite times. He'd never met anyone quite like her. She had risked everything for him. She was filled with determination and kindness that transcended his experience.

She had an instinct for helping people and was strong and fiery with it.

And he knew, without a shadow of doubt, that those strange blue eyes of hers would forever be etched in his mind.

The carriage slowed as it turned into the long sweeping drive of the Turner Estate. The manor house stood proudly amidst the rolling green hills and ancient oaks. Built of elegant honey-coloured stone, the symmetrical façade and tall windows glinted in the late afternoon sun. Ivy covered the west walls, intertwining with the wrought-iron balconies that adorned the upper floors.

The meticulously designed gardens featured stone ornaments and lead statues with arbours and secret corners perfect for quiet contemplation, connected with a winding path that invited leisurely strolls. Pretty viola faces and peonies filled the vibrant flower beds, nodding in the gently wafting air.

The carriage rolled to a stop in front of the imposing front door. It was flanked by two haughty-looking stone lions. Two footmen stepped forward to open the carriage door. Albert didn't wait for Elias. He was out of the carriage and striding across the stones, holding out his hat to another servant.

"See to Elias, will you? My day has already been ruined with babysitting."

The door was opened, and the butler, an older man with a permanently sour expression named Cassidy, stood at the threshold. He greeted the senior Mr Turner, seemingly giving his orders to the footman without saying a word to them.

Elias shuffled out of the carriage, his muscles protesting at having to move. He stood a moment on the stone chippings of the driveway, checking his equilibrium. He squinted up at the elegant exterior of his family home in the bright light. Clear blue skies and fluffy clouds—no dark smog from the city—and yet he would swap this for a few more moments in the company of Kezzie Doyle.

"Welcome home, Mr Turner," a footman said formally.

"Thank you, Jimmy," Elias murmured, carefully picking his way across the stones.

"Steady as you go, Mr Turner," Cassidy called out as Elias climbed the stone steps. "Welcome home."

"Happy to be home."

He allowed Jimmy to help him with his coat, wincing as the movement pulled at his injured side.

"We have your room ready for you, sir," Cassidy said. "You can enjoy a bath if you need or—"

Elias felt the weight of exhaustion from the journey. "Actually, all I want to do is climb into bed and sleep for days."

The click of heels behind him on the marble floor drew his attention. His mother Jane, looking as impeccable as ever, swept into the hallway. But it was the attractive woman behind her that made his heart sink.

When he'd awoken on the floor of the apothecary back room, he'd remembered three main things:

His name was Elias Turner.

He was 26 years old.

He was engaged to a woman named Henrietta.

CHAPTER 28

Bobby.

HER MOTHER, who had endured so much, who had barely clung to life after the loss of her sons, was gone.

Bobby's eyes burned with unshed tears as the reality of the words sank in. She couldn't cry. If she did, she feared that she might never stop.

She didn't remember the walk home. The world seemed a blur, echoing with the broken cries of her sisters. The news hit them all like a physical blow. Lydia wept openly, while Gertie clung to Bobby, her small body shaking with sobs. Bobby held them both, trying to be the pillar of strength they needed, even as her own heart shattered.

She had so much to think about. Another funeral. Her mother's body lay under a shroud in the corner of the room. She didn't know who'd fetched her home. Nor did she know what to do next. She'd let Mr Townsend take over because it had felt easier to let someone else take the lead. He reminded her that her father would want to say goodbye.

If he ever came home.

Darkness settled and the house was filled with a heavy silence. Bobby sat by the cold fireplace, staring into the darkness, trying to make sense of it all. She had lost so much, and now her mother was gone too. The weight of responsibility pressed down on her, but she knew she had to keep going. For Lydia, for Gertie, and for the memory of the mother who had loved them all so fiercely.

The gentle knock drew her attention. For a moment, she wondered if she'd imagined it. But the body in the corner was motionless. Heart thumping, she crossed to the front door and cracked it open.

Liam stood on the threshold, threading the brim of his cap through his fingertips. She blinked rapidly, trying to hold back her tears.

"Hello, Liam," she husked.

"Bobby..." The regret that rang in his voice almost broke her.

She shook her head quickly. "Please don't say it."

His mouth bent in sympathy. "But I am sorry, you see. Your mother was a good woman. She was always kind to me when she had no cause to be."

Bobby bit the inside of her cheek. His compassion too much. She couldn't give in. Not yet. "What do you want?" She asked thickly.

"I, um, I went to the Talbot," he began.

Her eyes slid closed. She'd forgotten all about the quest she'd sent him on to find her father. Her father still had no idea that Mary had expired right there on the factory floor, alone and exhausted. When he didn't say anything further, she opened her eyes.

He rubbed the back of his neck, shifting awkwardly from foot to foot. "Erm..."

"What is it?" Her eyes narrowed.

"George was there...at the inn, I mean," Liam said.

Bobby's face fell. "He's at the inn? He's alive? I must go! I must tell him about Mama!" She was down the stone steps and almost past Liam when he stopped her. "Liam, what are you–?"

"I told him about Mary, Bobby," he said. "I swear I told him what he needed to know. How some of the other men in the factory had helped me fetch her home for you all, carrying her through the streets like a… well, none of it was dignified now, was it?" His eyes lit up with crossness.

Bobby stared up at him. "You told him?"

"Aye, I did," Liam explained as gently as he could. "He…"

Bobby took solace in the struggle Liam was having to find the right words to explain what her father had undoubtedly used to convey his feelings towards the news. Bobby pulled her arm of out his hold, tugged the sleeve straight. Years of hearing the foul contempt that had dripped from the lips of George Luckett meant that she could accurately guess what her father had said to Liam.

"He's not coming home, is he?"

"I'll go back and try and speak to him again tomorrow night," Liam said earnestly. "He was very drunk, Bobby. My father didn't know right from left after a night on the barrel."

Bitterness burned hot inside her. They needed George more than ever. She had a funeral to organise and pay for. She had to find rent to keep a roof over the heads of her sisters. She couldn't even think about making sure they were fed.

"The barmaid said that he'd been sitting on the same stool all week. She'd found him asleep in the stables this morning, but he'd been seen coming out of the doss house other mornings by David Wilkes. He'll likely still be upset over the boys. You know how he adored them both and–"

Bobby held up a hand. "You don't need to excuse his behaviour. My sisters and I are all too aware of how much he loved his boys, whereas we were no better than something he'd scrape off the bottom of his boot at the end of the workday."

Liam didn't say anything further.

With a deep sigh, Bobby offered a brief smile. "Thank you for trying and for... for coming here tonight, Liam. That was good of you."

"It was nothing."

"No, you're wrong," she held up a finger. "It has shown me that we are truly on our own, rather than waiting for bated breath for the return of a spineless and cruel man."

Liam's dark brows rose.

Bobby didn't care that she was speaking disrespectfully. She didn't care that Liam might think less of her.

"Good night, Liam," Bobby climbed the steps without looking back. She closed the front door and leaned back against it.

They were all alone. No one to help save them. No one to take care of things for them. No Mary to soothe the worries away with a motherly kiss. No father to help work and keep a roof over their heads. A wave of panic clawed at her throat, threatening to choke off her air. She fought back against it. She knew with absolute certainty that all would be lost if she let it claim her.

She needed to be strong for all of them.

In the quiet of the night, Bobby made a silent vow. She would take care of her family. And she would honour her mother's memory by living with the same resilience and courage that Mary had shown every day of her life.

Together they would have to find a way to survive.

CHAPTER 29

Kezzie

"Are you sure you're going to be okay?" Rose paused in the open doorway.

Kezzie didn't bother to hide the eye roll. "Please, just go home. I'm fine, truly. I'm just a little tired. I shall clean up here and then finish the stew you made us last night."

"You're a terrible liar but I love you anyway. Good night," Rose brushed a chaste kiss across her cheek and then set out along the cobbled lane.

Kezzie watched as the old woman made her way along the street. The light was fading fast, but Rose lived nearby and wouldn't like any fussing over her more than she enjoyed receiving attention herself. Kezzie leaned against the window, her thoughts in turmoil.

The truth of it was that she wasn't alright.

She'd felt adrift ever since Elias had returned to his old life.

Perhaps it was because all her time had been occupied with caring for him.

Perhaps it was something more.

In the few days since he had left, she had tried various activities to occupy her mind and distract herself, but nothing seemed to work.

Deep down, she knew that she had made a promise to herself never to fall in love, and she hadn't – yet she couldn't seem to take her mind off Elias. She wondered if it was because, unlike her usual patients, she had no way of checking on his welfare. He hadn't told her where he lived. It left her with no means to visit him.

Once Rose had vanished from her line of sight, she turned from the door, intent on tidying the shop after a busy trading day.

She had just finished when a light tap against the window startled her from her reverie. A woman wearing a cloak, the hood drawn up to obscure most of her face, stood there in the twilight.

The frisson of fear dissipated when Kezzie recognised the profile of Eunice Joy, who was glancing nervously along the cobbles. She had half a mind to turn her away. The shop was closed, and she was exhausted but she recalled the distress Eunice had been in the other day. Wondering if she needed something because her husband had hurt her again, Kezzie let her in, quickly closing and locking the door behind her.

"Eunice, this is an unexpected surprise."

Eunice brushed the dark green velvet hood back off her hair, her red locks gleaming in the oil lamp light. Her cheeks were pink from exertion. "I know you've closed up for the night, but I needed to see you alone, you see," she said, a nervous energy quivering around her.

"It's fine," Kezzie replied, her curiosity piqued. "I was just finishing clearing up."

"Goodness, and now I've interrupted you. How terribly tiresome of me."

Kezzie dismissed her words. "I'm glad to see you. I've been worrying about you after the other day."

"You're a kind-hearted soul, Kezzie Doyle."

A smile brushed her lips. "How can I help you?"

Eunice hesitated, embarrassment flashing across her face. "I wanted to apologise for my behaviour the other day," she began. "I'm afraid I wasn't quite myself."

"There's no need to –"

"But there is you see," Eunice insisted. "You were very kind to me."

"Then you're most welcome," Kezzie inclined her head. "How is your wrist?"

Eunice shrugged, holding the appendage out though she didn't bother to pull her sleeve back this time. "It's healing."

"That's good news. I'm very glad."

"You have a way with people," Eunice said. "Like you're the keeper of secrets."

Kezzie thought about the man who had been hidden in her back room for days while she had shielded him from the police. She smiled, unsure what else to say under the strange look the other woman was giving her.

Eunice took a deep breath. "My husband isn't a good man," she said, her voice trembling. "I think you know this but, in case there was any doubt in your mind, I should say that he's cruel and he's cold, and… and he's sleeping with the servants," Eunice finished in a rush.

Kezzie couldn't contain her astonishment.

"I found him in the servants' quarters. He had his trousers around his ankles, spluttering about how it was my fault… that I was the one who…

"Goodness me, it was so terrible, Kezzie. The poor young girl was nigh on hysterical," Eunice snapped her mouth shut, tears glistening in her eyes. "I can't take much more of his abominable behaviour. It's such an embarrassment for me, and I…" Her lips rolled inward as she fought to maintain her composure. "I need your help."

"But what can I do?" Kezzie asked, puzzled.

Could she tolerate someone as flighty as Eunice staying under her roof? She'd grown used to her own company over the years but having Elias in the building had brought her comfort that she hadn't realised had been missing.

Was that all that she was missing? Companionship?

Or did Eunice need something to help the young maid rid her body of the consequences of her boss forcing himself on her?

Eunice's gaze darted around the shop as if she was afraid of being overheard. "Are we truly alone here?"

"We are."

"Because what I'm about to ask you could get us both into a lot of trouble if we're found out."

Kezzie waited impatiently.

Eunice swallowed. "I've read about such things that a wife can buy to rid herself of certain... problems."

Kezzie's face softened in understanding. She understood there were thousands of women in this city who couldn't afford to feed another mouth. Prostitutes who faced this situation as part of their job. "Pennyroyal tea. You can gently boil it in some milk. My grandfather used to make it with sage in, too." She turned, only to be stopped by Eunice's sudden grip on her forearm.

"No, I don't mean... that is, I don't need anything like that for the girl," she said quickly. "I need, that is, I read about something called dogbane. Sometimes, it's known as Rosebay."

Kezzie paused, eyes searching the other woman's face, as icy fingers of dread slithered along her spine.

Eunice rushed on into the silence that stretched between them. "Perhaps some hemlock, or a more modern alternative such as tartar emetic."

"Poison," Kezzie clarified. "Those are all poisons, Eunice."

Eunice moved the hand on Kezzie's arm, waving it between them to waft away the words that fell between them. "Everything is poisonous in the right quantities, my dear. Even a novice like me knows this."

Kezzie searched the woman's guileless face. "If I did have such a thing in my shop, what do you intend to do with it?"

Eunice stilled.

Her eyelids swept downwards, and she at least had the decency to blush. "Kezzie… my husband is a very wealthy man. Divorce is simply not an option for me. He would see to it that I was stripped of everything. He would think nothing about tossing me into a gutter. Men like him, they only have to click their fingers and they will have a thousand beautiful women flocking to meet their needs, out of which he will have the cream of the crop to choose from."

"You mean to…"

Eunice nodded. "I have suffered at his hands for years, Kezzie. I cannot take it much more. I fear for my life for he flies into the most terrific rages. You saw what he did to me, and that was because I bumped the table when I stood up. No one would miss Arthur Joy if he was gone."

Kezzie placed herself squarely in front of Eunice. "What you're asking is not only criminally wrong but also morally wrong, too."

"He's a dreadful–"

"I know!" Kezzie cried, irritated by the other woman's insistence about the dubious nature of the ghastly Mr Joy. "But I made an oath. A solemn promise to do no harm to others, Eunice. I take that oath very seriously. It's been something that has been drummed into me since before I took my first step."

Eunice straightened. "But you would have given me something to rid me of a pregnancy."

Kezzie blinked, unnerved by the swift and deadly change of tone, by the finality and almost accusing nature. "That's different."

"Is it? Because that too is against the law. I'm certain that the police would be very interested to know that you were going to sell me such a product."

Kezzie's brows met. "There are many abortifacients widely available in this city, Mrs Joy. Everyday products can be bought over the counter for working-class women who might have been assaulted or who are already struggling to feed ten children. I will also admit that you're not the first wife in here looking for a way out, nor are you the first to threaten me with the police."

Eunice's mouth pursed, irritation rolling off her.

Kezzie continued. "I want to help women as I know that we don't get a fair crack of the whip in marriage or indeed in life but... I can't help you take a life, even knowing how abhorrent your Mr Joy sounds. Now," Kezzie stepped around Eunice. "Unless you require anything else, I will say goodnight to you."

The long-drawn-out sigh from behind her filled the shop as Kezzie turned the key and tugged open the shop door. She understood her disappointment, of course. The demise of Mr Joy would surely be the answer to all her problems, leaving her a wealthy widow, free to live as she chose. She allowed Eunice a moment to compose herself, the bell tinkling into the taut silence.

Eunice walked across the floor, the movements stiff and awkward. She paused in the open doorway to flip up the hood of her cloak. Her eyes glittered with barely concealed fury.

"To say I'm disappointed in you, Miss Doyle, is an understatement. I doubt very much we'll meet again."

She exited the door with grace, her cloak streaming out behind her as she vanished into the dense fog.

CHAPTER 30

*E*lias

Elias lay in his wide, comfortable bed, the opulent bedroom bathed in the soft glow of the morning sun that peeked around the edges of the heavy damask curtains framing the tall windows. The walls were adorned with rich, deep green wallpaper, and the grand four-poster bed with its embroidered cream linens dominated the space. A mahogany wardrobe and matching dresser stood against one wall.

It was the bedroom of a wealthy man in his grand country home, yet he never felt comfortable there. The fire snapped and crackled in the hearth, signs that somebody had been into his room while he slept. Exhaustion still pulled at his limbs, but the pain in his side had lessened slightly. However, it was the ache in his heart that was hardest to bear that morning.

Upon his arrival the day before, there had been much fussing and attention that had grated on his nerves. Henrietta had broken from her usually coolly detached demeanour, fussing over him in a manner that felt cloying rather than loving. He'd wondered how much of it was a show for his parents. She had seemed put out that he hadn't been up for company. She had chased the maids out of the salon, determined to steal a few moments alone with him.

"Where were you?" She'd demanded as soon as the door was closed.

Elias made a show of being in a great deal of pain, clutching his side. "I was attacked, as I'm sure you're aware."

She fluttered across the blood-red carpet, brushing his arm, touching his face like she was checking he was real. "I've been frantic with worry, my love. Who hurt you? Did you see them?"

"I don't know," he mumbled. "I can't remember."

He was grateful that he at least had the excuse of exhaustion and had retired to his bedroom. He'd feigned sleep until he was left alone to brood.

He was renowned for being practical and brusque, traits that had stood him in good stead when running his father's empire. His decisions were always clear-cut, guided by logic and reason, not by the whims of the heart. Even now, in the cold light of morning, Elias found his thoughts consumed by something other than business.

Kezzie Doyle.

Inside, he felt guilty for concealing Henrietta's existence from Kezzie. He knew well enough that a woman like Kezzie would have valued the truth, yet he hadn't wanted her to look at him any differently.

Which was foolish. She hadn't looked at him in any way other than the way a doctor would view a patient – as someone they needed to care for.

Why, then, could he not shake the apothecary from his thoughts?

The mere thought of her brought a disconcerting flutter to his chest, an unfamiliar sensation that he found both exhilarating and troubling. He had always been a practical-minded man, which is why he found these intrusive thoughts highly irregular. He was only marrying Henrietta because his father had instructed it, not through any great love or romantic gesture. Henrietta was a wealthy orphan, polite and level-headed, precisely the sort of woman required to sit at the side of a businessman of his magnitude.

She was everything a man in his position should want: composed, intelligent, and capable of managing the societal expectations of a wife. While theirs had never been an arrangement of the heart, he nevertheless respected Henrietta. She was an educated woman who could handle herself in most situations, standing up against the drivel that her father sometimes spouted. She was also incredibly beautiful, and he was more than aware of the admiring glances she seemed to draw whenever they were together.

A clean, sensible arrangement that met his father's approval.

Yet, despite her many qualities, Elias felt as if he had quite lost his mind over Kezzie. Perhaps it was a hangover from the attack, a lingering after-effect from the trauma. Doctor Fenton had worried about the head injury, after all.

But Elias the logical, cut-throat businessman had fallen in love with a woman his father would never approve of.

A soft knock at the door interrupted his thoughts. It was his valet, a wiry little man named Hopkins. Elias felt a valet was an unnecessary indulgence. After all, when he was in the city, he managed to dress himself. Still, Elias wasn't one to do a man out of an honest day's work.

"Good morning, Mr Turner."

"Morning, Hopkins," Elias replied. "What time is it?"

"A little after ten, sir," the valet pressed open the heavy curtains.

Elias winced when the light fell on him, and the shaft of pain split his skull.

"Could you – could you close those, please?" Elias held up a hand to try and block the light. "I will be staying in here today."

Hopkins hesitated. Elias heard the clinking of the china plates before the hall boy carrying a breakfast tray appeared in the doorway. "I'm afraid your father has requested your presence in the library, sir."

Elias bit back the sigh. Of course, he did. Albert Turner wouldn't be concerned about Elias's return to full health, only about the fact that there was business to attend to.

Hopkins took the tray and carried it across the floor. He waited until Elias had adjusted himself in the bed so that the tray could sit across his lap, and he was leaning back against the pillows.

"Thank you," Elias said. His stomach protested against the contents of the tray, but he didn't have it in him to be rude to the other man. "Where's my father?"

Hopkins crossed to the window, opening it a little to let in some fresh air. "I believe he's in the salon, dining alone, sir."

Elias took a sip of water, dreading the conversation he was bound to have with his father. He wondered how much more of a mess had been made in his absence.

"Miss Henrietta had a tray in her room," the valet offered, predicting Elias' next question. "Your mother is still in bed. She doesn't wish to be disturbed until she has rung for her maid."

It sounded to Elias as if everything had continued as normal when he'd been recovering. All except the knowledge that Henrietta had decided to stay the night in the family home.

"When did Miss Henrietta arrive?"

"I believe she's been here for the week you've been missing, sir. She was most fretful."

Elias offered him a weak smile. "She was certainly happy to see me last night, wasn't she?"

"We all were," Hopkins added quickly.

Elias wasn't sure the servants worried about him beyond knowing that he was to inherit the land, money, and everything that came with it. He was certain that an employer as crotchety as Albert Turner wouldn't be deemed worthy of servant loyalty. He paid the minimum wages to his staff, cutting corners where he could, doing just enough to present a façade of success and wealth to the people who attended house parties at the manor house.

But the truth was, his father was broke, and there was no money. Elias hadn't wanted the match with Henrietta—he had been thrust towards her repeatedly simply because she was a very wealthy woman, and this would answer all his father's problems. On paper, it made a very good match. Elias reluctantly agreed to it once he'd seen the state of the company's accounts.

The valet busied himself, setting out the clothes for the day as Elias nibbled on the dry piece of toast.

Beyond the window, the sky was clear. Clouds rushed by, and he could make out the leaves folded back against the brisk winds. He should like to fetch Kezzie here. To show her a world away from the smog. To walk with her through the gardens and watch the wind in her hair. The sky was almost the same blue as her eyes.

Strange, he mused, when he had to be prompted to do these romantic gestures for Henrietta. He couldn't deny the connection he felt with Kezzie, so different from the society ladies he was used to. She was grounded, kind, and resourceful. He felt a genuine affection for her that he could never feel for Henrietta, despite her beauty and education.

"Will there be anything else?" the valet asked, breaking into his thoughts.

Elias pushed himself up further in the bed, feeling his

muscles protest. "Thank you, yes. I would be grateful for a hand dressing this morning."

If Hopkins was surprised by the unusual request, he didn't show it.

"You can take the tray, too."

"But you've hardly touched it, sir."

"I'm... not hungry but please do thank Cook for sending one up."

"Very well, sir."

Dressing was an effort, even with the extra set of hands. Twice, Elias had to sit on the edge of the bed and wait for the wave of nausea to pass.

"Perhaps I ought to send for the doctor, Mr Turner?"

Elias shook his head. "I intend on coming right back up here as soon as I have spoken with my father. Besides, the doctor will only tell me to rest."

"I could get Mr Cassidy to speak to your father..."

Elias straightened up. "No need."

"But sir–"

"My father won't take no for an answer." Elias pointed to his jacket and waited for the valet to hold it behind him. "Let's just get this over with."

Elias made his way along the landing, a headache already forming behind his eyes. The walls were adorned with ornately framed portraits of the moody Northumbrian coastline and stern-faced ancestors he'd never met yet owed a lot to. He made his way slowly down the wide staircase, the curved bannister gleaming in the soft light that filled the hallway.

He reached the bottom of the stairs and turned towards the library. The double doors stood open, revealing the room beyond.

It was one of Elias' favourite rooms. Floor-to-ceiling shelving packed with leather-bound books, soft leather seats tucked into the nooks and a vast fireplace, framed by a bone-white marble mantle. A fire simmered low in the hearth. Gold mock-Grecian pillars soared on either side, joining the filagree coving. The room was exquisite, built to the exact standards of his great-grandfather in a show of wealth, but it was the pleasant smell of dusty tomes and serenity that the room held that Elias loved the most.

He entered the room, his gaze settling on his father sitting at the desk in the centre of the room. If Elias was master here, he would have returned the desk to its original site right next to the tall windows so that he would take in the stunning gardens beyond as he worked.

He was certain his father barely noticed it was daytime. A cluster of papers scattered the desktop, a frown of concentration etched on his father's face so that he looked every part the astute businessman.

"Good morning, Father," Elias said, his voice steady despite the throbbing pain in his head.

"It's barely morning," Albert retorted without looking up.

Elias had to hold his tongue. Clearly, a beating and being stabbed were minor inconveniences in his father's eyes. He made his way to the sideboard and poured himself a coffee from the silver pot.

"What is so urgent?" Elias asked, taking a sip of the strong brew.

Albert finally looked up, his expression hard and unyielding. "I have firmed a date with Henrietta."

Elias stared at him. "You've done what?"

Albert's attention returned to his work. "Time waits for no man, Elias. You vanished and that poor girl was beside herself with worry. I had to do something to calm her down."

Elias set the cup on the side, fury pulsing through him. "You mean you were more concerned that the wealthy fish might come off the hook."

Albert leaned back in the high-backed chair; his mouth tensed. "You were apprised of the situation before your little sojourn into London. You know that Henrietta is essential to ensure the stability of the business."

Elias barked in disbelief. "I nearly died. What would you have done if I had?"

"But you didn't," His father's eyes narrowed, calculating. "You were compliant with the plan. You understood the stakes. Has something happened since to change your mind?"

Elias stalked across the floor, more to escape his father's insightful stare. He kept his back to the room, looking at the garden without seeing the riotous colours on display. Albert Turner might lack the entrepreneurial spirit, but he made up for it with an astute mind for cutting corners and sniffing out the last penny. It meant that Elias had learned to conceal a lot from his father over the years. Albert tended to bully people into getting his own way. Even at full strength, Elias had to tread carefully.

"Elias?"

"What?"

"Henrietta is a fine woman – you said as much yourself."

Elias dug his thumbs into his eye sockets until he was seeing stars, trying to assuage the pounding in his skull. "I know what I said."

"Then what is the problem?"

The problem was that his life was being steered, and he had no control over it. Before the attack, such a matter hadn't concerned him. After all, he knew that the match would be sensible. Henrietta's wealth would shore up the company and protect the future of the Turner business. She was beautiful and could string more than a few words together in a sentence, which was better than some of the other socialites that had been flung at him in the past.

But now, things were different.

He was different.

He looked back at his father, at the suspicion swimming in his eyes. How could he explain the feelings he was having for a woman he barely knew when he didn't quite understand it himself? Albert Turner had married his mother simply because she would look good on his arm. He'd admitted to Elias that he knew that she would produce handsome children that other women would want, therefore perpetuating a strong line for future Turner lineage.

To his father, marriage was clinical and deliberate. There was no talk of love or being happy.

Would Elias be content with a loveless marriage arranged for financial gain?

The alternative would be to knowingly put his parents out on the street. They would surely lose everything: no more fancy clothing, no more house parties. His mother had no skills for working, and his father had no trade to keep a roof over their heads. What of the servants and others who relied on the Turners for their income?

Despair slammed into him.

He wanted to shout, to rail against the unfairness of it all, but he knew it would be futile. His father was unyielding, a man who valued duty and tradition above all else.

He faced the challenge in his father's stern expression. "There is no problem."

Albert gave a curt nod. "I thought not."

"Will that be all?"

"Don't you want to know when you are getting married?"

"Very well," Elias said quietly, his voice laced with resignation. "When is the date?"

"Two months from now. The arrangements will be made, and everything will be taken care of. Do not disappoint me, Elias."

. . .

Elias nodded, the family's expectations pressing down on him. "I understand."

"Where are you going?"

Elias was walking towards the doors. "Back to bed. If it hadn't escaped your attention, I am still nursing a significant injury."

"But Henrietta is here to see you."

Elias paused, his hand on the door. He sighed. "At your invite, not mine."

"She is your fiancée, Elias."

"Yes, father."

"She deserves better from you. Do your duty. At least until the ink has dried on the marriage certificate."

Elias stared at his father, a man who had always been more of a tyrant than a parent. "I will be a good husband to Henrietta."

Albert nodded, satisfied. "You have two months. Make the most of them."

CHAPTER 31

*B*obby

"I KNOW you're in there, you mewling pigs!"

The front door shook from the relentless pounding of the odious rent collector, Billy Bateman. He continued to spew obscenities. Bobby crouched behind the sofa, her heart thudding as she tried to keep a scared and whimpering Gertie quiet. The banging on the front door continued, each knock like a hammer blow to her frayed nerves. Lydia sat beside her, hands clamped over her ears, her eyes wide with fear.

"I know you're in there!" Billy's shouts pierced the thin walls of the house. "Do you think you can hide from me? The rent hasn't been paid in two weeks! I'll have you all out on the street! I want my money!"

Bobby had known that this was coming. She'd managed to evade the rent collector, but he'd surprised them all by turning up in the morning. The few meagre savings they had went to their mother's funeral. There was nothing left for her to sell. She'd tried explaining this to the rent collector once. He didn't care about their plight. He'd issued an ultimatum: pay up or get out.

"We're going to be late for work again," Lydia whispered, panic edging her voice. Being late meant more fines at the end of the week, something they couldn't afford.

Bobby nodded. Thoughts raced for a solution. They weren't allowed any leeway for the loss of her mother, or her father abandoning them. In the ensuing silence, she couldn't hear anything over her pulse thundering in her ears.

"I think he's gone," Lydia started to stand, but Bobby pulled her back down.

"No, wait," she whispered. "Let me make sure he's gone."

She crept to the window, peering through a small gap in the curtain. There was no sign of Billy. With a nod to Lydia, she signalled it was safe. In silence, they hurriedly gathered their things and slipped out the door, making their way to work with as much haste as they could muster.

The roads were busy, but not with the factory workers. Instead, it was filled with people already going about their day. Sleek, gleaming carriages weaved between the scruffy carts; the well-heeled folks raced past the shuffling unfortunates. As the factory buildings loomed ahead, worry turned to cold dread when she saw that the huge black iron gates were already closed.

Bobby wrapped her fingers around the cold bars, gnawing on her bottom lips as she fought back the tears. They certainly couldn't earn if they couldn't get in.

The foreman struck out across the wide empty yard. She wondered if John Simpson had been waiting for them before she remembered that he only cared about numbers. He might have shown her some compassion the day her mother died, but that care had been short-lived once the girls were on their own.

"You're late," His expression was as stern as his tone.

"Sorry, Mr Simpson," Bobby called out. "Won't happen again, sir."

"You said that yesterday," he stopped a few feet from the gate. "I need reliable workers, Bobby. Not ones who show up half a day late and don't pull their weight."

"I know. I'm…" She wanted to let him know she was doing her best but knew he wouldn't care. Bobby bit her lip and could only nod, her throat tight with emotion.

"We'll work hard," Lydia called out. "The rent collector, he was at the door! We couldn't leave until he'd gone."

John Simpson scanned the three girls and then looked back at the factory.

"Please, Mr Simpson!" Lydia pressed. "We're sorry, aren't we, Bobby?"

"We really are!" Gertie lent her voice to her sisters.

There was a moment when hope flared, when she saw the indecision flash over Simpson's face. Then he shook his head.

"I took a risk giving you half a day for Mary's funeral. I have a quota to meet." The weight of his disappointment hung over them like a dark cloud. "I'm going to have to let you go."

"Wait! Mr Simpson, please!" Lydia implored but the foreman was striding across the yard, head down.

"Bobby? What do we do now?"

The austere lines of the factory blurred through her tears as hopelessness crashed over Bobby. Gertie sniffled quietly beside her. Her sisters looked to her for help. Seeing the terror in their eyes being mirrored back at her reminded her that she had to be strong, for their sake, if nothing more.

"We'll be fine," she assured them, wiping at her tears with her fingertips. "Come on. We can't stay here."

Leading her sisters away from the factory, they headed towards Whitechapel Market. The streets were bustling with barrow hawkers and muffin men, their shrill voices piercing the air to catch the attention of the people in the marketplace.

"Turnips! Penny a bunch!"

"Best Yarmouth bloaters! Fresh out the sea this fine morn! Get 'em while they're fresh!"

Middle-class ladies in their fine dresses walked beside their gentlemen callers. Servants, easy to spot in their smart black uniforms, flitted from stall to stall, pressed for time but still looking to strike a bargain.

The girls moved silently through the bustling crowd. The aroma of coffee and roasted meat tantalised their senses. Bobby tried to ignore the gnawing hunger, swallowing the saliva that filled her mouth at the sight and smell of the sizzling meats. She noticed how her sisters looked longingly at the costermongers' stalls, piled high with bread and vegetables.

They all needed to eat.

Bobby studied the crowd. She spied a wealthy-looking woman with a maid behind her, laden with a basket filled to bursting. Swallowing her pride, she stepped in front of the woman.

"Please, ma'am, we're in desperate need," Bobby said, her voice trembling as she stuck out her hand. "Could you spare some alms for my hungry sisters?"

CHAPTER 32

Elias.

YOU HAVE TWO MONTHS. *Make the most of them.*

HIS FATHER'S words had wormed their way into his mind until they'd become a mantra to him. Two months until he was legally bound to a woman that he didn't love.

He remembered the first time he'd met Henrietta Winters. A dinner party at the duke's lavish home. Henrietta had been sitting not quite opposite him. She was by far the most striking woman there. She'd handled the attention with aplomb as if she had been born to it. She'd made an effort to be seated with him as they'd shared a coffee before the men had split off for cigars and a game of cards.

When his father had learned of her considerable financial status, he'd thrown substantial effort into worming his way into Henrietta's life, before pushing his son at her.

Elias had resisted at first. It wasn't the first time his

father had tried to matchmake his only son, seeking to strengthen the family finances. But once Elias had seen the sorry state of the business, laid bare before his eyes in the London office on a soggy morning, he'd relented and allowed his father to make the arrangements.

At the time, Elias had gone along with the game. After all, he was at the age where it was expected for a man to marry, to carry on the Turner line. And Henrietta was beautiful. So, it hadn't been a hardship. She could be quick-witted, and he understood that she too seemed calculated in her motives.

Being married to Henrietta was a duty. Nothing more.

He stared at the papers spread across his cherrywood desk, the figures and charts blurring as his mind wandered. He'd found it hard to focus on anything since the attack. The headaches that had plagued him had lessened somewhat, though he still had to move carefully, or his wound would remind him that he'd been stabbed.

YOU HAVE TWO MONTHS. *Make the most of them.*

Was that his father's way of inviting him to be a young man, to sow his wild oats whilst he still could? Marriage to Henrietta would mean that her monies were transferred to him. She would benefit from the security of marriage. She would be given a fine surname and marry into a long line of renowned inventors.

He was aware that some men kept a mistress, a lefthand wife, as some men termed it. It had often struck him as coarse and disrespectful. But now… He perhaps understood a little better why many marriages were matches of convenience rather than of the heart.

Had his father meant to taunt him? Could Albert Turner know that his son was embroiled in a love affair that only seemed to be in his mind?

. . .

He rose from his chair and walked to the window, staring out at the neat lawns and the bountiful gardens. In the distance, trees raced up the rolling hills of the estate.

He had spent much of his morning forcing his thoughts back to work, so it was a welcome relief to let his mind wander to Kezzie: her gentle touch, her determined spirit, and those clear blue eyes that seemed to see right through him.

How could he be so smitten with someone so far removed from his world?

"Mr Turner?"

Elias hadn't even heard the butler enter the room behind him, so he jolted enough to jar his wound. He let out a pained breath as the butler apologised profusely.

"I thought you might like to know that Miss Winters is leaving us."

"When?"

"Now, sir. She requested the carriage this morning."

Frowning, Elias hurried from the study. The front door stood open, and he saw the waiting carriage out on the driveway, with Jimmy patiently holding the door open for Henrietta.

"Henrietta!" Elias called out.

. . .

SHE PAUSED AND TURNED, a gloved hand on the handle.

"WHERE ARE YOU GOING?"

SHE SMILED DEMURELY. "I have some errands to run, Elias."

He hesitated, then gently pulled her away from the carriage. "Were you going to leave without telling me?"

"You were working," she replied. Her lashes swept downwards. "I have no desire to be in the way here. Your parents were kind enough to extend an invitation whilst you were away. Now I must return to my life."

Elias swallowed hard. "Have I offended you? With my absence?"

The dark lashes swept up, the coy smile was back. "Not at all, sir. I understand you've been unwell. I'm only sorry that your father seems to have hurried you back to work before you were ready." Uncaring that they were in full view of the servants, she laid a hand on his arm, her fingers brushing the back of his hand. "Now that we have the wedding date set, I have several appointments I must see to."

Elias wanted to pull away from her touch. As if sensing this, her fingers tightened on his arm.

"You won't have to worry about decorum for too much longer, my love," she whispered. "Soon we will be waking in each other's arms, and no one will bat an eyelash. Now kiss me and let me go. They won't hold the train forever."

Elias bent to brush his mouth to her cheek, but at the last second, she turned her face for one of her sultry kisses that had once sent him dizzy with arousal. Today, it made him feel lower than a lizard's belly.

"Goodbye, my love," she whispered.

He handed her into the carriage but didn't wait for it to turn out of the drive before he strode back through the front doors.

He returned to the library, gathering up his papers. He summoned the butler using the narrow gold rope next to the hearth.

"You rang, sir?"

Elias tapped the edge of the papers against the desktop and placed them in the desk drawer. "When the carriage returns from the station, don't let them turn the horses out. And please have Hopkins pack an overnight bag. Nothing fancy so no tails. I'll eat at the hotel."

"Sir?"

You have two months. Make the most of them.

He had to know. He needed to see if his memory was distorted or if his feelings for the apothecary were genuine. Whether his father intended to be cryptic, or Elias was interpreting it that way for selfish reasons, he had to find out, one way or another.

He glanced up at Cassidy. "I'm going back to London."

CHAPTER 33

Bobby

THE HANDS SNAKED out of the darkness, wrapping themselves around her, mocking laughter filling her ears as one of those hands trapped the scream in her mouth.

"Hello, pretty," Billy Bateman stank, his putrid breath grazing her cheek. "I told you I'd be back for you."

Bobby struggled against him, flailing her legs, and digging her nails into his hands, while Billy barked out directions to the other two men who were trying to catch her sisters. Both had scattered into the darkness just as Bobby had been snatched up.

"Stop buggering' about and get them, will yer! Stick them in the wagon!"

Bobby thrashed about, her ears straining to hear. Billy had pinned her head too far back to be able to see what was going on. Her sisters' scream rent the air, their racing feet echoing off the walls.

"Leave us alone!"

"Go away!"

Bobby used his momentary distraction to sink her

teeth into the fingers pressing against her mouth. He bellowed in pain, the stars bursting in her eyes as he hit her. He grabbed at her again, plucking her up into the air, pulling her close to him. This time though, his grip was painfully biting.

"Stop yer kickin', you little witch," he breathed into her ear. Her screams turned to fearful whimpers as his one hand started to explore her body, gripping her breast through the rough material of her dress. "Oh yes, you'll earn your keep back in no time. I told you that ol' Billy always collects, didn't I? I might sample a bit of the treat now," he laughed, though the sound quickly turned into a gurgle.

Pain exploded through her as she was dropped to the ground. The sickening sound of bone on bone was muffled by the sound of scuffling feet. In the darkness, she squinted to make out what was happening.

The black cart that they'd seen as they'd approached the house was still in the street, the horse prancing nervously as the people around them scrapped in the middle of the road. Oaths, muffled and vicious, drifted through the fog, until Gertie rushed out of the swirling mists, straight into Bobby's arms.

"Hush, hush," she soothed, pulling her towards the safety of the front door.

Running feet.

More curses.

This time, Billy Bateman screaming blue murder and vowing vengeance on Bobby Luckett if he clapped eyes on her again.

Lydia, eyes wide and watery was next, hurrying forward with her arms outstretched. Bobby caught her, too.

Liam and Charlie appeared, both men puffing from their exertions.

"Liam? What are you doing here?"

"Are you alright?" Liam asked at the same time.

"Fine, I think," she looked down at her both Gertie and Lydia.

"Who was that?" Charlie asked, looking along the road where the cart raced away.

"Billy Bateman," Lydia spat.

The rent collector must have had enough of a reputation that no further explanation was required.

"They were going to put us in that cart," Lydia snarled. "Horrible men!"

"What for?" Gertie sobbed.

Bobby shook her head. She dreaded to think what might have happened to them, where the three of them might have ended up if Liam hadn't saved them. "It doesn't matter."

"You can't stay here," Liam told Bobby, his voice firm. "It's too dangerous."

"I know," Bobby admitted, her face still stinging from where Billy had struck her. "Though I don't know where. We've got nowhere to go. We've not paid the rent for nigh on three weeks…"

"I could go to the lodgings where I live, and see if they have a room there," Liam offered. "I don't know if they have but it could be a start. It's getting late and Billy will probably come back for you with more men."

Bobby shook her head. "No, we can't impose on you anymore."

She considered her options, which were few. She could go to the Talbot Inn to find her father, but she knew that would be futile. George Luckett had already made his choice to abandon them.

"Bobby–"

Liam's tone turned her legs to jelly. "We'll be fine," she said quickly, even though she wasn't so sure. She had lost her job and now her home. "You've done enough for us. I could never repay you."

"I don't need a repayment, but you've just reminded

me," Liam said, digging into his jacket pocket and pulling out a brown paper packet. He held it out to her.

"What's that?" she asked.

"Take it," he prompted her.

She did, recognising the envelope that the pay from the match factory came in. She held it out to give it back to him. "I can't take your wages, Liam."

"It's not mine," he pushed the envelope back to her.

She looked at Charlie, but Liam said, "It's from John Simpson."

"The foreman?" Bobby couldn't keep the surprise out of her voice.

"The very same," Liam nodded. "He pulled me to one side today after the shift ended. I think he knows that we're friends and he asked me if I knew where you lived. That's how I came to be here just now, and it was a good job I did, wasn't it?"

Bobby nodded, but she frowned, her smile fading. She opened the envelope, a small gasp escaping when she saw the amount of money inside it.

"Why would he do this?" she asked.

"Everyone knows he was sweet on your poor old ma," Charlie said.

"He was?" Lydia asked, exchanging a look with Bobby. They had no idea; until the day she'd passed, he'd never shown a lick of compassion towards any of them.

"Aye," Liam nodded. "There's talk about how the two of them were close to courting each other at one time, but I don't know if that's true or not."

"It would explain that," Charlie indicated the envelope.

"How much is in there?" Lydia asked.

"Enough for a room at least for a week," Bobby replied absently, wondering which angel had sent this to them.

"I know of some lodgings down Whitechapel," Liam said. "I could walk you to them, if that would help."

Bobby looked back at the house, the place that had been their home. The walls now seemed to close in on her, memories of happier times mingling with the dread of recent events. It was hard to leave all that she had ever known but it was no longer safe for them, not with Billy Bateman's imminent return.

She turned back to Liam, gratitude shining in her eyes. "That would be best."

Liam nodded, a reassuring smile on his face. "Let's go then. We don't have much time."

They gathered their few remaining belongings and left the empty house quietly, the echo of Billy's threats still ringing in their ears. Bobby settled a shawl over Gertie's shoulders, worried that the long day had already worn the young girl out.

"Here," Liam scooped her up.

They made a raggedy bunch, walking along the half-made pavements in the dark. Before long, Gertie had fallen asleep on his shoulder. She wished that she could sleep with such abandon. Instead, her mind drifted to what was going to happen to them all next. They had a little bit of money, certainly, but unless they could find more work, they would soon be right back where they were now. Maybe she would try the market stalls in the morning.

Lydia and Charlie walked ahead of them. Close enough to be friendly, not too close to be inappropriate. She realised then that her sister would soon be old enough to marry, to build a life of her own. Bobby feared what the future would hold for them all.

"Thank you," she said softly.

Liam walked in silence for a few minutes. "I could help you out. I've a bit put by for a rainy day."

Bobby shook her head. "I couldn't let you do that. Besides, you've already done so much for us."

"It's no bother," Liam shrugged. "I'm happy to do that for you."

The way he held her gaze set off a thrill of anticipation in her chest. He carried her little sister effortlessly. He'd saved them all tonight. The world, with the clickety-clack of hooves on the road, intruded on her brief bubble of contentment.

She didn't have time for romance. She needed to get her sisters settled because while Liam could be nice, as her husband, he could also turn on a whim. She'd lived too long in Mile End to know that a man ruled his house in any way he saw fit.

As her husband, he would have the right to kick her sisters out, and she would be powerless to stop him.

"We'll be alright," Bobby murmured.

She squeezed the wage packet tighter in her hand. With the unexpected kindness from John Simpson, it reminded her that there was still a glimmer of hope.

Liam shrugged. "At least this way I'll know where you are, and I can keep an eye on you."

"You're a good friend, Liam," she told him, hoping he would get the message without her hurting his feelings. If he was disappointed, he didn't show it. "But I want to do this for my sisters. We've got a good start, right enough. I'm certain I'll be able to find work and we'll be fine. You'll see."

CHAPTER 34

Kezzie

KEZZIE WALKED BRISKLY through the darkening streets, the damp chill biting through her cloak. Darkness had crept over the city faster than usual, and she shivered, pulling her cloak tighter around her shoulders. She didn't usually like to make her deliveries so late at night, but her last delivery had taken much longer. Consumption had taken its cruel hold on May O'Brien, and Kezzie knew that she could only make the poor woman comfortable, nothing more.

Rats scattered along the edge of the streets as she hurried past. The sounds of the city echoed out of the labyrinth of alleys—distant laughter from merrymakers, the low hum of the river. Her blood thrummed with memories of that terrible night so long ago.

Black eyes and mocking laughter.

She usually tried not to let it encroach on her day, but some nights, when the moon was high and the wind brought in the sea air, she couldn't help it.

She turned into East Alley, drawing solace from the

golden glow in the windows of her shop. Relief washed over her as she reached the door, but then the shadows to her left morphed into the shape of a man. She swallowed the scream that threatened to escape, knowing that to show weakness wouldn't help.

"Who's there?" she called out, her fingers sliding into the basket and wrapping around the hilt of her knife.

The broad shape stepped into the pool of light from the window, and her heart began to thrum for a different reason. Grey eyes watched her carefully, his dark hair combed back from his face. "Elias," she sighed, "you scared me. What are you doing here?"

"Waiting for you," he replied.

He wore a fine suit and a long wool coat. A red scarf kept the chill off his throat.

She held his stare, the light throwing the sharp planes of his face into prominence. She was the first to break the stare. She frowned, tucking the knife surreptitiously back into place. "You know full well how dangerous these streets are at night. Shouldn't you be somewhere else?"

"I wanted to see you."

Her pulse tripped at the simple statement. She glanced up, frowning. His expression remained serious.

"How have you been?"

She laughed then; the sound was sharp in the stillness of the street. "That's usually my question." She fumbled with her basket and keys, her fingers trembling. She surrendered the basket to him when he offered to help her. "Thank you," she murmured.

She slid the key into the lock. Her nerves tingled with awareness as he followed her into the shop. The warmth of the interior sent shivers racing over her skin. She brushed the hood back from her face, busying herself with the oil lamps to bring more light into the room. Slowly exhaling, she turned to face him.

He had healed, she noted. The bruises on his face had

faded to almost nothing. "You're looking better," she said softly.

"Thanks to you," Elias replied, his eyes never leaving her face.

Kezzie felt a flutter in her chest, a mix of relief and something more. She tamped whatever it was down firmly. "What brings you here, Elias? It's late."

"Where were you?"

"I was just making a delivery," she said huskily. "May O'Brien is very ill."

"I'm sorry to hear that," Elias said, stepping closer. "You're always helping others."

Kezzie's heart skipped a beat. She had spent the last few weeks trying to push thoughts of Elias out of her mind. He had a life. One that he'd not cared to share with her. She'd accepted that she wouldn't see him again. But seeing him here, standing in her shop, brought all those feelings rushing back.

"It's my job," Kezzie replied, trying to sound nonchalant.

"It's more than that," Elias said, his voice low. "You're a kind and caring person, Kezzie. I've seen it first-hand."

Kezzie felt her cheeks heat up. "Thank you," she said, looking down at her hands. "Though there are some who wouldn't agree with you."

"Well, there's no accounting for taste."

She smiled at that. Her breath quickened when she met his intense gaze once more. She had to distract herself. She delved back into the safety of her work. He was a patient. Nothing more could happen.

The cut on his eye was still an angry red, but it was healing nicely. Kezzie drank her fill of him, aware that he was searching her face just as intently.

"The bruising has cleared. Any headaches? Blurry vision?" she asked, then added hastily, "You look well." She clamped her lips shut, aware that she was babbling.

Elias set the basket on the counter. He faltered,

frowning into the basket. He reached in and slowly drew out the short, lethal-looking blade. "Is this what you were reaching for outside?"

"This is Whitechapel," she said by way of a simple explanation. "You can never be too careful."

He conceded the point with a rueful nod. "As well I know."

"Have you remembered more from the attack?"

He set the knife back into the basket. "Not even what I was doing the day of it. According to my diary, I had a meeting on Commercial Road. I cannot recall it."

"But everything else is there?"

He nodded slowly. "Mostly," His brows crunched into a deep frown. "You mentioned headaches. They've been quite troublesome. And my ribs still hurt," he said. "I was wondering if you have any more of that strange green paste you used."

He was lying.

She might not know much or be as educated as he appeared to be, but she knew people. He was hedging around something. "You should go to your doctor," she told him. "They have fancy tests that can check for things that I can only guess at."

"He tells me that there's nothing more they can do, and I must give myself time."

Kezzie's brow arched. "There's your answer."

"Aren't you sworn to help those in need?" His eye dwelt on her lips. "An oath, I believe you said you'd made."

A line appeared between her brows. He was teasing her, playing back the words she'd used when he was first lucid and trying to leave the shop before he was able to. She'd been consumed by thoughts of him but, now that he was here, she was unnerved by the reaction she was having to his presence. It made her voice sharper than necessary. "You got here under your own steam, didn't you? You don't appear to have a fever, nor are you delirious."

He tilted his head. "Are you alright?"

How could she explain to him of all people that she'd been moping about the shop these past weeks, glum and morose to the extent that Rose had chased her out earlier today, just so she could have some relief from her sour mood?

No Elias to care for. Worrying about Eunice and her threats.

"I'm fine," she said. She would give him the paste and then send him on his way. "How is the wound near your ribs?"

His hand went to his side. "Painful," he admitted.

She sighed. "You'd better come on through."

She briskly swept the curtain aside, the glow from the lamp she held aloft swinging abruptly around the room. She lit two more candles and busied herself setting up the room.

"Can you lift your shirt?"

When she turned, he had done as she asked. Her mouth went dry. She reminded herself that Elias was a customer. That she'd touched his exposed skin more than once. She swallowed, trying to control the jackhammer of her heart.

Instead, she focused on the angry red splotch high on his side. She frowned as she peered closer at it. "That doesn't look as well healed as the rest of you. You've not been resting."

"My father doesn't believe in recuperation." His eyes were fixed on a point behind her head when she stepped closer to him. She pressed her fingers into the site.

He sucked in a breath, let out a low moan.

"Does it hurt?"

"More than you know." The tone he used drew her eyes upwards. For a moment, her heart stopped before thumping crazily against her ribs, making her dizzy. His heated gaze, stormy and grey, dropped to her lips.

Kezzie pulled herself back to the task at hand. She yanked open several drawers and began dumping the ingredients into her pestle. The subtle smells of plantain and yarrow filled the air as she mixed them, the familiarity of her work smoothing out the jagged edges of her nerves.

She heard him moving about the room behind her. A glance over her shoulder told her that he was exploring – sniffing at jars, reading labels, and the like.

"How has business been?" He asked casually. "How is Rose?"

"Rose is well, thank you. And the business ticks over, the same as it always does."

"And what of young Bobby? How is her sister?"

Kezzie paused. "I haven't seen her since she was last here."

"I was curious to know how she fared."

"I haven't seen her on my rounds," Kezzie replied. "I'm certain it wouldn't take too much looking to find out how she was though. Not much changes around here and I know most people."

She pressed the ingredients harder into the pestle, realising she'd missed this easy camaraderie.

She'd missed him.

And therein lay the danger. Her feelings of alarm turned to anger. She couldn't have him here. She didn't want to feel anything for him. Love led to marriage. Marriage led to children. And children would lead to his inevitable death.

And she couldn't live with that knowledge.

She stopped pressing and turned to look at him. "Why are you really here, Elias? Because you can get this type of medicine from your doctor," she motioned over her pestle.

He set the jar in his hand on the side and walked towards her. His eyes shuttered as they swept over her. "I told you," He drew to a stop a foot away from her. "Whatever is in there works much better than anything the doctor could give me."

"Yes, but why are you here? In the dark, no less. You could have sent a maid or someone else to collect it?" She scraped the paste into the jar as she spoke. "Surely it would have been more convenient for you. I'm certain your father wouldn't be happy knowing that you're loose in the city once more, though if I were from a family as renowned as yours, I'd be ashamed to be seen in Whitechapel, too. I'm almost positive that the heir to Turner Enterprises should be much more careful where he decides to shop. You didn't have to risk coming here at night again, just for a paste that you can buy from a druggist much closer to Belgrave!"

He was a Turner. It was Rose who'd pointed out the newspaper article buried deep in the back of the Star newspaper.

Elias Turner: Reunited with his family.

Nothing of the attack, nor where he'd been hiding out. Just a small piece of smudged ink tucked away, though it had been vague enough to pique her interest. Unable to help herself, she had scoured the newspapers ever since, desperate for any titbits about him, his family, his life.

What she found filled her with everything she needed to know about him. A powerful family of inventors. Educated men of science.

Status.

Wealth.

Privilege.

All the things she didn't have. All the things that meant her world and his would never mesh. In a way, it confirmed what she already had ascertained from their conversations. From his clothing. From his elocution. Everything that meant daydreaming about Elias Turner was simply a wasted effort on her part.

She still couldn't get him out of her mind.

She thumped the cork lid into place and shoved it

towards him. Elias didn't move. When she raised her eyes to meet his, amusement shone there.

"What? What are you smiling at, for Heaven's sake?"

His lips twitched but he took the jar. "How often should I apply this?"

Kezzie frowned at him, confused by his evident glee. "Twice a day. Re-apply after washing," she muttered. "There's enough to last a week if you use it in the right quantities."

"Very well. How much do I owe you?"

She folded her arms and glowered. "Tell me what is so funny."

His sigh was soft and resigned. A dimple flashed in his chin. "I came here at the end of the day because I recall how Rose felt about my presence here. I wanted to avoid her if I could and speak with you alone."

"Why?"

"Curiosity, mostly," he admitted.

Her frown deepened and she shook her head. "What about?"

"Whether I'd imagined this reaction to you," he husked. "This intoxicating rush that courses through me whenever I'm near you."

Her audible swallow was the only sound in the room though she was almost certain he could hear how her pulse thundered in her ears.

"I didn't imagine it. I've never felt like this before. And I'm amused because I'd convinced myself that it would be one-sided. That a woman as incredible and talented as you would be far too sensible to be interested in me. Then I find out that you've been searching for information about me." His hand reached up to brush a strand of hair from her face gently. Her skin tingled where his fingertips had touched. "Which tells me that you're curious enough about me, too."

CHAPTER 35

*B*obby.

GERTIE WHIMPERED IN HER SLEEP.

The sound drew Bobby's gaze away from the grimy window, and she soothed her little sister, murmuring sweet things until she settled once more. Lydia slept soundly on the other side of her, the three of them huddled under one thin blanket in an effort to keep warm.

The dilapidated room was at the top of the building, barely more than four walls and a roof. Water trickled down one wall, leaving a dark damp stain that spread across the crumbling plaster and dirty floorboards. She could have lit the fire in the little black iron stove that sat in the corner of the room, but she wanted to make John Simpson's money stretch as far as she could.

As Gertie's breathing evened out once more, Bobby leaned her head back against the wall, peering at the sky beyond the window. Even now, in the dead of night, the sound of the city wasn't quiet. All around them, life could be heard through the thin walls and on the floors below them, families packed in tightly to maximise the rent earned.

She watched as the sky began to lighten. She unfolded her limbs stiff from the cold as she stood up.

"I'm hungry," Gertie complained as she woke up, her small voice plaintive in the dimly lit room.

"Here," Bobby offered them the last half of a slice of bread. Gertie stuffed the small amount into her mouth, chewing heartily while Lydia eyed her sister worriedly.

"What about you?" Lydia asked.

"Don't you worry about me," Bobby said, forcing a smile to her mouth. "I'll get something from the market today. You two are the ones who need your strength, standing out on the streets and selling the watercress. Get your baskets and let's go. Not a moment to waste if we're to be earning."

Bobby had learned to ignore the constant gnawing in her belly. Thinking about how hungry she was only seemed to make things worse.

She sent the girls down the road to the water's edge to pick watercress that they could sell at the marketplace. It was a small way to earn some money, but it required them to go out and pick it first. The three of them ventured out into the early morning fog, and Bobby watched the two girls make their way down the street. Alone, she held her worries close to her chest. John Simpson might have been kind and his donation generous, but if they carried on the way they were, Bobby knew she would be knocking on the gates of the workhouse before too long.

She pulled her shawl tighter around her shoulders. Dew drops beaded on the worn wool, chilling her further. The coalmen and drays filled the streets, the smells of manure mingling with the damp morning air. People emerged through the gloom, shuffling past her, their grimy faces set with acceptance of their fate.

It was a short walk to the marketplace, already

teeming with stallholders and shoppers. Vendors shouting their wares and customers haggling for the best prices filled the bustling square to bursting point. She began to make her rounds, checking at the stalls to see if anybody needed a hand that day. One by one, each shook their head slowly. Most people were too poor to be able to offer anything, working hard as they barely had enough to feed their own families.

By the time she had been refused by all the stallholders, hours had passed. Her stomach growled deeply. Bobby took a deep breath and held out her hand, beginning her usual routine.

"Please, could you spare a penny? Please, sir, any alms for the poor?"

People strode past her as if she were invisible.

Disdainful glances were accompanied by muttering under the breath as they hurried away. Shame burned her but she kept her hand out. Some spat on her, calling her filthy names, but she kept in mind that she needed to find enough to pay the rent and to buy the girls a little something to eat. The smells of fresh bread and roasted meats filled the air, driving her hunger to the point where she felt nauseous.

Not everyone was unkind. An older woman, dressed neatly in a black uniform, paused, and handed Bobby a coin. "Here, child. It's not much but that's all I can spare."

Bobby pressed her hands together in supplication. "God bless you, miss," Bobby said, her gratitude genuine.

At the end of the day, Bobby checked around her before she paused to count the coins held in her palm. She divided the pile into two, slipping half into a pocket before she began making her rounds at the market stalls, hoping to bring down their prices as they were desperate to get rid of anything left over at the end of the day.

She managed to scavenge a slice of bread and a meat skewer. It wasn't much, but it would feed them for tonight. She hurried along the streets, head down to make herself as small and invisible as possible, mindful of the pickpockets that might be watching her as she walked.

She darted down the narrow alley to the front door and let herself inside. She hurried up the narrow steps, mindful of the ones that creaked or were too rotten to stand on. She let herself into the tiny room at the top of the stairs and was relieved to see Gertie and Lydia sitting together on the straw mattress in the corner, both under the thin blanket.

Bobby smiled warmly at them both. "Look what I have," she held the bag aloft.

Gertie's eyes lit up. "Food?"

Bobby dropped to her knees and divided the food into three equal piles. As usual, Gertie gobbled everything up without swallowing, it seemed. Lydia nibbled delicately. Bobby savoured each morsel, chewing slowly to make the pleasure last just a little longer.

"Here," Lydia said.

Bobby took the coins that she held out, giving her sister a thankful smile.

"I don't know what you're thanking me for," Lydia scowled. "We earn five times that in a day at the factory. How can we ever hope to get out of this place if that's all we can earn?"

Bobby swallowed her food, carefully choosing her words. "You and I can get a job in a factory, but what about Gertie?"

Lydia wasn't to be steered off the subject this time. "I'm sure if I went back and spoke to them at the factory, they would take us back. And there are other factories too, all over the city, as you well know."

Bobby didn't bother to disguise her sigh. "You're right, of course. I was hoping to keep the three of us together. I worry that if all three of us can't get a job together, then I won't be able to keep an eye on you."

"I don't know why you care so much about us," Lydia

muttered. "Father didn't care enough to stay, so why should you?"

A line appeared between Bobby's brows as she looked at her sister. She settled her hands on Lydia's shoulders and was shocked to realise she was crying. Wordlessly, she gathered Lydia close and began to rock her sister as their mother once did when they were upset. "I'm sorry Father left and that I wasn't enough. You know that I tried to go to the pub and that even Liam and Charlie have tried to make him see sense, but I'm telling you now I will never leave you, Lydia. I will be here for as long as you need."

"Promise?"

Bobby nodded. "I promise. I will not leave you and I will not stop until I find something that means the three of us will be alright."

As they huddled together once again under the thin blanket, they listened to the sounds of the city outside.

They would survive this.

One day, she would find them a better life.

CHAPTER 36

Kezzie

"You timed that well," Kezzie said, a warmth blooming inside her as Elias stepped in through the door. The day had been long, yet the tingle of anticipation that he might visit her had fizzed in her belly. The streets had grown quieter as dusk settled over the city. "I was just about to close up for the day."

Elias' smile told her that he'd planned it just that way. "Have you eaten? I smelled the most delicious roasted meat scent and found the source – an old street seller had these on her barrow." He held aloft a paper bag darkened with grease off the pig's trotters.

Elias's visits had become a regular occurrence over the past two weeks. Always at the end of the day, always when she was alone. He made sure to arrive bearing a gift of some kind – a bouquet of wildflowers or hand-wrapped chocolates.

Tonight, it was a delicious meal.

She took the bag from him, keen to keep the grease from seeping into the wooden surface that he was about to set it on. The smell from the bag made her mouth water, and her stomach reminded her that she'd not eaten since that morning.

"Lock the door and come on through," she instructed. She knew that his being here alone with her was wrong and that she shouldn't be encouraging him. After all, where could it go? They were from two different worlds. But, just like a parched man finding water, she drank her fill of him when he stepped through the heavy velvet curtain.

He removed his black overcoat and hung it on the back of the door. "How was your day?" He asked, his usual greeting.

She ripped into the bag and dumped its contents onto a plate she kept in the cupboard for this very reason. "Busy. Jane Clementine called by to let me know that the swelling I made the ointment for has subsided on her husband's leg. He's happy because he gets to go back to work. She's happy because he is no longer under her feet and griping in her ear."

Elias laughed as he plucked up a hunk of meat. "I don't know who to be happier for."

Kezzie watched as he tore into the meat, thinking about what his peers would think of him standing in a backstreet Whitechapel apothecary, eating with his bare hands, instead of at a candlelit table bulging with gleaming silverware. He surprised her constantly.

"What about you?"

He slurped up a dribble of juice, catching it with the back of his hand. "Nowhere as interesting as yours, I'd say. Facts and figures. The usual."

She'd asked him the same question each time he visited, and every time, he gave the same vague answer. She sighed inwardly but didn't press further. She didn't want to ruin the connection that they appeared to be building.

She knew he was holding back, but she tried not to let

it bother her too much. Their conversations followed a familiar pattern—her sharing details of her day, him responding with evasive remarks.

Yet, despite this, she found herself looking forward to his visits, treasuring the moments they spent together. She would regale him with entertaining stories until he had tears rolling down his face, while he responded with something trifling. It irked her, though she couldn't quite explain why. She fell silent, turning the trotter in her hand thoughtfully.

"What is it?" he asked, picking up another meaty chunk and watching her through his lashes.

She forced a smile. "What do you mean?"

He wiped his mouth, looking around for something to clean his hands on. He accepted the cloth she passed him.

"You look melancholy, as though a rain cloud has just spoiled your sunny day."

She turned away, uncomfortable with the scrutiny. He seemed to have a knack for gauging her moods, whereas she couldn't read him at all. She wondered why he seemed determined to withhold information about his life yet continued to visit her. What was worse was that she'd come to look forward to his visits.

"It's nothing," she murmured, eyes downcast.

He stepped around the table between them. "Don't do that. Don't say it's nothing when it's something."

"Why do you come here?"

He jolted, surprise flickering across his face. "Well, I… I enjoy your company. I would like to think that you enjoy mine, too."

She should follow their usual pattern and talk about her day instead; about all the visitors she'd had that day and the peculiar local characters that were a part of the pattern of her world. He would listen attentively and nod when the matter turned serious.

But there was something that had been bothering her.

Because, despite his evasiveness, she felt an undeniable bond forming, and she was scared because of its intensity.

"These visits... the lovely gifts that you bring, although I'm very appreciative, it leads me to think..." She took a deep breath to try and summon her courage. "You are spoiling me."

"You deserve to be spoiled."

She waved a hand, determined to say what had been niggling deep in the back of her mind each time he'd visited. "It feels like you're courting me, Elias."

He held her gaze, his expression gentle but guarded. "What that be so terrible?"

She dropped the meat onto the plate and snatched up the cloth he'd used. "We come from different worlds. We can't have a future together if that is what you were hoping. You don't know me, not what happens to people who get too close to me—"

"Kezzie, stop," He caught hold of her hands, smiling down into her eyes.

She knew she should protest, to make him see the impracticalities, the impossibilities. But the sincerity in his eyes silenced her doubts.

He drew her hands up, and brushed his mouth across her knuckles, one hand at a time.

The rest of her words evaporated off her lips as her blood turned syrupy and all sensible thoughts scattered out of her head.

"I don't have all the answers to the questions I can see floating in those incredible eyes of yours," he murmured, tending to the backs of her hands with his mouth. The pads of his thumbs traced the same path. Her insides turned to molten liquid. "Can't we just enjoy what we have now? Must we look so far ahead?" He reached out, gently cupping her chin so that she had to look at him.

Elias reached out, gently lifting her chin so she had to look at him. "I spend my days thinking about you," he admitted, his gaze locked on hers. "I can't stop. I don't want to stop."

Kezzie held her breath as he leaned in.

He hesitated for a fraction of a second, seeking permission, waiting for her to push him away. To end his advance.

But she couldn't.

Then his mouth was on hers and she was swept along in a torrent of feeling, of heat, of sensations that made sense only to them. She melted into the kiss, savouring the sensation of having him claim her mouth as his, and only ever his.

When he tore his mouth from hers, it pleased her to hear his breath was just as ragged as hers. He leaned his forehead against hers, his eyes shut tight.

"You're important to me, Kezzie. More than you know."

Wrapped in his embrace, still tingling from his kisses, Kezzie knew he spoke the truth. She clung to the fragile hope that it would be enough.

CHAPTER 37

Kezzie

KEZZIE WATCHED as the black carriage melded with the sea of other carts and cabs making their way along the busy road of Commercial Street. Even this late in the day, the road was still a cacophony of activity, and soon enough, the cab that Elias was in vanished within the sea of vehicles.

She struck out along the pavement, the buzz of her pleasant afternoon giving way to the suspicions that inevitably crowded in on her mind whenever Elias left her.

She knew the only reason Elias had accompanied her out that day was because she had pointed out to him that he was treating her as if she were a dirty secret by only visiting her at night.

He'd baulked, almost offended by the suggestion and had promised to take her out during the day. She tried not to take offence when he chose a beautiful park on the outskirts of the city. They had strolled along the winding walkways, careful not to touch, even though young couples meandered arm in arm, with young ladies under parasols and their guardians a few feet behind them to keep the outing respectable. It was highly improper for her to be out alone with a young man and without an escort, and yet Kezzie couldn't care less.

But now, as the light slid into darkness, the niggling doubts returned.

She turned off the main thoroughfare and walked along the narrow, sullied streets, the rundown buildings sagging against their neighbours. The leaning structures diminished the light, making it seem later in the evening than it was. She wove her way around the detritus that cluttered the footwells, past the shuffling souls of native Londoners.

She knew Elias was hiding something from her.

That nagging sensation had not left her, not since before the night he'd kissed her. Not for the first time, she wondered if it was because of her lowly social status. The idea of being meeting clandestinely filled her with shame. She seemed to spend her hours longing to see him and was conflicted with wanting to push him away from her to keep him safe all at the same time.

Like a man pressing his face against the windows of an opium den, she spent her days thinking about all the reasons Elias Turner was bad for her, and then the limited time they spent together dreaming about the possibilities of a future with him as his wife.

She turned into East Alley, her thoughts a tangle of emotions and was surprised to see the shop still open for business.

Kezzie walked back into the shop to find Rose still there.

"Why are you here so late?" Kezzie asked without preamble.

Rose quirked a brow, giving her a look that told Kezzie her thinly disguised excuse for leaving the shop for the whole day hadn't passed muster. "I wanted to finish off this sprain oil."

Kezzie could smell the red sage, rosemary, and lavender that still scented the air from where the herbs had been simmering in the almond oil to make up the treatment.

"How was your day?" Rose asked.

Kezzie unwound her shawl and hung up her bonnet in the back room, wondering if she should continue with the ruse that she'd gone to meet Marjorie Topham. One look at Rose's face, however, almost dared her to lie. "My afternoon was wonderful, actually," she said, unable to help the smile that slid over her face.

Rose scoffed. "It'll end in disaster, Kezzie, mark my words."

Kezzie didn't want to argue, but Rose had been warning her since she realized Elias had been visiting in the evenings. She busied herself cleaning away the products that Rose had used, willing back the tears.

Rose's soft sigh reached her before the older woman said, "I don't wish to see you unhappy, Kezzie. I'm glad that you're willing to look past this hex you seem to think you have."

"Don't," Kezzie interrupted, unwilling to delve into a fight after her pleasant afternoon.

But Rose was not to be put off this time. "He's a man of substance. It's folly on his part to think this is the right match. Will you give up this business to be his wife? Or will he live here as your husband, giving up the society life that he no doubt enjoys?"

Kezzie gripped the edge of the counter, the action sending the tears that filled her eyes tumbling down her cheeks.

"It's been a month you say he's been coming here. You deserve more, Kezzie."

Kezzie turned away, hiding her face. "I don't know

what to do, Rose. I care for him, but you're right. Our worlds are so different."

Rose came up behind her, placing a gentle hand on her shoulder. "You have to think about your future, dear. You have to be realistic."

Kezzie nodded, wiping her tears with the back of her hand. "I know. But it's hard."

Rose squeezed her shoulder. "I know it is. Just promise me you'll think carefully about what you're getting into."

"I do, every moment of every day," Kezzie whispered, her voice thick with emotion.

Rose clicked her tongue, leaning down so that her face appeared in Kezzie's line of sight. "It will all come out in the wash, hmm?"

Kezzie inhaled, using the heels of her hands to wipe her eyes. She gave Rose a watery smile. "Thank you for staying on later."

Rose nodded, taking down her coat and hat where she'd hung them on the coat stand in the corner of the room. She wasn't saying anything Kezzie hadn't already thought of herself, but hearing the words out loud only reminded her that it was reckless.

"I'll be here in the morning first thing so you can make your deliveries."

As Rose left for the night, Kezzie stood alone in the shop, her heart heavy with uncertainty. She thought about the afternoon with Elias, the way he had looked at her, the way he had made her feel. When she was with him, she threw all caution to the wind.

She turned the big iron key in the lock and finished clearing down. Then she turned out the lamps and made her way up the narrow staircase at the back of the shop.

The upstairs of the shop hadn't changed much since her grandfather's day, and Kezzie didn't mind. She had no desire to offend her ancestors by changing things around. She settled down to eat cold ham, cheese, and a hunk of fresh bread for her supper, her mind churning with the events of the day.

Strolling along with Elias, she had almost fooled herself into believing what was happening between them was real. But hearing Rose that night confirmed what she'd secretly known all along.

Elias couldn't mean to give up his life.

Nor could someone like him live in Whitechapel with her, any more than she could give up her work or her home. Each time she'd voiced her concerns to Elias, he'd simply leaned in and brushed a light kiss over her mouth to change the subject.

The next day, she woke early to the clanging of the coal merchants and the night watchmen making their rounds. The warm weather of the day before had filled the streets with heavier fog than usual; it clung to the buildings, making them appear ethereal through the mists.

There was already someone waiting at the door when she stepped into the dim shop interior.

"Good morning, Sally," Kezzie greeted as she let in Sally Briggs, who needed elderflower ointment. They were just finishing up when Rose walked into the chiming of the bell.

"Good morning, Sally!" Rose called out. "What brings you by?"

"My Jack's hip is playing him up something chronic," Sally held up the ointment for Rose. "This ought to do the trick though. Goodbye to you both."

"Goodbye, Sally," Kezzie and Rose echoed, and the bell rang into the silence as Sally left.

It appeared Rose was still cross with Kezzie. Kezzie went to the older woman and wrapped her arms around her. For a moment, Rose resisted but, when Kezzie simply held on tighter, she relented, her arms folding Kezzie into a comforting hug.

"I don't like it when we're at odds," Kezzie said.

"Neither do I," Rose said, setting her away. "Now, what are we doing today? Did you see the list of deliveries?"

"I did," Kezzie replied. Together, they packed up her basket—filled heavier than usual because she'd taken the afternoon off yesterday—and Kezzie left with a promise to fetch back some fresh bread so they could make sandwiches for their supper.

She walked through the streets of London, shrouded in the gloomy fog. She headed to Mile End, knocking on doors, and tending to her usual customers. She then made her way back towards Whitechapel, remembering her promise to fetch food for lunch. She cut through the marketplace, which was thronged with busy people. Hawkers and market stallholders filled the air with their cries, each competing over price and volume.

Just as she was about to reach the other side where the bakery was, a bedraggled hand appeared in front of her. The grimy girl dressed in filthy rags begged apathetically for alms.

Kezzie dug into the purse at her side, pausing when she saw the girl's expression shift from desperation to recognition.

"Bobby? Is that you?"

CHAPTER 38

Bobby

"Rose!" Kezzie greeted as she stepped into the apothecary and held open the door for Bobby and her two sisters to follow her in. "This is Bobby, the girl I told you about. That's Lydia and the little one is Gertie. They're Bobby's sisters."

Bobby stood in the middle of the shop, the scents of herbs and chemicals strangely comforting after the unpleasant aromas she'd grown used to. Gertie pressed herself to Bobby's side, and she could feel Lydia standing close behind her.

The past few hours had whizzed by.

She'd not even noticed Kezzie in the marketplace. She wasn't sure when she'd stopped noticing the people, their condemnation, and their disgust as they looked down their noses at her. To her, they were just a possibility of a tiny bit of humanity, a chance to scrounge a few coppers to be able to feed her sisters. That was why she kept at it, even when the damp cold air meant she'd lost all feelings in her fingers and toes.

She didn't need a looking glass to know how far she'd fallen from where she'd once been. It had been written all over Kezzie Doyle's face.

Horror.

Disbelief.

Pity.

Kezzie had wasted no time in accompanying Bobby to round up her sisters, to walking with her to the tiny hovel of a room where they'd been living and collecting up the few belongings they'd kept for cooking and such like, before she'd walked them all through Whitechapel to her shop.

Even now, as Bobby stood gazing around the interior at the array of brown and blue glass bottles, the brown and cream masonry jars, the displays of pretty perfumes and lotions arranged on the wide counter, harshly whispered words like 'waifs' and 'strays' and 'workhouse' reached her ears and Kezzie's patient reply about the hovel she'd just been in that the girls had called home.

Bobby was too tired to care.

"Here, girls, please," Kezzie pushed the two plates piled with food that she had bought from the barrow sellers in the marketplace towards them. "Come and eat."

Lydia didn't need to be told twice. She fell on the plate and grabbed up handfuls of meat and bread, stuffing them into her mouth. Gertie responded to Kezzie's gentle encouragement by turning her face into Bobby's skirts.

Bobby, motivated by the pointed look that Kezzie was sending to the woman she'd called Rose, peeled Gertie off of her side and coaxed her across the shop floor. Eying the two strange women, Gertie gingerly took the piece of bread.

"It's fine," Bobby whispered to her little sister. "Kezzie is the kind lady who made the magic medicine that saved your life. Remember how I brought it to you, in that pretty green bottle."

Gertie nodded slightly. Eyes wide, she nibbled at the bread.

"Take something for yourself, Bobby," Kezzie held the plate out.

With her mouth watering at the thought of food, she picked up a meat skewer. It was still warm when she bit into it.

"Better?" Kezzie asked Gertie as she finished the last morsel.

"I think it's the best thing I ever tasted," she admitted.

Kezzie laughed. "Then you better have some more."

"Thank you," Lydia said around a mouthful of food. "Truly, miss. Thank you."

Kezzie returned the plate to the counter. Her sigh was full of concern as her eyes travelled over the dishevelled girls. They settled on Bobby.

"What happened?"

Bobby looked down, her hands twisting in her ragged dress. The simple question made her eyes sting with tears as hopelessness flooded her.

"Ma died. Dropped dead in the match factory," she husked, unaware of the tears that tracked through the filth on her face. She laid it all out for the apothecary, who remained silent as she recounted the events that had led the three of them to beg on the streets, struggling to stay together and avoid the unscrupulous people who wanted to exploit them for their own nefarious ends.

"There's no sign of your father?"

Bobby shook her head. "Not in weeks, miss. My good friend Liam believes he's found work outside of the city."

"Typical," Rose harumphed under her breath.

Kezzie shot her friend a dark look and then began to clear away the greasy papers. "What have you been doing for work? How have you been feeding yourselves?"

"We were lucky enough to have been given some money by one of the foremen from the factory," Bobby said.

"We think he was a bit sweet on Ma," Lydia added.

Kezzie's lips twitched. "Well, that was generous of him."

"Very generous, miss," Bobby nodded. "It meant that we had a place to go so that the rent collector…" Her throat tightened, choking off the words.

Lydia rubbed a hand down her back. "He tried to drag Bobby off. Said he was going to put her to work."

"We had to leave there," Bobby explained, shame filling her. "John Simpson's money meant that we had a bit of leeway, but I've not been able to find any regular work that brings in enough money to pay the rent and buy us food."

Kezzie and Rose exchanged another look. Bobby wondered what it would be like to have a silent language like that with someone else.

Kezzie balled up the paper and dropped it in a bucket in the corner. She turned to face the three girls; her hands fisted on her hips as she looked at each of them.

"Do you all read?"

They nodded in unison.

"What about writing?"

"Bobby and I can, Gertie still needs to practice her letters a lot," Lydia offered.

"Good. That will help. Now, I don't like shirkers and Rose here cannot abide laziness. We also won't tolerate any backtalk from any of you. What we say goes, yes?

"You are not to steal either, from anyone. I am not sure how much I can pay you yet, I haven't had a chance to do the sums but if you pinch a single thing then you'll be out on your ear. I have no qualms marching you to the police station on Commercial Street myself and I happen to be on first-name terms with the policemen there. Do I make myself clear?"

Bobby frowned at her, confusion clouding her mind. "Miss?"

"First things first, we need to get you bathed and into

some clean clothes. I can run along to the Salvation Army and see if they have any old clothes that might fit you because those rags you're wearing are only fit for the fire," Kezzie tried to herd the girls towards the door in the corner that led upstairs, though the girls merely huddled together. She spread her hands at them as if the answer should be obvious.

"You're going to be living here...with me."

CHAPTER 39

*B*obby

"What about this one?" Kezzie asked.

"Angelica," Bobby said.

"Correct, and what is it used for?"

"Flatulence and indigestion. It can also be used in a tonic to treat colds and sweeten other remedies."

Kezzie nodded and moved on to the next jar on the shelf.

"Feverfew," Bobby stated. "Used for nervous disorders and can be applied in salves for insect stings and bites."

"Very good," Kezzie smiled. "I can see that you have been studying hard."

"Yes, miss," Bobby said. "I find it all fascinating, truth be told."

This statement seemed to warm Kezzie, her smile broadening as she stepped to the counter. She held up one of the little muslin bags gathered in a basket on top of the counter.

"Fennel seeds," Bobby pointed. "Remedy for heartburn,

constipation, and it can be used to ease the symptoms of cystitis as well."

"I'm impressed, Bobby. You have a natural aptitude for learning. You're like a sponge, soaking it all in. I don't think I took to it all quite as easily as you have."

Bobby was still getting used to life on East Alley.

A life of praise.

A life without the gnawing pains of hunger and dread of what would face them that day.

Under George Luckett, learning was seen as a waste of time and energy. It had taken the three girls a few days to settle in. Bobby waited for their stroke of good luck to turn sour, but, so far, her life seemed to have changed for the better.

Kezzie and Rose encouraged her. Every spare minute of the day when she wasn't cooking or cleaning, Bobby was allowed to have her nose in a book. There were many books to choose from on the shelves in the rooms upstairs. Bobby pored over their pages, carefully deciphering the ancient language to better understand the old methods, keen to learn everything she could while she could.

To delve into the history of what was prepared here in the shop fascinated her. To learn how strange herbs and seeds were brought in on the ships and fetched from the docks to be made into recipes to help those in need here. To understand how Kezzie's grandfather had built his knowledge from his travels and training all those years ago.

It wasn't just medicinal remedies that were made in the apothecary. Lavender was tucked into pillows to aid sleep and ease digestive complaints. Lemon balm was used as a gentle sedative. The pots of marigold cream and ointments stacked on the counter, rich and soothing, were well-loved by those wanting to soothe their sore skin.

Marshmallow infusions made from the root were

used for relief from coughs and insomnia. Chamomile flowers for their calming effects could be used for stomach upsets and mouth ulcers, but also as a rinse to lighten blonde hair. Even now, as Bobby moved around the shop reciting the contents of the jars and their uses, Kezzie was measuring out juniper berries for a customer who needed a steam inhalation for a particularly nasty cold.

"I can see that you've been studying hard," Kezzie said, and Bobby wondered if it was pride that she could hear in the other woman's voice.

"Thank you, miss," Bobby murmured. "Though it's much easier to learn when my belly isn't growling."

Kezzie's strange blue eyes shone with delight. "I suppose it is."

Kezzie had made it a daily practice to test Bobby on her knowledge of the herbs, spices, and roots that filled the shelves in the shop. It made Bobby study harder because she wanted to prove to Kezzie that her kindness and generosity were not going to waste.

Bobby wasn't sure which angel had brought Kezzie into her path in the marketplace. Even the recalcitrant Rose was starting to thaw towards the three girls.

Her life was so very different now. She kept wondering when she would wake up from this dream.

Kezzie had somehow managed to find Lydia some honest work cleaning for one of the townhouses three streets over. Her sister left early in the morning and was back just before supper, telling tales of the wealthy woman who treated her servants better than most, according to the rest of the staff in the household.

The doorbell jingled as the front door swung open and Bobby's eyes fell upon the skinny young girl who stood nervously in the doorway. Her dress hung in rags, her eyes round and scared in her dirty face. It felt strange to know that a few short months ago that was her, seeking a remedy to save a life, and now Gertie was upstairs healthy and fit, peeling vegetables ready for their supper.

"Welcome to Doyle's," Kezzie said. "I'm going to let my assistant help you today," she added playfully.

Bobby was surprised by the news but determined to do her best. She had been in the shop every day and was confident that she could at least mimic that she knew what she was talking about.

"Come on in," she encouraged, pleased to see that her voice wasn't quaking as much as her belly was inside. "How can I help you today?"

"We've got rats," the young girl retorted quickly, though she didn't venture any further into the shop. "Lots of rats. My pa sent me for some poison."

Bobby looked at Kezzie for confirmation, who nodded.

"We have some arsenic in pellets," Bobby stated and turned towards the shelf that held the boxes, but the young girl stopped her.

"No, miss," she amended quickly. "He said strychnine."

Bobby hesitated, but Kezzie took over, asking pertinent questions and the girl answered confidently, though she looked deeply uncomfortable being in the shop at all. When Kezzie was certain that the girl only wanted a small amount of the poisonous grains, she carefully weighed them into a bag and sent the young girl on her way. She dropped the coins into the drawer behind the counter and turned to Bobby.

"Well done on your..." her voice faded off. "What's the matter?"

Bobby shook her head, watching the young girl through the shop window as she raced away and disappeared around the corner. "It's just that... Never mind," she said quickly, feeling a little foolish.

"No, please," Kezzie gestured. "Tell me what put that strange look on your face?"

"I suppose it's just I will never understand people. I

mean, the girl's father sent her out for poison and pest control and yet his daughter doesn't have any boots on her feet."

⁓

"How did you know I was here?"

Bobby closed the shop door behind her, stepping down onto the cobbles. The day had been warm, the sun barely piercing through the fog, but as twilight loomed, the air was tinged with the scent of fire smoke and the pungent aroma of waste that filled the gutters.

Liam appeared to have come straight from work. He had dirty hands and an oil streak along his cheek. He whipped off his black cloth cap and stuffed it into his pocket, running a hand self-consciously over his dark hair.

He grinned lopsidedly. "Jack Briggs. He was stinking out the factory with some fancy ointment for his hip. His wife told him she'd seen you behind the counter here." He ran a gaze over the front of the shop. The weathered exterior turned black from the city fog seemed to hold a quiet dignity. The glass in the muntin windows was slightly warped, distorting the light that enhanced the mystical appeal.

The faded lettering, once a vibrant gold, had worn off the signage though the shop had stood for so long in this neighbourhood, that it didn't need announcing to anyone other than those in need.

"I wasn't sure where you went," Liam said, swinging back to her. "When I knocked on the door and your old neighbour told me that you'd gone, I wasn't sure what to think. It was only when Sally brought Jack his stuff that he mentioned this is where you were."

Bobby's face pinched with regret. "I'm sorry if you were worried, Liam. Truth be told, everything has been a bit of a rush these past few weeks. With Lydia finding a new job and Kezzie pushing me into studying for my new job here at the shop, I haven't had two minutes to myself."

He nodded, his gaze dropping to the floor. He toed one of the cobbles in the lane. "I'm glad you're safe."

"I am," she said. "We all are."

His gaze came up and he squinted at her. "You sure? You're not... under a spell or anything?"

Bobby snorted with laughter. "She isn't a witch. Kezzie happens to be a very talented healer.

His expression turned dubious. "You call her Kezzie?"

Bobby's smile was quick. "She insisted. Miss Kezzie or Miss Doyle sounds far too formal for how she is in real life. She's nothing like the people around here will have you believe."

Liam nodded, and she could tell he was a little surprised by this news.

"I mean it. They call her a witch and say that she's in league with the devil, I know, but she's really nice. You're from down Mile End, and you know the good work she does around there."

"I've also heard what people say about her, and I was wondering if you'd thought about that. You don't want to be tarred with the same brush as her, do you?"

A reluctant smile tugged at Bobby's lips. "I couldn't care a fig what people think about me down in Mile End. None of them were around to lend a helping hand when my father disappeared. That is, no one except you, Liam."

His expression shifted and she sighed softly. "And here I go again, feeling like I've let you down."

He quickly shook his head. "You haven't let me down, Bobby. I'm not sure you ever could. I'm just worried about what might happen to you if you stay here any longer than you need to."

"Nothing will happen to me here. Kezzie is teaching me skills that will stand me in good stead for years to come. I want to be the best apothecary's assistant I can be, tending to the sick and helping those who can't help themselves, just like Kezzie does… like you once did for me."

"So, you're staying here?"

"I am. For as long as she'll have me. My sisters… we're all safe here."

His mouth twisted in disbelief.

"As my friend, I want you to be happy for me, but if you can't, well then… so be it." She stated primly.

Liam made a sound of regret. "And now I've annoyed you," he murmured. "And that wasn't my intention. Life is tough enough around here, Bobby. I just don't want you making things worse for yourself if it can be helped. You're in the company of someone that many people don't like. How can you hope to live well under the pall of a Doyle?"

She stepped closer to him and laid a hand on his arm. "Bless you for being concerned about me, but I promise you, I'm much better off here than I ever was in Mile End. I just hope we can still be friends."

"We are friends," he said softly. A smile lingered on his face as he studied her, and Bobby knew he wanted more from her than she was ready to give at the moment. He opened his mouth as if about to say something further, but Bobby stepped back, breaking contact with him. "I must be off. There's still so much to do before we close up. It was Kezzie who spotted you through the window and said I could come out to see you."

Liam glanced towards the windows once more, but the distorted glass prevented him from seeing inside. "Will you do me a favour?"

Bobby hesitated, then gave a little nod.

Liam dug into his pocket and pulled out a small paper packet. "Will you give this to your sister? Charlie is a bit soft on her and was beside himself with worry when he heard that you'd all gone. If you can pass this along, I'm sure he'd be grateful forever."

Bobby laughed and held out her hand. "I'm sure Lydia

will be glad to hear from Charlie. God knows she's bent my ear about not seeing him for the last three weeks we've been here."

Liam looked as if he was about to say something else when his eyes moved beyond her to the street. Through the swirling mist, a figure was walking towards them. Bobby recognised the familiar shape straightaway, even before the figure hesitated upon seeing the two of them standing outside the shopfront.

"Good evening, Mr Turner," Bobby called out. "I shall let Kezzie know you're here."

She turned to Liam. "It was good to see you, Liam. I'd hope that you might call by to visit me again soon, but I do understand if you don't want to."

"Take care of yourself, Bobby."

Bobby refused to watch him walk away.

Liam was her last link to her old life, and it was the only link she would preserve if she had the choice. But she reminded herself that she was doing all this so that she could build something better for her future.

CHAPTER 40

*E*lias

He had made a mistake.

A huge miscalculation.

One that he knew he would be paying for the rest of his life.

Elias wound his way through the fog-choked lanes of Whitechapel, his footsteps echoing along the cobblestones, his mind in turmoil.

He knew that he had taken his father at his word – two months to sow his wild oats, to live the life of a man unencumbered by responsibility or marriage. So, he sought out Kezzie once more, to indulge himself in one last dalliance before he became a married man.

In doing so, he discovered that Kezzie Doyle was so much more than he had first anticipated.

She was warm, kind, and giving.

She was quick, clever, and funny.

She was everything that he could ever dream of in a woman and more. But getting to know her more had only shown him what he would be missing when he took Henrietta as his wife.

Because, as selfish as he was being so far, he couldn't tarnish her reputation and ask her to be his mistress.

The duality of his life gnawed at him.

He felt guilty for misleading her into believing that he was a free man in the first place. This truth had been eating away at his conscience. Throughout business meetings and society dinners, thoughts of Kezzie had been like a siren's call, taking up space in the recesses of his mind. Every new day was like a countdown to when he would have to say goodbye to her and to his chance at happiness.

He'd begun to dread it.

He considered himself an honourable man, and his actions in the past few weeks had been nothing short of dishonourable.

This made him feel worse.

He'd wiled away hours coming up with all the reasons he needed to marry Henrietta.

To preserve the family name, to maintain a standard his parents were accustomed to. Each time he tried to focus on his family and responsibilities, he stumbled. Every time Kezzie had tried to steer the conversation towards their future, he distracted her with a kiss.

He was in a tortured state of limbo.

Tonight was no different.

He was being a coward, hiding from his duties. Even now, as he walked towards the apothecary shop, with the sounds of the city settling down for the evening around him, his mind was filled with all the practical reasons not to do what he was about to do.

He was going to let his father down. He was going to break Henrietta's heart.

Because, as much as he'd tried to conceal the truth, he knew that he was in love with Kezzie.

In this truth was the knowledge that was more

powerful than his doubts: he was prepared to give up his life of comfort and wealth if it meant spending the rest of his days with his apothecary.

He wouldn't be the first Turner to live his life as a pauper.

He walked along the murky streets, past the blackened buildings and mud-filled gutters, past people who hobbled along with the weight of the world on their shoulders. He tried to picture how it would be when he lived around here.

He turned into Brewer Street, with East Alley up ahead of him.

His heart began to thump nervously. First, he had to confess to Kezzie that he was an engaged man. He'd been selfish and thoughtless, that much he did know. He could only hope she would find it in her heart to forgive him. He had lied to her, deceived her in the worst way. Not even a confession of being driven wild by his love for her would go halfway to explaining this madness. He was prepared to beg for her forgiveness before asking for time to break the news to his family and to let Henrietta down gently. Turning his back on his obligations and the Turner family legacy would cost him dearly but he knew she was worth it.

He wanted a life here with Kezzie, as her husband.

He wished he could be as carefree and spontaneous as she was, unconcerned with the opinions of others. Impulsive and unencumbered, she lived her life as she saw fit.

He'd spent a few days rehearsing what he was going to say, both to Kezzie and to his father. He turned into East Alley. The fog swirled around him. The familiar shop sign barely visible through the murkiness.

The mistake he made was not being strong enough or brave enough to live his life in truth.

That was going to end today.

He hoped that he could borrow a little of her strength when he faced his father's wrath. But for today, he would break the news to her that he had lied to her. He had been promised to a woman to strike a financial bargain, but that he loved Kezzie.

That he wanted her, if she would have him.

Elias was a man of logic and science.

He took in a steadying breath and pushed open the door. The man of rational thinking was about to lay his cards out and let his life fall into the hands of fate.

CHAPTER 41

Kezzie

KEZZIE PAUSED mid-pacing when the ringing of the brass bell filled the silent shop. She couldn't help the warm smile that bloomed on her face as Elias's head appeared around the edge of the door.

"Elias," she said, "I was hoping you would come tonight."

He took his time shutting the door behind him, and she didn't miss the way he seemed to wipe his hands on the edges of his overcoat.

"Good evening," he said hesitantly. "Where is everyone?"

She glanced around the shop and realised that it wasn't quite set up as it usually was. She had sent Rose home early and dispatched Bobby upstairs to entertain her sisters for the evening. The counter was clean, and everything had been stowed back into its place. The activity had kept her hands occupied but hadn't slowed down the stormy thoughts in the slightest.

"I was hoping to talk to you alone," she replied. "Lock the door and then come through to the back?"

"Very well," he exhaled shakily.

She drew back the curtain, frowning at him over her shoulder. "Is everything alright? You seem a little out of sorts."

"Yes," he said briskly, amending himself at her frown. "That is, it will be. I'm glad that you are alone. There's something I need to talk to you about."

Kezzie set the lamp on the side and lit two more so that there was a soft glow that filled the room.

Elias paced around the edge of the room as she took a seat at the small table and chairs that she'd placed inside the room for their regular evening rendezvous. The day had passed slowly as she quietly rehearsed what she needed to say to him tonight. Her heart wanted to break with the pain, thinking she wasn't going to see him again.

"Elias, you're going to wear a hole in the floor," she pointed out, echoing Rose's sentiments from a few short hours ago. "What is on your mind?"

Elias came to a stop in the centre of the room. He hesitated, his mouth opening and closing several times as he tried to find the words.

Concerned, she flowed to her feet. "Whatever is the matter?"

His gaze dropped to his shoes, and he shook his head. "I don't deserve your compassion. I don't deserve your concern. I've lied to you, Kezzie. I've lied to you for weeks now and I'm not quite sure of the words to find that sufficiently say how sorry I am."

Cold fingers of fear slid into her chest and stole her breath. "What do you mean by that? When have you lied to me?"

Grey eyes clashed with her blue ones. "I love you, Kezzie. I came here tonight to tell you my truth. That I am in love with you, but I am not the man you thought I was."

Her eyes narrowed as she searched his face, waiting for the punchline of a joke that never came. She shook her head. "What are you talking about?"

"My memory returned to me – not fully – but enough for me to know, to remember enough about my previous life on the day that I left here."

Her heart began to beat in a different way, and she knew she wasn't going to like the next words that came out of his mouth.

"I'm engaged to be married to a lady called Henrietta Winters," Elias said.

The world seemed to tilt a little underneath her feet. She stumbled backwards, gripping the edge of the table at her back.

"You're engaged?" But even as the words left her mouth, even before he nodded slowly, she knew them to be true.

It was that nagging voice in the back of her mind, urging her to ask questions about his life. It was the knowledge that he was side-stepping the more personal questions she would ask him about his day.

It explained the peculiar way he looked at her during the times he thought she wasn't looking.

For weeks, she had known that this moment would come. They couldn't have a future – the Doyle legacy put paid to it. Tonight, she was prepared to trot out all the reasons she could think of why she shouldn't be with him.

Before either of them got hurt.

But it was too late.

Her heart was breaking even though she should have been relieved because he could never have been hers in the first place.

Because she loved him, too. It had always been a futile dream, yet she couldn't help herself. She had attached herself to him when he'd not asked it of her.

He'd never promised her a thing.

"I should never have let it get this far," he explained,

eyes pleading for her understanding. "God knows I tried my hardest to stay away from you, but it was impossible to stop. You fill me, Kezzie. My head, my thoughts, my heart…"

Never in her wildest dreams did she think that he would already be promised to another woman. A shaft of pain lanced through her. In the fissures of her heart, anger bubbled.

Safe, ferocious, cleansing fury.

"If you're engaged to be married to this woman, how can you say those words to me? How can you say that you're in love with me whilst you go home to another woman and say the same words to her?"

Elias shook his head briskly and took a step towards her.

Kezzie backed up against the table behind her, her hands out to prevent him from coming any closer to her.

"It's not like that," he pleaded. "My engagement is a matter of duty, not love. My father arranged it. The Turner family needs her money…"

"So, you're a prostitute?" she finished for him. "The price of your hand might be higher than what they charge at the docks, but that makes you no better than someone using this poor woman for your own ill gains."

A muscle ticked in his jaw. "You're right, of course," he said tightly. "It's difficult when you have a father like mine."

"You're blaming him for your lies?"

A breath exploded out of his mouth. "You're twisting my words, Kezzie."

"Am I? Or am I just highlighting the unvarnished truth for you?"

Elias shook his head. "I know you're trying to make me feel worse than I do, and I'm sorry. I truly am."

"I should have seen it," she flung her hands wide. "I knew it. Deep down, I knew that you were hiding something. Rose warned me, too! What an idiot I've been, so wrapped up in trying to keep you safe from the curse and this whole time, I was the one being strung along!"

"What curse?" He frowned.

She whirled on him, her eyes blazing. "Why did you even bother coming back here, Elias? If you knew all along that you weren't free to marry, why did you lead me down the garden path?"

He advanced on her, eyes boring into hers. He kept walking until she was pressed flat against the wall, his hands planted on either side of her head. "Because I could no more stay away from you than I would deny myself the air I breathe.

"I wanted to see you, Kezzie. I was sick of talking about the mundane, the monotonous. I wanted to hear about something other than reports and projections, shipping, and government!"

His gaze moved to her mouth, parted by her ragged breathing. "I wanted to know if what I felt for you the first time that I saw you was real, or a figment of a fevered mind. I'm in love with you. I've come here tonight to tell you that I'm going to call everything off with Henrietta. Break from my family. I want to live here with you. I want to be your husband."

Kezzie let loose a bark of disbelief, filled with pain. Using both hands, she shoved him back away from her so that she could gather up her scattered thoughts. "And I'm expected to roll over in gratitude because the mighty Elias Turner declares his love? You know so much about me, yet I know very little about you. If you are ashamed of me, then why did you persist in this… this…Whatever this was between us!"

"I told you, I–"

"Please just go, Elias. Leave me in peace."

"No, Kezzie. I came here tonight to–"

"You're engaged," she reminded him, struggling to maintain her composure. "You have responsibilities. That is your life. You're level-headed and conscientious."

"What about what I need?" Elias asked, eyes filled with anguish. "What about what *we* need?"

Kezzie shook her head, tears stinging her eyes. "It doesn't matter. You must be practical here."

"Practical," Elias repeated bitterly. "That's all I've ever been. But meeting you changed that. You've shown me there's more to life than duty and obligation."

Kezzie turned back to face him, her eyes glistening. "And what do you expect me to do? You should have confessed all of this from the start and allowed me to make my own choice."

"I didn't imagine for a minute that I would love you as much as I do. I didn't think it possible that I was capable of such feelings."

She pressed her lips together to curb the trembling. Pressed ruthlessly down on the hope that swelled inside. "Do you think your father will allow you to marry a lowly apothecary like me? Someone who lives in the shadows and tends to the paupers and the homeless for free?"

Elias stepped closer, his hands gentle as they cupped her face, tilting her chin up to meet his gaze. "I don't know what he'll do," he said honestly. "But I don't care about duty. And I won't let you go without a fight."

She wrapped her hands around his wrists, felt the blood under her fingertips. A heart that she knew the beat of as well as her own. A heart that she'd nursed back to health.

Her eyes slid closed. She leaned into his touch, her body vibrating under it. It would be so easy to give in to this sickness that she was gripped in. For a moment, she allowed herself to imagine a different life, one where she and Elias could be together without fear or obligation. Until the day that the curse that had stolen her parents found its way into her world once more.

Because then she would be alone.

And he would be dead.

"I can't," she whispered.

She opened her eyes and caught the hurt that lit up in his eyes. She hardened herself against it.

"Kezzie, please–"

She drew herself up, schooling her expression into a remote one, dragging the mask of detachment into place. "No, Elias." She stepped around him. "There is no future between us."

"How can you say that?"

With a little space between them, her fluffy mind cleared. "It's the truth. I wanted you to come tonight to tell you it was over."

His mouth opened, then closed. He shook his head.

"Every man a Doyle woman marries dies young. They have one child – a girl – that is left to be raised alone. I made a promise to myself that this curse would end with me. You must leave. Go back to this Henrietta, where you belong," she added into the ensuing silence. "Go now."

"No! I refuse to leave you this way, Kezzie. I can't stop thinking about you. I don't want to stop."

Her resolve wavered, her feelings threatening to overwhelm her. "Elias, please…"

He strode across the room, drawing her up by the arms and crushing her mouth under his. Passion, hot and fast, consumed her. It would be so easy to give in. To take him in any way she could.

"Tell me you don't feel the same," he challenged as he broke the kiss. "Look me in the eye and tell me you don't care. That I mean nothing to you!"

"You lied to me. You were right. You are not the man I thought you were," she said dully, her heart shattering into pieces. "You mean nothing to me."

CHAPTER 42

*B*obby

"I suppose you're wondering what's going on," Rose commented, breaking into Bobby's thoughts.

Guiltily, Bobby quickly turned away from the window where she had been watching Kezzie make her way along East Alley, a laden basket hooked over her arm. She pulled a face and shook her head. "I wasn't thinking anything of the sort, Miss Rose," she said.

Rose gave her a look of disbelief. "Pull the other one, it will play a tune."

Bobby chuckled as she made her way back behind the shop counter.

"You don't need to look so worried about her," Rose told her. "That girl's been through worse and she came through it right enough." She handed Bobby a bowl filled with a fine powder. The scent of chamomile and lavender filled the air, the ingredients for the batch of soothing balm they were making.

"It's nothing to do with me," she said, but the knowing

look that Rose gave her told her she wasn't convinced by her denial.

Bobby knew something had happened: the mysterious Mr Turner hadn't been seen at the shop for more than a week. He had been a regular presence in the evening. Kezzie had always seemed lighter and more cheerful after his visits, and it seemed his disappearance had left a void. She was curious to know more, but this was more out of concern rather than gossip.

"She doesn't seem very happy anymore though, does she?" Bobby said quietly.

Rose's soft sigh conveyed more than words ever could. "She'll be fine. She's had her heart broken, but she's a stubborn mule, just like her mother."

Bobby added the powder to the bowl on the counter and passed the empty vessel back to Rose. "You knew her Ma well?"

Rose smiled wistfully. "I did. We became friends as young girls and stayed close until the day she died. I miss her now as much as I would a limb."

They focused on the task at hand, blending the herbs, adding fresh rosemary and mixing it into the base of beeswax and almond oil. Bobby's mind was occupied with what she could remember hearing about the lovely Ada Doyle. She knew that Kezzie's mother had been murdered.

"Did they ever find the man who killed her?"

Rose's hands stilled. For a moment, Bobby worried she had overstepped the mark until Rose said, "We know who did it, yes, but... the police would not take the word of a child over that of a man."

Bobby digested this, thinking of how she had been ignored so much as a child, too. It made her feel a deeper affinity for Kezzie and for the life she had carved out for herself.

"Doesn't matter now anyway," Rose said bitterly. "He's

been gone for years. Hopefully, he's somewhere at the bottom of the sea and long gone."

Bobby didn't wish to cast bad luck on someone, but she knew that her sentiment would be the same if the man who had killed her mother had got away with it.

"Anyway, that Mr Turner won't be coming back here," Rose said.

"You sound glad about that," Bobby teased her.

"Not glad, no. She hasn't told me the details, but it sounds like her wanting to push him away over this stupid curse was a waste of..." She caught herself and flicked Bobby a quick look.

"It's okay," Bobby reassured her softly. "I know all about the supposed curse."

They worked in silence for a few minutes before Rose spoke again. "Do you believe in it?"

Bobby considered her answer before she spoke. "I think Kezzie is magical, but I don't think she is cursed. She has far too much kindness in her."

Satisfied, Rose nodded.

"I'm not sure that man was right for Kezzie. They're from different worlds, you see. Kezzie won't change to fit in anywhere where she's not welcome. That's what makes her so unique. She's always walked her own path," Rose turned to her, "a bit like you."

"Me?" Bobby looked up, surprised.

"Yes," Rose nodded. "What happened to that young man Gertrude told me about, the one who was sweet on you and helped you get that place before you came here?"

Bobby felt the blush drift across her face. Rose and Gertie had formed a strong bond already, and she should have known that Gertie would have shared this news. She knew it was futile to try and deny it. "He was my friend, nothing more."

"Was?"

Bobby nodded. "He's not been to see me since I sent him away."

"And why did you send him away?"

Bobby stalled, her mouth twisting.

"Bobby?" Rose prompted.

"My ma once said that my father was a happy young man when they first met, and that he changed after they got married. He was a hard, cruel man."

"I see," Rose said, "and you're afraid that this Liam will turn out to be the same as your father?"

Bobby didn't answer, though her silence spoke volumes.

Rose sighed. "The trouble with you young 'uns is that you are all too scared of your own shadows. Here," she held out a pot of hand cream. "Gertie mentioned that this Liam always has trouble with his hands. This is very good for cracked skin. Why don't you take it to him, and use it as a way to start a conversation? That way, you might be able to make friends with him again?"

Bobby shook her head, remembering the last conversation she had with Liam. She'd left the invitation open for him to return. The fact that he hadn't told her all she needed to know.

Rose pushed the pot into her hands anyway. "You know as well as the next person that life can change on a sixpence, Bobby. And we need all the friends we can get in this life. Go and make your peace with him. At least this way you'll know one way or the other what kind of man he is."

Bobby looked down at the pot of cream in her hands, her heart pounding with indecision.

Sighing, she set the pot down on the side. "I want to finish this batch," she said, "and besides I'm not sure it's possible to mend what has been broken."

CHAPTER 43

Elias.

Elias leaned against the window of his father's study, staring out across Belgrave Square. The square was a far cry from the frantic activity he'd observed in Whitechapel. It had a leisurely atmosphere, with the occasional elegant carriage drawn by sleek, well-groomed horses. Gentlemen in top hats and ladies wearing the height of Parisian fashion exited the carriages and gracefully entered their opulent townhouses.

Even in the late afternoon sun, the pale Portland stone houses presented an imposing facade, adorned with intricate carvings and black, wrought iron balconies. Large windows along the brickwork were framed by heavy curtains. Gas lamps lined the streets, and their glass globes would soon bathe the square in a soft, muted light that spoke of wealth and privilege.

Behind him, his father and the company accountant were deep in discussion. Elias had tuned out a while ago, bored and disheartened by the incessant monotony of his father's greedy nature. The study they were in was majestic, with rich mahogany panelling lining the walls. The shelves were filled with leather-bound books and various artefacts from his uncle's travels, giving the room an air of scholarly sophistication.

"Elias, are you listening?" Albert demanded.

Elias looked over his shoulder, meeting his father's stern gaze. The wide mahogany desk that dominated the room was cluttered with papers and ledgers. The accountant, Mr Ferguson, was a delicate man with a pale complexion and a nervous disposition. He sat across from Albert, staring up at Elias with a furrowed brow over his spectacles.

"Of course," Elias lied. His mind had been miles away, wallowing in self-pity.

"This business concerns you too," Albert reminded him, his eyes glinting with irritation.

"Mm-hm," Elias turned back to the window, his jaw tightening. He could feel his father's frustration mounting, punctuated by a long-suffering sigh. He watched a couple through, linked arm in arm, smiling over a shared joke as they made their way down the quiet street. It only deepened his sense of despair.

The accountant cleared his throat. "Once Miss Winters' funds are transferred, things will look a lot healthier."

"And when is the earliest that we can access them?" Albert asked impatiently. "It's less than a week to go until the wedding."

Elias listened as they calmly and clinically dissected Henrietta's funds like a pair of vultures. It made him feel sullied, as Kezzie's accusing words about prostitution echoed in his head. Thoughts of her caused him physical pain, and he dug his thumb and forefinger into his eyes, uncaring of the tender skin around the injury there. He didn't much care about the funds, but he couldn't sit back and let them feast on the bones of Henrietta's inheritance any longer.

Elias turned abruptly. "I wonder if I might speak with my father in private, Mr Ferguson?"

The accountant hesitated, dividing a look between father and son. He set down the papers in his hand and stood, leaving the room without further ado.

Albert watched his son carefully, narrowing his eyes. "What now?" he asked, his tone clipped.

"I cannot do this," Elias said, letting the anger into his voice. He indicated the desk with a wave of his hand. "I cannot listen to another minute of this. You are talking about directing this woman's funds before we've even said our vows. It smacks of avarice."

Albert rolled his eyes. "Not this again. We've been through this before."

"Yes, this again," Elias insisted.

Albert slapped the papers in his hand on top of the desk. "You have seen the state of the business accounts, have you not? Must I remind you once more that you agreed to this proposal?"

"Under duress," Elias pointed out, "well, no more. I simply won't marry her."

Albert stared at his son before exploding with fury. "Of course, you're going to marry her! Have you lost your mind?"

"No, quite the opposite, in fact," Elias said, holding his father's enraged stare. "I went along with this farce because I thought it was the right thing to do. But Henrietta deserves more from me than just granting me access to her funds or having her money misappropriated."

"Misappropriated!" Albert spluttered. "How dare you! The money will be used for—"

"I don't care what it is used for!" Elias yelled back. "I am not watching you squander away more money on poor business decisions. It's already started with you wanting to invest in railways in America. I told you, it's a shaky decision at best."

Albert's eyes narrowed dangerously. "Perhaps that

bump on the head knocked all the common sense out of you," he growled. "Either that or your little witch has hexed you."

Elias stilled. "What did you just say to me?"

Albert smirked, drawing out the moment with a smug look. "Do you think I don't know where you've been sneaking off to all these nights? I know exactly where you've been, my boy. I said to sow your wild oats so you would get her out of your system. Perhaps I underestimated how gullible you are. And if you think I would welcome some harlot like her under my roof and into this family, you have another thing coming."

"Father," Elias warned, his voice low and dangerous.

Albert merely laughed mockingly. "I am not going to let you break off this engagement because you have these grand illusions that you are in love with some skivvy from Whitechapel."

Anger lit his eyes so they blazed. "What if I am in love with her? What then?"

"Once the wedding certificate is signed and the money is in the bank," Albert said, "I don't happen to care where you choose to dabble. But you will not do anything to jeopardise this deal before it is done."

"You can make all the demands you want to, Father," Elias said as reasonably as he could. "Henrietta deserves better than to have everything taken from her and I'll have no part in it."

Albert's face grew redder. Elias found himself holding his breath as he waited for the next insult to be flung out. Instead, Albert strolled around the edge of the desk and dropped unceremoniously into the leather chair, which creaked in protest.

Calmly, Albert leaned back in the chair and stretched his legs out in front of him, linking his fingers across his middle. "You *will* do as you are told," he said icily, "or I'll see to it that your little witch's cavern in East Alley is burned to the ground."

Elias went cold.

He didn't want to believe his father was capable of such ruthlessness. He could call the man's bluff, but Kezzie was Elias's Achilles' heel, and Albert knew it. He also knew that Elias wouldn't risk harming a hair on her head. "If you touch her, I will never forgive you."

Albert's eyes went flat. "I don't need your forgiveness, son. I just need your compliance."

Elias took a deep, shaky breath as he searched for a way out of this. Elias had brokered many a deal, manoeuvring his opponents into a corner so that they had no choice but to agree to his terms. It pained him to know that he had clearly inherited these traits from his conniving father.

Albert smiled a cold, triumphant smile. "You have your mother's dramatic tendencies which make you predictable. You will marry Henrietta. You will attend the engagement dinner and fawn over her as if she is the best thing since the invention of the wheel. You will play the part and you will march that girl down the aisle. And you will stay away from East Alley until then. Do you understand?"

Rage fumed inside him. He'd never known he was capable of such murderous loathing until just at that moment.

∽

"Miss Winters to see you, sir," Cassidy announced.

Elias glanced up from the book that he had in his lap. He'd quickly opened it to maintain the ruse of reading as he heard the footsteps approaching outside the library, but his surprise at seeing Henrietta was genuine.

"Henrietta!" He rose fluidly to his feet.

"Hello, Elias," she said, pausing to hand over her gloves to the butler.

"Did we have an arrangement to meet that I've forgotten about?"

Henrietta tutted. "Do I need an appointment to come and visit my fiancé?"

Elias allowed a small smile. "No, I suppose not. Cassidy, may we have some tea, please?"

Cassidy inclined his head and left the room silently. Henrietta marched further into the room, stretching out her hands to the fire that simmered in the hearth. "I can't wait for the day when they can put one of these inside a carriage," she said with a smile over her shoulder.

She wore a deep blue satin dress that was cinched at the waist. Her hair was artfully arranged so that the strategic curls framed her pretty face. She was breathtakingly beautiful, with a quick smile and intelligent eyes. He had to remind himself that he should be grateful that at least he wouldn't be married to a dullard.

"Why are you really here?"

Henrietta turned with a knowing smile before she let out a breath and shook her head. "Very well. You saw straight through my ruse. Your father wrote to me, with a rather interesting letter."

Of all the things, he'd expected her to say, that hadn't been one of them.

Jimmy, the footman, carried the tray into the room and Elias dismissed him so that they could be alone. The brief interlude allowed him to gather his thoughts a little more and he could only wonder as to what games his father was playing this time.

He fixed her a cup of tea and carried it over to her. She accepted it and sipped at it daintily, waiting until he had filled a cup of his own and taken the seat opposite hers.

"Your father alluded to the fact that you might be having second thoughts. He instructed me to visit with you, to reassure you that our union will be a wise choice."

Elias knew that he shouldn't be surprised. After the explosive argument yesterday afternoon, it seemed that

Albert had wasted no time in ensuring the odds that Elias was going to go through with this sham marriage.

Henrietta set the cup down and made the short walk to join him on the sofa. Elias couldn't be sure if she had deliberately chosen to sit so close to him but as their thighs met, he knew that the contact was more than an accident. It was a suggestion of what she was offering him. She took his hand in hers, a smile crinkling around her eyes. Elias felt a pang in his heart, wanting to let her know that his heart belonged to another, that he could never love her in the way that she deserved.

"I know that we don't know each other very well," she said gently. "But I want to assure you that I am going into this with my eyes wide open. I know that it will take time for the two of us to get used to each other."

He studied their linked fingers. The smooth skin of her hands was in direct contrast to the strong, capable fingers that had touched him so often whilst he was healing.

She didn't know the extent of their lies. That his family was broke.

To the outside world, it appeared that the Turner family had it all – money, wealth, fancy houses, and fancy dinners in them.

It was all a lie.

Within months, everything that his uncle had built would collapse without her wealth. He had to remind himself that he was offering Henrietta something, too – status, family, stability.

She prompted him to look at her. "If times were a little different, perhaps we could have spent more time together alone. We could have got to know each other the way a man and a woman should before committing to a lifetime with each other." She paused, her pink tongue moistening her lips, drawing his gaze, before she spoke again. "You might not love me now, Elias.

Your heart might belong to another and, if that was

the true reason for your father's letter, I want you to know that I don't hold any malice towards you. We are all fallible creatures, after all. By joining your family, it means that we are beginning to build something strong together. This is the start of something rewarding and valuable. I do hope that you can see it."

Elias wanted to tell her then and there that he couldn't love her, that his heart belonged to another and that he would never be able to be the husband that she deserved. As if to dispel any doubt of her feelings towards him, she leaned forward and laid her open mouth on his.

CHAPTER 44

Kezzie

"Agnes!" Rose exclaimed warmly once the brass bell had quietened down. "What brings you to our quiet part of town?"

Agnes Powell had a permanently stern expression of a woman who didn't mince her words. Along with her husband, she ran a successful drug shop in Marylebone. Much like Kezzie, Ronnie Powell came from a long line of chemists interested in helping others. Kezzie wasn't sure if Agnes liked the notoriety or the income that she'd married into.

She wore a dark green dress with a modest neckline, and the full skirt reached down to her ankles. Small pearl buttons ran up to her throat, and she wore a matching mother-of-pearl brooch. Her smart jacket featured a high collar and decorative buttons, cinched at the waist to enhance her silhouette. She carried a small wicker basket over one arm, though it was currently empty.

"Good afternoon, Rose, Kezzie," Agnes nodded briskly. "I do hope I'm not disturbing you."

An array of pots, jars, and matching lids were scattered across the counters. They had had a brisk morning of trade and hadn't yet had a chance to catch up. Kezzie tried not to bristle at the disapproval creasing Agnes' features.

Kezzie wiped her hands on her apron. "Not at all, Agnes. What brings you by?"

In the past, the Powell's had called upon Kezzie for more unusual ingredients that strayed from the typical ones a druggist would use. It was known in the area that Kezzie and her recipes did not follow traditional methods, with her grandfather mixing a blend of modern and homoeopathic remedies effectively.

Agnes didn't smile. "My call is business-related, though I have no need to buy anything from you today."

Kezzie raised her brows. "I see."

"There's a warning being circulated amongst the druggists and the chemists in the city. It's filtered down from Manchester."

Kezzie's frown deepened. But it was Rose who asked, "What kind of warning?"

"There's been a flurry of purchases of certain products. Someone is buying them up in large quantities, leading to a city-wide shortage. Antimony and prussic acid mostly," Agnes said grimly.

Immediately, Kezzie felt a ripple of concern.

"Who is buying poisons?" Rose asked.

"I'm not too certain. We sell a lot of it, as you can well imagine, being situated where we are in the city, so we haven't noticed too much more of an increase in demand. I know that you are slightly off the beaten path back here. Not everybody knows that you're here, so I am simply passing along the message for you to be on your guard," Agnes explained.

As required, they kept records of everything that was purchased, including the date, the person's name, the quantity of the product, and what it was they were purchasing. Kezzie hadn't noticed, nor could she remember, anyone trying to buy enough poison to do any great harm.

Apart from one person.

"Should we be on the lookout for anyone in particular?" Kezzie asked.

Agnes shook her head briskly. "I have no further information other than we are to be on the lookout for anybody trying to purchase poison in great quantities. Apparently, chemists from other cities are also on alert because of the increase in purchases."

"Well, we appreciate the warning," Rose said. "As you said, we are not on the usual circuit and mostly serve local people. The benefit of this is that we can spot any discrepancies quickly and put a stop to them."

"Well," Agnes smiled, but it didn't quite reach her eyes, "I shall leave you to it then."

The doorbell clanged, and Kezzie watched Agnes hurry away along the cobbles.

"What do you think that's all about then?" Kezzie asked.

Rose shrugged. "It was kind of her to give us the warning, but I don't think it's anything to be concerned about."

Kezzie wondered what had happened to Eunice Joy. The woman hadn't returned ever since the day Kezzie had refused to sell her the poison. She pondered whether her emotional visit had any relevance to this situation, but then the door opened, and a young man staggered in, a limp child in his arms, putting paid to any further brooding.

It wasn't until later that evening, once the shop was closed and the street beyond was quiet, that Kezzie's mind returned to Agnes' peculiar warning. The girls were fast asleep in their beds, but Kezzie couldn't sleep.

She made her way downstairs, holding the candle out in front of her to illuminate the steps down to the shop level. Cold air swirled around her feet, sending goosebumps chasing across her skin.

She wasn't sure what was niggling at her mind, but checking the stock levels would surely ease her troubled thoughts. More than half an hour passed, studying the books, and weighing out the poisons, before she sat back, with cold realisation chilling her more than the evening air.

Actual stock levels were much lower than where her books said they should be.

She had been particularly careful in monitoring Bobby measuring out the poisons and writing it down correctly, so she was almost certain it couldn't have been a mistake.

Somewhere, somehow, there was a huge discrepancy in her stock levels of antimony.

CHAPTER 45

Kezzie

"You're being overly cautious," Rose said with a shake of her head. "Reading more into it than needs be. You have a new assistant. It's simple to make a mistake. Perhaps it was me," Rose added. "My eyes not being what they were when I was a girl."

Kezzie had already tried to ease her worries by telling herself the same thing.

She'd questioned Bobby more than once until she was certain the poor girl was about to cry. But Kezzie wouldn't settle.

"The amount that is missing could land all of us in hot water," she stated tersely. "I have every need to be concerned about this."

Rose expelled a breath as if she could blow the concerns away. "Then go to the police. Mention this woman's name. Tell them you're worried."

"How can I go to them and say that?" Kezzie exclaimed, horrified. "What if Eunice came to her senses when she left here? I haven't seen anything in the paper about a murder by poison!"

Rose quirked a brow. "When did you last read the papers?"

Kezzie's mouth flattened. "If you're going to call my bluff each time I raise a valid point…"

Rose chuckled, the sound echoing in Kezzie's ears as she slammed out of the shop and down the street. The rain had thickened the fog to a soup consistency. The sky was a murky grey, the fog pressing the coal smoke closer to the ground. Kezzie hiked up her skirts to leap over the deep, dirty puddles that had formed along the gutters and in the uneven pavement, ducking her head against the steady downpour. She wished she'd not been as impetuous as to come out without her woollen coat.

Whitechapel Road was alive with commotion despite the inclement weather. Vendors bellowed from underneath their makeshift oilskin awnings, their voices joining the chatter of the hagglers and the bellow of children as they danced in the rain.

Stalls lined the street, selling everything from fresh fruit and meat pies to clothing and used pots, repaired and repurposed for the working community who couldn't buy new.

Carriages rattled along the road, bouncing out of the muddy ruts formed by those wheels gone before them. Drivers hunkered deep into their coats; their faces obscured by the brims of their hats.

A steady stream of people flowed out of the train station ahead. In the doorway, tucked back against the wall and under the narrow eaves, Kezzie spied the newspaper stall.

Bill Saunders yelled out into the gloomy day, squawking about an escaped prisoner and bathers being attacked in the sea by a killer octopus.

"Kezzie Doyle!" the newspaperman's toothy grin expanded as she hurried up to him. "As I live an' breathe!"

"Hello, Bill, what a day!"

"Is it raining?" He shot her a wink. "I hardly notice."

"Have you got the *Sentinel*?"

"'Course, love, 'ere you go," He expertly rolled up the paper, held it out. "Thruppence, please, love. 'Ow's them nippers of yours? All settlin' in now?"

Kezzie handed him the copper coin, wondering when Bobby and her sisters had become 'hers'. She smiled anyway. "They're doing very well, thank you. Bobby is going to make an excellent apothecary one day."

"I 'ear that young 'un is courtin' someone from dan' Mile End?"

"Lydia, yes," Kezzie waggled the paper at him, turning to leave. "Thanks, Bill. Say hello to Myra for me!"

"Will do, love!" Bill waved her away, already bawling to the passengers hurrying out of the station, their heads bowing against the rain.

By the time she got back to the shop, the paper was stained dark and sodden, despite her tucking it against her body as best as she could.

She ignored Rose' knowing smirk as she let herself into the shop, walking straight into the back room. She stripped off her damp shawl and stoked the fire, poking at the coals until the flames hungrily flicked over them once more. As her shivering subsided, she spread out the papers, hoping that they'd dry in the warmer air. Most of the print was smudged, rendering it illegible. Two of the pages tore as she was turning them.

"Anything?"

She had been so focused on her task, scanning the articles she could see, that she'd not heard Rose come in behind her.

Kezzie looked back at her. She shook her head. "Not from the bits I can still read."

Rose gave them some privacy, drawing the curtain across, leaving Bobby to deal with the customers. "I was only teasing. It'll be me or Bobby that has made a mistake. You're working yourself into a lather over nothing."

Kezzie dragged her eyes up from the paper. "All it takes is someone using one of our bottles, and we will be in so much trouble. What will happen to you if they arrest me? Bobby and the girls need me–"

"And if I lay golden eggs, we'd be rich," Rose rubbed a hand between her tense shoulders. "You're adding two and two together and coming up with twenty."

Kezzie sighed softly. "I know. It's just… what if I knew something and said nothing?"

"Would it make you feel better if we reported this Joy woman? But we got someone else to do it?"

Kezzie looked back at the paper, contemplating that idea. She had Eunice's lodging address in her ledger. It would be simple enough to…

Her heart stuttered in her chest as a familiar name caught her eye.

She must have made a noise because Rose leaned in. "What is it? Do you see her?"

Pain twisted her stomach into knots as she scanned the article. Each word felt like acid dripping on her heart.

Engagement Announcement

Engagement of Mr Elias Turner to Miss Henrietta Winters

It is with great pleasure that Mr and Mrs Albert Turner of Belgrave Square announce the engagement of their esteemed son Mr Elias George Turner to Henrietta Winters.

. . .

Miss Winters, a woman of exceptional grace and charm, is renowned for her benevolent work in the name of her late parents. Mr Turner, a gentleman of notable standing and distinction, is actively involved in the family business, Turner Enterprises, and is highly regarded for his contributions to commerce and society.

The engagement will be celebrated in a private gathering on September Thirteenth at the Turner family residence with many close friends and associates in attendance. The union is eagerly anticipated by all who know them.

The wedding is scheduled to take place the following day at All Saints church, Belgrave.

Mr and Mrs Turner extend their heartfelt thanks for the warm wishes and many congratulations they have received.

CHAPTER 46

Bobby

It seemed to Bobby that each of the Byrne boys had the same quick smile and sparkling green eyes. And each was just as charming as Liam.

Except, Callum, who was currently watching her out of his one remaining open eye and looking at her as if she was the devil incarnate. "That burns like blazes," he muttered.

"It's meant to," Bobby murmured, "It's vinegar to clean the wound." She threaded cotton and passed the tip of the needle through the candle flame.

"And where exactly do you think you'll be sticking that?" His eye wheeled wildly to his brother, seeking support.

He got none. "Sit at peace, will you?" Liam muttered to him, dubiously.

Bobby tried to ignore the little fizzes of pleasure that burst inside her whenever Liam's gaze met hers. She couldn't quite pinpoint if he was happy to see her, as he was still annoyed that his younger brother had cut open his eye after consuming a belly full of beer down at the Talbot.

Bobby held the needle ready for Kezzie, but when the needle wasn't picked up, Bobby glanced at the other woman. Her gaze was fixed on a spot on the floor in the corner, her mind far from the back room of the apothecary shop. "Miss?" Bobby prompted.

Kezzie sucked in a breath, blinking several times. She quickly apologised and took the needle from Bobby, speaking kindly to Callum, who squirmed and whined as Kezzie brought the needle through the skin to close the wound.

Bobby knew enough to realise that Kezzie wasn't fully focused on the task. Usually, she took her time to calm her patients so they would sit still for the procedure. Today, she appeared to be simply going through the motions.

Not that Bobby blamed her.

Rose had let slip the previous evening that Kezzie had seen an article announcing the engagement of the mysterious Mr Turner and had filled in the rest of the gaps.

Of course, she would be distracted. Anyone with eyes could see that her boss lit up whenever Mr Turner was near her. She was in love with him, and now he was marrying another.

Kezzie applied the lavender gel to the three stitches, murmuring instructions for Liam to ensure that his brother kept the wound clean for as long as he possibly could. With that, she promptly left the back room, and a few seconds later, Bobby heard her footsteps as Kezzie ascended to the upper floors.

"Is it done?" Callum whimpered, his eyes still shut tight.

Bobby patted his shoulder and gave him a reassuring smile. "It is. Until next time when you're too drunk to stand up and fall into a wall again."

Callum belched and shook his head. "I'm never touching another drop for as long as I live."

Liam chuckled and helped his brother down off the table. "And I'll be a monkey's uncle if that ever happens. How much?"

Bobby refused payment from him. "I will cover the cost of what was used. It's the least I can do after everything you did for me," she finished with a warm smile as she followed the pair out into the shop.

Liam steadied his brother through the open door, watching Bobby carefully. She wasn't sure if he was about to say something profound, but at that moment, Lydia bustled past them both.

"Liam!" Lydia exclaimed. Her hair was neatly pinned back into a pleat at the back of her neck. She wore a smart-looking plain black dress and black leather shoes, looking nothing like the street urchin he'd helped only a month or so before. "Is Charlie with you?"

"No," Liam said. "I had to bring this wee dolt here to get his eyeball stitched back up. I shall tell Charlie I've seen you."

"Thank you," Lydia said warmly. "I can't be seeing him until my next half day off, which is a week on Sunday. Needless to say, I'm very much looking forward to it."

Liam tugged his cap and gave Bobby a little nod.

Lydia watched him go. "What was that all about?"

"What was all about?" Bobby had to drag her eyes away from the street and Liam's retreating back.

"I do wish you two would sort yourselves out," Lydia clucked her tongue impatiently. "Everyone here can see that you're sweet on each other."

"Hear, hear," Rose muttered from in the corner.

Bobby wasn't about to get into a denial game with either of them right at this moment. "Did you get it?"

Lydia nodded and held out the paper parcel, the string dangling from her extended fingers. "Make sure that it doesn't get any damage, or it'll come out of my wage. It's the same size as mine, as that's all that Mrs Sweet had in the stockroom. Mind you get it back as soon as you're done with it, too."

Bobby took the parcel and gave her sister a grateful smile. "I will."

"I'd best get back. I left them all having their lunch." Lydia flew back through the door and out along the cobbles.

Rose was watching the exchange from behind the counter. "What's going on? What's in there?"

Bobby considered the parcel resting in her palms. "Nothing exciting. Just an idea I had last night. Could I be excused to pop upstairs and see Kezzie?"

Elbows on the counter, Rose's thin grey brows arched inquisitively as she pursed her lips. "Not until you tell me exactly what's going on."

CHAPTER 47

Kezzie

THE PALE FRONT of the townhouse in Belgrave Square gleamed under the soft glow of the street lamps. Elegant carriages lined along one side of the street in a neat row. Their occupants emerged in a flurry of silken satins, their animated chatter drifting through the cool evening air. Footmen stood on either side of the front door, others still helping the ladies down and guiding them inside the brightly lit house.

Kezzie hurried through the pools of light, keeping to the shadows as much as possible. Following the instructions, she darted down the narrow alley at the rear of the house.

Here, the atmosphere was remarkably different.

The servants were engaged in a frantic dance, cigarette smoke thickening the air. She cut through them, her heart pounding as she prayed that Lydia would be waiting where she said she would be.

Perhaps it was a morbid curiosity that had brought her here.

Ever since she'd seen the engagement announcement in the paper, she realised that up until that point she had been waiting for Elias to walk back through her shop door and declare his undying love for her. But such romantic notions didn't happen, at least not to people like her. Still, here she was, stepping into the lion's den.

Lydia emerged from the shadows, her eyes alight with excitement. "The housekeeper here is Mrs Blackstone. She and my housekeeper, Mrs Sweet, are firm friends, but you are under strict instructions not to speak to the family."

Kezzie swallowed nervously.

When Bobby had presented the borrowed maid's uniform earlier that day, Kezzie had been horrified, even as the plan had been laid out. Lydia could ensure that she had access to the house. Perhaps if she could just talk to him, he would change his mind...

Kezzie had refused the very idea.

She had lit into Bobby for interfering in her life. Bobby had set the parcel on the table, an apology dying on her lips as she fled back down the stairs.

But the uniform had sat on the table, almost mocking her along with Bobby's last words, "Aren't you a little bit curious about what she looks like?"

And so, Kezzie had gone against her better judgement, following the need to know who it was that had captured Elias's heart so entirely and replaced her. Now, dressed in the maid's uniform, Kezzie followed Lydia into the back door of the house. The servants' quarters were a hive of activity, with maids and footmen hurrying about. The clatter and chaos of the kitchen filled the air, scented with the steam of roasted meats.

Lydia explained as they walked, "There are only two footmen and one maid usually at the Turner residence, as well as a cook and a butler. Mrs Sweet isn't impressed with such a small household staff, which means either the Turners are tight-fisted or they are not as well-off as they'd have you believe. They've had to draft in extra staff for tonight's party. Hang your cloak up there," Lydia pointed to the row of pegs high up on the wall.

"Right, this is as far as I dare take you. That's Mrs Blackstone up ahead. I'm certain she'll give you your orders. Good luck!" Lydia disappeared as quickly as she had arrived, leaving Kezzie to navigate this world of strangers on her own.

The housekeeper, Mrs Blackstone, was an austere woman with a no-nonsense attitude. She barked out instructions to various staff who raced about. Kezzie's doubts plagued her until the sound of it reached a fever pitch. Only the footmen were allowed in the dining room to serve: the maids were to fetch and carry the dirty dishes down the narrow back stairs, ensuring that the refilled silver platters were placed back in the serving hatch.

It felt like she'd been in the house, marching up and down the narrow stone steps, for days.

The sit-down meal concluded, and the guests began to spill out into the main salon. Following instructions, her heart in her throat as the salon began to fill with more guests, Kezzie felt out of sorts, exposed among these people despite the starched black uniform and white cap that weren't much of a disguise. But she needn't have worried: no one paid her much attention, allowing her to keep to the shadows as she had done for most of her life.

Hidden in plain sight, shielded by the other guests, she heard rather than saw Albert Turner's booming voice carrying across the crowd of people. Standing on her tiptoes at the edge of the room, she caught her first glimpse of Elias's father.

He was a robust-looking man with a flushed face and neatly combed thick grey hair. Dressed in an elegant dinner suit, he looked every bit the successful businessman she had imagined. The sedate woman at his side was undeniably Elias's mother – she had the same striking colouring and structure.

Heart thumping with nausea, she pressed her fingers to her lips as the applause continued when the happy couple stepped through from the dining room and into the salon.

Elias looked dashing. He was dressed the part, with his starched white collar standing out against his olive skin. He had a smile fixed on his face. Her heart ached at the sight of him, his hair styled neatly back off his face.

Had she hoped he'd be heartbroken? Instead, he was smiling, turning to draw the woman at his side further into the room.

Kezzie's heart stopped. Mouth slack, the sounds of the room seemed to shift under her feet.

She stared at the stunning bride-to-be.

She turned away, her vision blurring through tears. She pushed through the sea of people as the weight of realisation crashed over her.

Not just because the other woman was breathtakingly beautiful in a deep, wine-red satin gown, but because she recognised her.

CHAPTER 48

Kezzie

SHE SHOULD HAVE SAID SOMETHING.

She stood in the back room of the apothecary shop. An array of herbs and powders was spread out across the counter, though she could no longer remember what she'd started making early that morning. She had hidden away for most of the day until Rose turned the key in the lock and demanded to know what was wrong with her.

The silence stretched on. Bobby, Gertie, and Rose all stood in the room behind her.

"Tell me, what was I meant to do?" Kezzie asked the wall, her voice trembling. "Was I supposed to run up to the happy couple and wish them all the luck in the world?"

Today was his wedding day.

Humiliation and anger vibrated through her blood.

She couldn't remember the walk home from Belgrave Square. She hadn't slept all night, driven crazy by the endless thoughts that rolled through her mind like a spinning kaleidoscope.

She gripped the edges of the counter. "I was only meant to be there to have a look," she reminded them all quietly.

She hadn't noticed the tears slipping through her lashes until they plopped onto the counter, mixing with the dried herbs and dust.

"You should've said something to him—anything," Rose began, but the sudden pounding on the front door startled them all into silence. With an impatient sigh, Rose peeked through the curtains.

"Kezzie," Rose's tone pulled Kezzie's attention around. "You'd best come out here to deal with this."

She stepped through the curtain, leaving Bobby and Kezzie to exchange a puzzled look.

Kezzie wanted to shut the world out. She wasn't sure she had it in her to deal with another crisis right at that moment. But she didn't have that luxury.

She wiped her eyes, sucked in a deep breath, and expelled it in a huff. When she stepped through the curtain, her heart leapt into her throat. For a moment, she was transported back ten years.

She was the same young girl standing there, staring up at the crisp navy uniforms and the shiny buttons of a police uniform. But the policeman standing before her was no longer young—he had streaks of grey flashing out from his temples. The smile he gave her seemed genuine.

"Miss Doyle," Mr Jenkinson nodded politely. There was a younger version of him standing near the door, watching them all nervously.

"Hello," Kezzie husked, stepping further into the shop.

"I'm terribly sorry to disturb you," he said. "I know the door was locked."

"It's fine," Kezzie made her way behind the counter, almost like pulling on her armour. "How can I help you today?"

He cleared his throat. "I'm certain you've heard the rumours by now. It seems that each druggist or apothecary we've visited in this town is more apprised of this situation than we are." His tone indicated amusement rather than annoyance, and Kezzie's estimation of him rose. His predecessor wouldn't have liked being on the back foot. "We're on the lookout for anyone who is buying up poisons in great quantities."

Kezzie's blood ran cold.

The antimony discrepancies. She'd forgotten all about them. *Is that why the police were here?*

"Agnes Powell actually informed us of this the day before yesterday," Rose nodded.

She avoided meeting the weight of Rose's gaze which she could feel boring into her from the other side of the room.

"That's good," the policeman nodded. "We have reports of a significant increase in purchases of antimony. Given your position and your knowledge, we wanted to see if you had any information that might help us track down who's been making these purchases."

"We keep meticulous records of all sales, especially those involving dangerous substances," Rose informed them primly. "We'd be happy to provide you with those records."

The policeman's face crinkled with a deep smile. "That would be very helpful, thank you. We're visiting as many people as we can today because we have more information that emerged from the station. There's been a survivor."

"A survivor of what exactly?" Rose asked.

Kezzie was grateful, as her mouth was too dry for words.

"I'm sure you've guessed by now that we're looking for someone who is poisoning people. This case was an attempted murder," the policeman replied gravely. "This criminal is clever. We think she's been working a scam for a good few years now."

"She?" Rose asked.

The officer nodded. "Yes, a woman, as most poisoners are," he reached into his pocket and pulled out a piece of paper. "She scams men into marrying her. The husbands die suddenly on their wedding night or just after, leaving her to inherit everything. This witness has been a breakthrough in the case. We have an image, sketched from the description that the survivor was able to give us." He held out the piece of paper towards Rose.

Kezzie stared at it as if it were a snake. The face was distinctly female, with a pert nose and a full mouth.

"If you have any information or if you recognise her—"

Kezzie had stopped listening.

The thunder of blood in her ears drowned out the rest of his words. The image might have been in black ink, but she knew those features anywhere. She'd seen them standing right here in the shop, berating her for not supporting her in the effort to get rid of her abusive husband.

She had also seen them less than twelve hours ago, dressed in a fine wine-red gown, standing next to Elias.

Her hands shook as she took the piece of paper. The likeness was uncanny.

"Miss Doyle? Have you seen this woman?" Mr Jenkinson asked.

"Kezzie?" Rose's voice cut through the fog in her mind.

Kezzie blinked, trying to focus on the policeman's words.

"Do you recognise her?" He pressed.

Kezzie swallowed hard, forcing herself to meet his gaze. "Yes," she whispered. "I know her. I know her as Eunice Joy. And I know exactly where she is."

CHAPTER 49

*E*lias

"How is it all going downstairs? Is everything shipshape?"

Elias wasn't particularly concerned about the answer, but he thought that the enquiry was perhaps what a groom about to get married would ask.,

Jimmy, the footman who had been commandeered as his valet for the day. "Shaping up to be quite the day, sir," he murmured, smoothing out the back of his vest. "Your father has drafted in several staff for the day, of course, which seems to have added to Mr Cassidy's woes."

"I see," Elias's lips twitched. "We must be sure to thank Mr Cassidy for the extra work this day has caused for everyone."

"It's no trouble, sir. Miss Winters has already been down to the kitchens and thanked us on your behalf."

Elias held his arm at shoulder height to allow Jimmy to attach the cufflinks to his shirt. "Miss Winters was in the kitchens?"

"Oh yes, sir," Jimmy threaded the cufflink through. "Cook has everything under control, of course, but it appeared that Miss Winters wanted to make sure everything with the dishes was perfect for your day."

Elias hadn't had much experience with brides, but perhaps it was normal for the bride to be downstairs with the servants on her wedding day. That said, nothing appeared normal about this wedding day. Henrietta had no family to speak of and so had spent the night in Belgrave Square on the opposite side of the house.

She was much older than many other blushing brides.

Elias held the opposite arm up and then allowed Jimmy to help him with his jacket. Jimmy used a black bristle brush, swiping at his back and shoulders to remove any flecks of lint remaining and ensure that his morning coat was immaculate.

He inspected his appearance in the mirror. He had given much thought as he was growing up to his wedding day. His life had been business and finance. But he didn't think his wedding day would be one filled with resentment and dread.

He sighed and nodded at his reflection. "Let's get this over with then, shall we?"

He was partway along the landing when the commotion downstairs became more audible. He rounded the top of the staircase and heard the loud, angry voices clashing in what sounded like a heated confrontation.

As he began to descend the staircase, his father's protests grew in volume. Elias froze when he saw several dark police uniforms standing in the foyer. They looked absurd standing amongst the explosions of flowers and orange blossom that covered every surface.

"What is going on here?" he called out.

Albert, too incensed to pay any heed to his son, continued berating the policeman in front of him. "This is utterly ridiculous! I've never heard anything so absurd in all my born days!"

"If you could just let Miss Winters know that we are here to see her," the policeman in front of him said evenly.

"I will do no such thing! This is my son's wedding day. Have you no compassion?"

"I'm certain if you calm yourself, sir, and listen to what I am trying to tell you, all will become clear, and you will be grateful—"

"Hello?" Elias injected enough steel into his voice to cut through the melee. "Can I help? What is going on here?"

"This imbecile is laying the most atrocious accusations against your fiancée, Elias," Albert spoke to him though his eyes did not deviate from the police officer in front of him.

The policeman's attention was now on Elias. "Mr Elias Turner?"

"That's correct," Elias said, noting how the policeman seemed relieved at his confirmation.

"We need to speak to Miss Winters as a matter of urgency."

Albert waved his hands furiously. "They won't tell me what the issue is regarding, and they won't leave until they've spoken to Henrietta."

Elias surveyed the group in front of him. "Jimmy," he said to the footman at his heel. "Could you please fetch Miss Winters? Ask her to come as quickly as she can and let her know the urgency of the situation."

The policeman inclined his head in gratitude as Jimmy and two maids raced up the stairs.

"Could you please let me know what this is about?" Elias asked.

"All in good time, sir," the policeman said. "My name is Mr Jenkinson. I am from Whitechapel Police Station over on Commercial Street. We're here on a tip-off and we just need to ascertain a few facts—"

"Whitechapel?" Albert exploded. "If I find out this has anything to do with that witch from East Alley, there'll be hell to pay, I swear!"

"Enough!" Elias said sternly. "Not another word, Father, or so help me—"

"Elias?" Henrietta descended the stairs, though her steps faltered when her eyes moved beyond Elias to the sea of navy uniforms at his back. "What is this?"

There were two seconds of stony silence before it seemed that the hallway erupted into movement.

Three police officers strode up the stairs beyond Elias and surrounded Henrietta, who began protesting before they even reached her.

"Eunice Joy, we are placing you under arrest for the attempted murder of Jeremiah Trevor on the 4th of March this year. We would also like to question you regarding similar charges from Coventry, Manchester, and Leeds. If you would like to come with us—"

Frantic, Elias tried to make sense of the situation, but his voice and questions were drowned out by the commotion in the hallway.

Henrietta, resplendent in her white gown, struggled against the two men as they propelled her forward down the remainder of the stairs and out across the black-and-white tiled floor of the townhouse. "Mr Jenkinson," Elias called out. "What on earth is going on?"

"What's going on, sir, is that Miss Winters is wanted in connection with the attempted murder of a man she married three months ago in Coventry. We have tested the food and found that the sandwich she prepared him at bedtime was laced with antimony."

"What is that?" Elias asked, trying to comprehend the unfolding chaos.

"It's a toxic element used in small doses as medicine but lethal in higher amounts."

"She's already married?" Elias asked, his mind reeling.

"What we are discovering, if it is to be considered true, is that she has a history with at least three other marriages in the last five years to her name. It appears that we have a woman who has been murdering the men in her life and claiming their life insurance before she moves along to her next victim."

Elias' mind stuttered as he stared at the policeman.

"Preposterous," Albert spluttered. "Henrietta is a wealthy orphan in her own right. What makes you think you have the right person?"

The policeman drew out the piece of paper.

On it was an image.

Elias looked at it.

Henrietta was staring right back at him.

"In this picture, her name was Clarissa Beckwith. She portrayed a widow involved with a charity for the underprivileged. She quickly befriended a wealthy benefactor called Jeremiah Trevor. This was drawn by his son. A renowned artist," he added. "If we have the wrong woman, we'll return Miss Winters right back to you."

"How did you track her down to my home here?"

Mr Jenkinson tucked the piece of paper into his breast pocket. "Miss Winters, calling herself Eunice Joy, tried to buy some antimony to poison her abusive husband from an apothecary shop in East Alley," he gave a pointed look at Albert. He placed his hat back on his head, sniffing indelicately. "You owe that *witch* a thank you, Mr Turner. She might have just saved your life."

CHAPTER 50

Kezzie

"I'll make it quick," Mr. Jenkinson said, stepping into the interior of the apothecary shop.

Kezzie tried to compose her face into a calm expression, even though her heart crashed about in her chest.

"I thought I'd stop by on my way home just to give you a quick update," he scanned the three women before finally settling on Kezzie, his smile sympathetic. "I know that you were keen to accompany us to the Turner residence earlier, but as I said, it really wouldn't have been appropriate."

Kezzie nodded mutely, thinking that the word "keen" was an understatement. She had been almost frantic when she realised that Eunice was more than a wife looking to be rid of her husband.

She was a serial killer intent on marrying the man she loved.

"Did you catch her?" Rose blurted out the question that Bobby and Kezzie were thinking.

"We've apprehended her, yes. She's currently at Commercial Street police station answering questions." He paused, his brows bobbing slightly. "She's not too happy about the situation. Of course, she's protesting her innocence. I believe word has been sent to Jeremiah Trevor to see if he's well enough to travel. If he can positively identify her, then that will go a long way to securing a conviction for his case at least. The journey is far from over."

"Elias is safe?"

Mr Jones nodded gravely at Kezzie. "Thanks to your help, yes. I'm not too sure that the senior Mr Turner was too happy about the interruption, but Mr Turner, that is Elias, appeared to take it all in his stride."

The tight vice of fear that had clamped around her chest all day eased at the news. "Thank you very much for letting me know."

"We have it on good authority that Miss Winters was getting underfoot in the kitchen this morning. Around the food," he added. "We are going to test the food, just in case, though I'm not sure she would be foolish enough to try anything quite so daring, but you never know with these people."

"Well, I never," Rose shook her head. "She's brazen, I'll give her that."

"One more thing," Mr Jenkinson said, and for the first time, he appeared a little uncomfortable, fidgeting with his hat. He cleared his throat and exhaled slowly. "Miss Winters has been quick to mention the name of someone who's been helping her. That is, she's been paying someone to steal poisons.

"She's singing like a canary because she thinks it will save her neck from the noose. I know you said that you kept accurate records…" His voice drifted off.

"Go on," Kezzie said, unnerved by his tone.

"It's Thomas Mooney," Mr Jenkinson replied.

Kezzie's legs wanted to give way. The name that

lurked in the depths of her nightmares, black eyes leering at her from the shadows.

"I thought... I thought he was dead?"

"No," he replied slowly. "He's very much alive, although as of this moment, he appears to have gone to ground again. We're not too sure how long he's been back in London. We do know that he was away on the ships. We also know that he served a prison sentence in a jail in York for a while."

"I always wondered how Eunice knew that this apothecary was here," Kezzie murmured.

"It won't be the first time that she has used someone local to tap into the network and utilise their knowledge," Mr Jenkinson agreed. "Sometimes, with these cases, once word gets out what has been happening, more witnesses come forward."

"What about Tommy? Will he be arrested?"

"At the moment, it will be his word against hers. We need proof that he has stolen—"

"He has," Kezzie said. "There's a discrepancy in my stock levels. I didn't want to say anything in case we were incriminated in any way, but I can prove that my stock levels are much lower."

"If you can come down to the station and make a statement to that effect," he offered.

"Of course," Kezzie said.

"We're not out of the woods yet, but I thought I would update you and once again thank you personally for your assistance. I know that in the past you and I haven't always seen eye to eye..."

Kezzie bobbed her head. "I think on this occasion we had the same goal in mind, Mr Jenkinson."

The police officer replaced his hat and bid them all goodbye.

The brass bell had fallen silent before Rose moved. "Well, that's that then."

Rose frowned at Bobby before she said to Kezzie, "But

he hasn't married her. Surely, that means that you and he can—"

"It means nothing of the sort," Kezzie interrupted her. "Bobby, if you can, run down to the market. I need some mint." She dug into the coin drawer and fished out two shillings. "Don't let them give you the stuff that's turning brown at the edges. I want it fresh."

"Yes, miss," Bobby said hurriedly and rushed out of the shop.

"Don't take your bad mood out on that poor girl," Rose told her in a tone that brooked no argument.

"I didn't," Kezzie protested.

"You most certainly did," Rose countered. "And I don't understand why you're still walking around like a bear with a sore head. Go and find your Mr Turner—"

"He isn't my Mr. Turner!"

"He won't marry her, even if she manages to free herself of these criminal claims. He knows what she is now. Which means he is free to marry whoever he chooses."

"Well, it won't be me," Kezzie said firmly, her throat tightening with the threat of tears.

"Is this still about that curse? I told you; it doesn't exist!"

"It does!" Kezzie shouted at the top of her voice. "I love him! I do, but it is pointless because I won't sentence him to an early grave."

"For pity's sake," Rose said crossly. "It doesn't exist, and I will tell you exactly why it doesn't. Because your grandmother is proof, Kezzie."

Kezzie halted, her brows crunching together. "My… grandmother?"

"Yes," Rose said on a deep exhale. "Your grandmother is proof that it can't possibly exist. Your grandfather died of dysentery on a ship and your father left because he was weak, leaving your mother and your grandmother. The fact that your mother held a torch for your father for so many years, waiting for the man to return, drove a deep wedge between your grandmother and your mother."

Kezzie stared. "I...Why am I only just hearing about this now?"

"Your mother swore me to secrecy. She didn't want you to meet your grandmother. They never saw eye to eye."

"But Granny died," Kezzie frowned. "Mama told me…"

Rose shook her head. "One day, you asked why you hadn't seen your grandmother, and if she was in heaven, and your mother went along with it."

Memories, sounds, voices… they blended into a riotous blur in her head.

"After she died, it seemed easier to just keep the truth hidden. Your grandmother wanted to close the business down. Even now, she thinks you're mad to keep at it."

"My grandmother is alive?"

Rose spread her hands. "Who do you think has been looking after this business from afar all these years? I don't have a clue how to run a business. But I think it's about time you met the woman who does."

CHAPTER 51

*B*obby.

Bobby stared at the fresh mound of dirt.

It was in a row of several more, so she couldn't be sure which one George Luckett was in. Her eyes travelled down the neat row of piles of black soil. Mists clung to the ancient yew trees clustered in the corner of the graveyard. Behind her were the grave markers of the wealthier people.

A pauper didn't get a fancy headstone like the one she'd managed to save for and put on her mother's grave. You were sent back to the parish you hailed from, and they had to stump up the cost of burying you. To save money, they did it in the most cost-effective way possible.

She'd informed Lydia and Gertie of his passing but hadn't told them of her visit here today. She would now that she'd seen the place for herself. That she'd checked there were no nasty surprises that would upset them.

That George Luckett was indeed gone.

She wasn't sure how she felt about her father's demise. Sad and, if she was being honest with herself, a little bit relieved. His death meant that he wouldn't just roll into Doyle's one day and demand that she hand her sisters over to him. It meant that they were all finally safe from his cruelty. But he was still her father. Which meant a loss of connection.

She shook her head as the sadness washed over her. She wished that things could have been different for them all. If she'd have found the apothecary job sooner, she could have saved her brothers. Perhaps even squeezed a few more years out of life for her mother before phossy jaw claimed her.

But it wasn't meant to be that way.

She couldn't say for sure how her father had died. It was thanks to her job at the apothecary that word had reached her that he was dead at all. She could only surmise that he'd ended up in a workhouse somewhere, otherwise they wouldn't have known where to send him back for burial.

She laid the small posy of asters atop the grave and hurried out of the graveyard. She waited for the cart to roll past her when she spotted him on the other side of the road.

With his hands shoved deep in his pockets, his cap pulled down low, he leaned against the grey stone wall. She faltered for a moment. He looked as though he was trying to blend in and didn't want to be seen.

Then he lifted a hand to her. Relief rushed through her. She crossed the road, pushing back the hood of her cloak a little more so that she could see him better.

"Hello, Liam. What...what are you doing here?"

He grinned self-consciously as he straightened up. "Your Miss Kezzie told me."

Her heart gave a nervous jolt. "You spoke to Kezzie?"

"Aye," he drawled softly. "I did. I'd heard about your Pa. I just wanted to make certain that you were alright. I went to the shop earlier. She told me that I could find you here."

"I thought that you were scared of her," she cocked her head, teasing him.

His shoulder came up and back down in a half-shrug. "She's not so bad when you talk to her. Callum thinks she's wonderful."

She shaped her lips into a smile. "How's he doing?"

"Better," he replied. "Not head-butted any more walls yet."

She chuckled. "That's good to hear." She smoothed her lips, pushing through her nerves, to ask the question that buzzed in her mind. "How have you been?"

He ambled closer to her. Up close, she caught the fine drops of moisture that clung to his clothing. The way his long lashes held them, too. She'd missed him, she realised now. She'd missed the conversations as they'd walked to work. The mild flirtations that, in hindsight, had been more than superficial to her.

She missed her friend terribly.

He removed his cap, pushing his fingers through his thick hair. Her brows lifted when she caught the nervous gesture.

"Do you want the truth?"

Her breath caught sharply in her throat so that she could only nod at him.

"I've stood at the end of East Alley more times than I've had hot dinners in the last month."

"Why?"

His mouth hooked up on one side, his dimple popping out on his cheek. "To catch a glimpse of you so that I'd know you were well. I saw you, more than once, through the window," His eyes roamed her face and settled on her mouth. As if he couldn't resist, his hand came up to briefly cup her chin. His hand fell back down again. "You looked happy, Bobby. Settled. Capable," he spoke softly to her. "Like you were right where you were meant to be."

"Why didn't you come in?"

He shook his head. "Because..."

"Because you're a fool?" She asked. "I was waiting for you to come and find me. I left the door open for you. I'd hoped you wanted to step through it. That I was worth stepping through it for." She laughed briefly. "I've picked up and set down a hand cream more times than you can count."

"A what?"

She waved her hand. "It doesn't matter. What matters is that you are here, in front of me. I've been waiting for you to come and find me, when I wasn't brave enough to come and find you to tell you that I miss you, Liam. Every day.

"Even now, when I'm doing an unpleasant task, you're here. When I don't know that I need you, here you are."

She saw the way her words landed, caught the slow wondrous smile that cruised over his face. The way his eyes lit up. "You missed me?"

Heat filled her cheeks. She tilted her chin up anyway, when she wanted to shy away from him. "Yes."

"Well, now, Miss Luckett," he drawled. "You've just made my whole year."

She smiled up at him. "Then my moment of bravery was worth it."

He searched her face. He put his cap back on and nodded. "Can I walk you back to Doyle's?"

"You want to walk there and back again when you live not five minutes from here?"

He offered her a crooked arm so that she could thread hers through it. "That's right. I should warn you though," he leaned down to speak quietly to her. "I have an ulterior motive."

She tipped her head up to look up at him as they started walking arm-in-arm along the pavement. "Oh? And what motive is that, Mr Byrne?"

"I didn't want our first kiss to be outside a graveyard," he snickered. "Because I do intend on kissing you before this day is out."

CHAPTER 52

*E*lias.

ELIAS STARED at the document in front of him. At the one name that proved everything that Mr Jenkinson had posited was true.

Clarissa Turner.

On a ship's manifest, due to have sailed to New York on the morning after he was meant to have married Henrietta.

Her real name was Lucy Reeves. She'd grown up in Exeter, the second eldest of seven children of a tenant farmer. She'd moved from service to factory, using her feminine wiles and good looks to trample over people to get where she needed to be next.

Her supposed wealth came from inheritance. Extortion. Blackmail.

Blood money.

The evidence was stacking up against her and it appeared that the Inspector was confident that he was going to secure a conviction against the woman he'd known as Henrietta.

He leaned back in his seat. He let out a breath slowly. "Miss Doyle saved my life."

The policeman drew the ledger back towards him, closed it firmly. He laid a hand on the surface and nodded gravely. "Three dead husbands plus Mr Trevor. You would have been the fifth in as many years. If not for his daughter-in-law taking ill during their dinner, Jeremiah Trevor would have eaten more of the meal that she'd laced with prussic acid. As it was, he'd consumed enough to make him gravely ill.

"We believe that his surviving the ordeal was the real reason behind her pushing for a quicker wedding date with your father. She clearly planned to take your money, use that for her passage fare and flee to America."

Elias huffed out a mirthless laugh. "The irony being that we have no money."

"To all intents and purposes, you do. To the outside world, at least," Mr Jenkinson conceded.

Elias passed his hands down his face. "Is that everything?"

Mr Jenkinson rose to his feet, sticking out his hand. "I think so, yes. We appreciate you coming down and speaking with us. You've been most helpful."

"It's the least I could do," Elias said. "I've been a fool for not seeing through her."

Mr Jenkinson held open the door for him, followed him through into the long corridor. "She tricked almost everyone, sir."

"Except Kezzie," Elias murmured to himself.

The police building was starkly utilitarian. Yellow plastered walls and scuffed floorboards from years of use. He followed Mr Jenkinson through another door where the space opened up into a larger room. Here, wooden desks were pushed up against the outer walls. Each one was cluttered with piles of papers and ink pots, ledgers, and an oil lamp for late-night working. Uniformed men moved about with purpose, tobacco smoke hanging low in the room. In the corner, he saw that the stove was lit, the top of it crammed with pans that had been discarded after their lunch break.

Mr Jenkinson led the way through the group. He just about reached the door when it flew open, and a tangle of men fell through it. Bellows of rage and flailing limbs barrelled towards Elias. He was mown down by the blue wave of officers, trying to control the prisoner at the core of the group.

Pain ricocheted through his body as he struck the floor, his head filled with the shouts, the yells, the scuffling. Instinctively, he rolled out of the way. The laughter. The jeers.

Something in his mind moved. Drew back those curtains all the way to the edges of his memories. A hand appeared, a gentler voice helping him to his feet.

But Elias was looking past the genial policeman, seeking out the source of the taunts. He blinked, unsure if he could trust his mind. In the middle of the crowd, a hulking beast stood. Unruly hair, partially tied back with a leather thong.

"Mr Turner? Are you hurt, sir?"

Elias stared at the ogre who glared back at him. "Who's that man?"

"One of the less savoury elements of Whitechapel," the police officer began but Elias didn't want to know his life history.

"His name?"

"Edward Rigden," Mr Jenkinson said carefully. "He's a local criminal. He was implicated in many crimes but never charged. Mostly because any witnesses either changed their minds or they vanished. He's not–"

"Rigger," Elias breathed. "That was the name I heard that night I was attacked."

"He… He was the one who attacked you?"

Elias dragged his gaze from the maniacal grin that

Rigger was giving him. "Yes, it was him. I remember everything."

~

Elias had worked himself into a frenzy by the time he reached Belgrave Square. The carriage hadn't even come to a full stop outside the grand townhouse before he was leaping out and stomping up the steps. He shoved open the front door, barrelling past Cassidy, the butler.

"Father!" he yelled, his voice reverberating through the opulent house. He ignored the startled looks he got from the servants. "Father! Where are you?"

Cassidy extended a finger, indicating the study door.

Elias straight-armed his way through the door. His father was sitting at his desk, a sea of paperwork spread out before him. He looked up, despair etched into his once-proud features. And for once, Elias didn't care.

"It was you, wasn't it?" Elias yelled, slamming the door shut behind him. "You are the reason I was beaten up."

Albert froze, staring at his son mutely.

"I went to Whitechapel to deal with your gambling debts," Elias seethed as he advanced on his father. "You asked me to try to reason with those animals. I remember everything about that day. Hunting about Whitechapel. Going into those places to meet with those men. I tried to pay them off for you, and they wanted to send you a message that you were to pay up. *I* was that message, wasn't I?"

Albert's hands shook, and the papers slipped from his fingers, fluttering to the floor.

"Don't you dare try to deny it, either," Elias raged. "I can see it in your face. I saw the man who stabbed me today. He was being dragged into the police station after being named in another crime by Tom Mooney, the man who stole from the apothecary shop. It will do you good to know that you were in bed with some very dangerous people, father."

Albert seemed to deflate before his eyes, his shoulders slumping as his austere facade crumbled. "Yes," he whispered. "Yes, God help me, yes. It was my fault."

Elias's words caught in his throat as he tried to drag up more insults to lash his father with.

"I thought they'd killed you," Albert admitted. "They sent me your pocket watch as proof. It was covered in your blood. They said you weren't dead, but… I tried to find you. God knows I ripped apart trying to find you. I thought I'd lost you. You are my only son…"

"No," Elias shook his head, refusing to be swayed by his father's defeated tone. "I was your meal ticket. You wanted me to marry Henrietta as soon as possible because you thought she had money. You skimmed over the many warning signs in your determination to marry me off and get your hands on her money.

"She had no status, no real past to speak of. No one knew her in London. She didn't even want you to put the announcement in the Sentinel and was furious with me when you did!"

Albert changed tack, desperation creeping into his voice. "Please, Elias. You have to help us. It's all gone. We have no money left, absolutely nothing. Even if we sell everything we have, we will end up on the streets and still owe money to everybody."

"Good!" Elias shouted triumphantly. "You deserve nothing! You deserve to know what it is like to work hard rather than to squander and borrow to your heart's content. You brought this on your head. You made your bed, now you can lie in it."

"You don't mean that," Albert cried. "I'm your father. What will this do to your mother?"

Elias shook his head in exasperation. "That will not wash with me anymore, Father. I'm done with you," he said, spreading his arms wide to encompass the room around him. "I'm done with all of it. You sent me to those jackals to clean up your mess, and they almost killed me. They stabbed me and left me in the street like I was nothing. I was nothing more than a message for you to sort yourself out and pay up the money that you owed. If not for Kezzie, I wouldn't be here today."

"Elias…"

Elias turned on his heel, his father's protests filling his ears. He walked out of the study, deliberately and slowly shutting the door on that part of his life.

The butler and two footmen hovered in the foyer of the house. They'd clearly overheard everything. Elias knew there was no way to sugar-coat what he was about to say, so he chose the most direct route.

"Mr Cassidy," he said, "I'm very sorry that your employment will be coming to an end so abruptly. If you can let me have everybody's addresses, I'll be sure to pay everyone's wages for three months in order that none of you will not be left high and dry. I'll be happy to provide references for everyone here to secure future employment."

Mr. Cassidy's face softened, and he inclined his head gratefully. "That's very kind of you, sir. And where shall I leave these addresses for you?"

Elias paused with his hand on the front door handle. With a half-smile, he said, "I'll be at Doyle's Apothecary in Whitechapel."

CHAPTER 53

*E*lias.

ELIAS PAID THE DRIVER, tipping him heftily for his help in ferrying him back and forth across London so quickly. He stepped back, waiting for the carriage to pull away from the curb and then scanned the bustling streets before him.

Whitechapel looked different to him today. The streets were filled with jolly people going about their business. Flowerpots adorned the shop fronts, their blooms nodding under the gloomy smog. Colourful window displays caught his eye as he looked along the damp street.

He stopped at one of the stalls and picked out a posy of fresh flowers. He overpaid the wizened old lady behind the barrow and received a toothless grin in thanks. He strolled along Brewer Street feeling lighter than he had in years. He turned into East Alley, his eyes automatically seeking out the familiar apothecary shopfront with its quaint sign swinging gently in the breeze.

He had no idea how the conversation with Kezzie would go.

After his discoveries that morning, after the illuminating conversations with the police and with his father, Elias felt as if he had been presented with a precious gift that he was not about to cast away.

The brass bell above the door rang as he entered the shop. Kezzie was standing behind her counter. His gaze clashed with her vibrant blue one. He took heart in the look of delight that passed over her face before she had the chance to pull her remote mask back into place.

For a moment, he contented himself with just being able to look at her. "Hello, Kezzie."

She nodded, her throat working as if she was trying to fight her emotions. Wordlessly, she walked through into the back room.

He waited for a few moments in the empty shop before deciding to follow her.

She stood off to one side, arms wrapped around her middle. "I just... need a minute," she sniffed.

"Very well," he murmured. "Would you like to be alone?"

"I'm not sure," she replied honestly.

He held out the small posy of flowers. "These are for you," he said. "A paltry offering in exchange for my life, but I feel it's a good start."

A watery smile wobbled across her lips. They continued to watch each other, unspoken words swimming in those incredible eyes of hers.

"How have you been?" he asked her gently.

She laughed, catching the tears that escaped the corners of her eyes. "I saw you the night of your engagement. I was there."

He wasn't expecting that response, but it did answer his question about how she knew where Henrietta was and how she had known to send the police to his house.

"I'm sorry," he said. "That must have been very difficult for you. You have to know that I didn't want to marry her. I did try and call it off, but..." He hesitated and then decided to go with the truth. "My father threatened you if I didn't. And I would rather live a lie than let anything bad happen to you."

She rolled her lips inwards, fresh tears filling her eyes. He ached to go to her and gather her in his arms, to soothe the conflict that he could see on her face. Instead, he balled his hands by his side, uttering her name in a whisper.

"I'm alright," she said. "Much better now that I've seen you."

The words fanned the flames of hope in his heart. "I saw Mr Jenkinson today. I had to go to the police station to make a statement, otherwise, I'd have been here sooner."

Kezzie slowly rotated towards him.

He continued, "He told me how Henrietta had been in the kitchen on the morning of the wedding. She was getting under the cook's feet. She claimed she wanted to prepare a special cake as a wedding gift for me. Our cook happens to be quite territorial over her kitchen and watched her like a hawk. Henrietta managed to distract her long enough to add some liquid to the batter. One of the maids noticed her doing it. The police said that they could test the cook to be certain. It seems she planned on feeding it to me on our wedding night. I came here to tell you that you saved my life, not once, but twice."

She pressed her fingers to her mouth to catch a sob.

"Henrietta had also booked a boat to New York the day after our wedding."

Kezzie frowned, bewilderment drawing her brows together. "Why did she do this? Try to kill you and concoct this elaborate escape plan? I don't understand."

"The same reason that she wanted to kill all of her husbands. Money," he said bitterly.

"So, she's done this before?"

"Five times that they know of. You helped catch a prolific poisoner," a look of loathing flashed over his face.

"The funny thing is she would have been bitterly disappointed."

"What do you mean?"

"My father thought that Henrietta was a wealthy orphan and believed that her riches would be the answer to all of his problems. Henrietta thought we were a rich family, and therefore the meal ticket to the next part of her sad life. Greed is an ugly trait," he shook his head, "and one that was almost the death of me."

"She was very convincing when she came here as Eunice Joy," Kezzie explained. "She portrayed a wife looking to get rid of an abusive husband. She even had a ring of bruises around her wrist, but when I think about it now, I noticed at the time that they were very small fingerprints. Not really big enough to be a man's hand. I refused her, of course, and she was very angry with me."

His mouth twisted. "That's hardly surprising if you thwarted her plan, though she still managed to get her hands on some antimony."

"Yes, stolen from my stock," Kezzie said quietly, filling him in on how Eunice had employed the services of Tommy Mooney. "The peculiar thing is Tommy Mooney was one of the men who was there the night my mother was killed."

"I know," Elias said gently.

"How did you...?" Kezzie began, puzzled. "Mr Jenkinson told you?"

Elias nodded. "He will be calling here to see you again in the next few days. He has some more news for you."

"More?"

Elias eyed her carefully. He couldn't be sure of her reaction to the next part of his story. "This is difficult for me to say but... the ringleader of the gang involved in your mother's death was a man named Rigger."

Kezzie's face went slack, real fear reflecting in her eyes. Mutely, she nodded.

"I know because I saw him. I didn't know of the

connection to your mother's murder. I didn't know that his full name was Edward Rigden before today. There was a scuffle at the police station, and I was knocked off my feet in the process. At first, I thought I was imagining things but when I stood up and saw him, my memory came flooding back. I identified him to the police as the man who stabbed me in the attack," Elias continued.

"He... he stabbed you?"

"He is the leader of a gang of pirates, thugs, and killers, it would seem. The fact that I identified him positively will go a long way in securing a conviction against him. It might not get him the noose that he deserves, but he'll be behind bars, Kezzie."

Her eyes drifted closed, tears rolling silently down her face. His heart cracked as he saw her standing there, as the ramifications of what had gone on sank in. The way their paths seemed to be linked inextricably, through separate attacks.

"Kezzie," he whispered. He closed the gap between them, stopping just in front of her, when all he wanted to do was scoop her up and never let her go. "Are you alright?"

Her eyes opened; her tongue pressed into her upper lip to control her emotions. She nodded. "It's over. It's all over."

"It won't be a conviction for the death of your mother, but it's something."

"Yes, it will be something. I don't know who killed her. I'll never know what really happened that night but… I know if I'd have stayed then I'd probably have met the same fate as she did."

His mouth moved, he nodded slightly. "Then I wouldn't be here. Nor would Bobby, or the girls. You kept this place going in her name."

She wiped her eyes with the heels of her hands. "You're right."

He waited and watched as she brought herself back

under control. To him, she'd never looked more magnificent.

"I still love you," he murmured. She met his steady gaze. "I never stopped."

She nodded, her lips trembling.

"You fill my mind every moment of every day, Kezzie. I have nothing left to offer you, other than my heart. My family's on the brink of bankruptcy. My uncle was an inventor, and his inventions generated all the income we had. When my uncle passed away, my father inherited everything.

"He is a terrible businessman. He's made a career out of trading on my uncle's name and has driven Turner Enterprises into the ground. I come to you as a penniless man with nothing more to offer but the promise that I will work hard. We could never enjoy the riches of society life." He caught her hand and brought it to his mouth. "I don't care about any of it. I will live in a hovel if it means I can be with you."

"Elias," she began.

"Wait, please, before you say no," he interrupted her, framing her face in his hands and drawing her in for a kiss. "Please, I love you, Kezzie. I will spend a lifetime making it up to you. You've saved my life more than once. If you're going to tell me my life will be shortened by this notion of a ridiculous curse, I don't care about that either. It will be worth it to spend however many days I have left with you."

She leaned into the hand pressed against her cheek, her eyes closing. When her eyes popped open again, her dark lashes formed a spiky frame around those expressive eyes. In them, he saw pent-up longing and unspoken love. "Elias, I..."

He kissed her again, trying to convey all the love and the regrets that filled him.

"I want to build a life here with you, or if not here, anywhere," he whispered, his forehead touching hers.

"You are my world. It won't be easy, but nothing worth having ever is."

Kezzie's eyes remained closed for long moments after he drew back, her fingers lingering on his wrists as if savouring the moment.

"Elias," she breathed.

Her eyes opened slowly, revealing those incredible, expressive, magical eyes that had haunted his dreams since the very first time he saw them.

"I think there's someone you should meet."

CHAPTER 54

Kezzie

SHE LEFT Bobby in charge of the apothecary, fielding a constant stream of questions from Elias as they rode in the carriage through the streets of Whitechapel towards Bayswater.

The houses here weren't as grand as the townhouses he'd grown up in, but they were as fine as any she'd seen. Little fragments of front lawns lined the street on either side. Well-kept pavements and maintained gaslights lined the avenue. Beech and oak trees separated the houses along the leafy avenue.

She tapped on the side of the cab to signal to the driver to stop. Elias clambered down, looking about him as she paid the driver and sent him a shy smile. "Almost there."

She could see the confusion and slight apprehension in the smile he returned. "This is all very intriguing, you know."

She sent a mysterious smile over her shoulder as she unlatched the little wooden gate in the picket fence. The red-bricked house was neat, with a well-maintained garden and curtains in all the windows. They made their way along the stone path to the porch, framed by climbing honeysuckle on either side. She rapped three times on the door.

She watched his face as she heard the footsteps on the other side of the door. The door opened, but rather than looking at the occupant of the house, Kezzie's eyes were on Elias. She watched as his confusion slid through to wonder and gave way to recognition.

Stormy grey eyes clashed with hers, his dark brows drawing together. "She has your..."

"We share the same eye colour," Kezzie smiled broadly. "Elias Turner, I'd like you to meet Isabel Doyle. Isabel is my grandmother."

⁓

"Of course, now that I know the truth, it should have been evident from the start. Rose had never run a business, yet she managed to successfully steer a complicated healing business and all the legalities that go with it overnight, it would seem."

Elias and Kezzie strolled hand-in-hand along the riverside. The sun was setting along the river's edge, sliding towards the horizon in a show of yellows and fiery oranges. She'd spent another pleasant afternoon getting to know her grandmother and could tell that Elias was as taken with her as she was.

"She's a remarkable woman," Elias stated, "Though I'm still uncertain how you came to believe that she'd died."

"Mama and Granny fell out over my father. Granny knew that he wasn't the right man for her. My mother was young, impetuous, and deeply in love. She tried to love him enough for the both of them, I think. He couldn't handle the constant stream of people, of having mother called up at all times of the night to help those in need. Granny said Mama cried over the ones she couldn't save.

"After my father left, Mama didn't want to go to Granny and admit that she'd been right. Rose said that neither of them would budge. They'd tried to speak, that's true, but each time had dissolved into a terrific argument."

"What happened to your father?"

"It was as Rose said, he'd died of influenza. He sent for my mother. Despite Rose and Granny telling her not to, she went. She tried to save him, but she couldn't," Kezzie said. "That was when things really broke down between them both. Granny allowed Mama to keep the building because she had no desire to be a healer. The work was difficult, and my mother was keen to get into the community and help others, whereas Granny wanted to sell up."

"Sounds like they butted heads regularly."

Kezzie nodded, her eyes drifting to the other side of the riverbank. Willow trees dipped their long fronds into the slow-rolling river. "I would quarrel with my Ma too, but things never got as bad as they did with Granny. Perhaps if she'd have lived until I was older but…" Kezzie wrinkled her nose as she thought about it. "I don't remember ever feeling like we could argue to that extent."

"Maybe falling out with her own mother taught her a little caution. Perhaps she didn't want the same thing happening with you both."

"Rose says that she often tried to persuade Ma to tell me the truth about Granny still owning the business, but that the timing was never quite right. She could be stubborn when called for," Kezzie flashed him a quick smile. "That seems to be a trait amongst the Doyle women."

Elias caught her hand, lifting it to brush his mouth across the back of it. "That's good to know, at least."

The sensation of his mouth on her skin set off butterflies in her stomach and she frowned, trying to get the rest of what she wanted to say out. "As it stands today,

Granny and I own the business fifty-fifty. Her money bankrolled the business for years until I came of age. She seemed quite proud of the fact that Doyle's has been turning a healthy profit for a number of years now.

"Rose had always insisted on handling the ledgers and dealing with the bank. She'd managed them by herself for so long, and it was one less thing for me to think about. It was only recently, when her health wasn't as great, that I'd started to take on more of it."

"And what of this curse that you lived in fear of for so long? How did that come about?"

She shrugged. "Who knows? It's true enough that there's only ever been one girl born into each family. Both my grandfather and father died not long after marriage, though in different circumstances. And healers have been feared for generations, so perhaps out of that."

She watched the kingfisher dart across the river, the streak of white when he broke the surface of the water.

"I met my grandmother only a few days ago. It was quite emotional for us both."

"I can well imagine," he said. "What next for you?"

Kezzie sighed softly. "Bobby has made a fantastic assistant. She has the option to find work elsewhere, but I hope she stays on with me. Granny and I have been talking about the possibility of buying a large house around here. A place where the sick can come to recuperate. I would like to nurse people back to health, to get them out of some of those houses that make their conditions worse. Perhaps even start a charity."

"Wouldn't that take a lot of money?"

Kezzie's eyes twinkled as she looked at Elias. "Well, you see, there's something else you should know. My granny happens to be an astute businesswoman. She has a bob or two in the bank."

Elias stopped. "For heaven's sake, don't tell my father. He'll be rushing us up the aisle quicker than you can say 'Bob's your uncle'."

She turned to face him "It means that your parents won't necessarily have to be out on the streets, if you don't want it that way."

Elias drew her towards him, not caring if anyone saw them embrace in public. He held her in his arms, feeling as if he was right where he was meant to be. "I don't want to think about my father right now. As far as I'm concerned, I'm done with him."

"You have a good heart, Elias," she laid her hand over his chest and looked up into his face. "You wouldn't want to see your parents turned out on the street any more than I would."

"I have a heart because you saved it, Kezzie."

Her smile was slow, satisfied, happy. "It was worth it, too."

"I'll remind you of that during our first argument," he teased, drawing her closer to him.

"We won't argue," she shook her head.

"We'd better argue," he lowered his voice and bobbed his eyebrows at her. "I hear that the making up is the most fun part."

Laughter, free and cleansing burst from her.

"I promise you this," he murmured into her hair, "I will spend my days trying to make you laugh like that. I am going to marry you, Kezzie."

She nestled against his chest, feeling a sense of peace she hadn't felt in a long time. "You know that I come with three children? I can't give them up."

Elias captured her chin, lifting her mouth up. "You'll never have to give anything up for me."

She kissed him back, showing him the promise of a shared future that she could finally embrace with hope in her heart where fear had lived for so long.

ABOUT THE AUTHOR

Annie Shields lives in Shropshire with her husband and two daughters.

When she doesn't have her nose in a book, you'll find her exploring old buildings and following historical trails, dragging her ever-patient husband along with his trusty map.

If you would like to be amongst the first to hear when she releases a new book and free books by similar authors, you can join her mailing list HERE

As a thank you for joining, you will receive a **FREE** copy of her eBook The Barefoot Workhouse Orphan

It is the prequel to the book In the Shadows of the Workhouse, where we meet William Finnegan and Connie for the first time.

Your details won't be passed along to anyone else and you can unsubscribe at any time.

The book is yours to keep.

ALSO BY ANNIE SHIELDS

In the Shadows of the Workhouse

In the heart of Brookford workhouse, darkness festers.

Portia Summerhill, the spirited new schoolmistress, arrives full of hope, eager to bring light into the lives of the forsaken souls trapped within its walls. Yet, as she delves deeper, a chilling truth emerges from the shadows.

Maisie Milne, a brave orphan on the brink of a new life outside the workhouse, whispers haunting tales of unspeakable deeds.

With time running out and Maisie's future hanging in the balance, Portia is drawn into a race against time, determined to unveil the harrowing secrets lurking behind closed doors. Will they unravel the truth before the clock chimes its final hour?

Step into a tale of dark mysteries and secrets lurking in the shadows of the workhouse.

Ghosts of the Mill

As Hawks Mill teeters on the brink of collapse, Lena Pemberton stands at the helm of a revolution, challenging every norm Victorian society has set.

Alone, she must navigate the treacherous waters where others believe a woman has no place at the helm. Her only hope lies with the millworkers, who urge her to seek the aid of an enigmatic engineer, Henry Wickham. He is a man of guarded emotions and a mysterious past. Lena needs his expertise to rescue the struggling mill, but Henry has encountered her kind before - profit first, safety last.

The Dockyard Darling

In the haunting aftermath of her father's sudden death, Ella Tomlinson finds herself at the mercy of her cruel stepmother,

Clara. Left destitute, Clara devises a sinister plan to regain her fortune by marrying the very doctor who tended to Ella's late father. As Ella uncovers Clara's dark secret, unsettling questions about her father's demise surface.

Desperate to escape a forced marriage, Ella seeks refuge with her estranged uncle in his lively tavern, hidden in the heart of London's bustling Docklands.

Here, she is plunged into a dangerous world filled with sailors, boatmen, and shadowy traders.

Printed in Great Britain
by Amazon